MW00399080

Mandi Blake

THE
Only
EXCEPTION

WOLF CREEK RANCH BOOK THREE

USA TODAY BESTSELLING AUTHOR
MANDI BLAKE

The Only Exception
Wolf Creek Ranch Book 3
By Mandi Blake

Copyright © 2022 Mandi Blake
All Rights Reserved

No part of this book may be used or reproduced in any manner whatsoever without written permission, except in the case of brief quotations embedded in critical articles and reviews. The unauthorized reproduction or distribution of this copyrighted work is illegal. No part of this book may be scanned, uploaded or distributed via the Internet or any other means, electronic or print, without the author's permission.

This book is a work of fiction. The names, characters, places, and incidents are products of the writer's imagination or have been used fictitiously and are not to be construed as real. Any resemblance to persons, living or dead, actual events, locale or organizations is entirely coincidental. The author does not have any control over and does not assume any responsibility for third-party websites or their content.

Published in the United States of America

Cover Designer: Amanda Walker PA & Design
Services
Cover Image Photographer: Macie Shubert of
Macie May's Photography
Cover Models: Olivia and Hunter DeFalco
Editor: Editing Done Write
Ebook ISBN: 978-1-953372-18-5
Paperback ISBN: 978-1-953372-21-5

Contents

Chapter One

Cheyenne

A loud thud woke Cheyenne from a fitful sleep, and she threw the covers off the bed. The old clock on the bedside table read 6:12 AM–a quarter of an hour before the alarm was set to go off.

Padding across the worn, brown carpet of her bedroom, Cheyenne listened for other noises. The locks on the trailer doors were flimsy, but anyone with eyes could see that there wasn't anything worth stealing inside. The drapes were worn, the porch steps rotted, and the "Beware of Dog" sign out front wasn't too foreboding without any sign of a real dog.

Poor Sport. She'd probably never know what happened to him.

Cheyenne took a deep breath, reached for the bedroom doorknob with a trembling hand, and opened it. It squeaked on the old hinges. Peeking out into the hall, all seemed quiet.

"Cheyenne?" Hadley called from her bedroom.

Cheyenne opened her sister's bedroom door to find Hadley lying on her back on the floor. Her long, dark hair sprawled around her, and her head was a mere inch from the dresser that took up most of the space in the small room. "I fell," Hadley said.

Cheyenne extended a hand to Hadley, sighing in relief. "You forget how to walk?"

Hadley stood, then bent to rub her calf. "I was putting on my shoe, and I got a cramp. I fell like a tree."

"What are you doing up so early?" Cheyenne was always the first to wake, and she often had to herd her younger sister out the door in the mornings.

Hadley brushed at her plain black shirt–the standard uniform at The Back Porch Bistro. "I thought I'd stop by and see Mom before I went in." It had been almost a week since Hadley had been able to visit their mom at the rehab facility.

"I'm sorry. I know you've been missing her," Cheyenne said.

The guilt hit all at once. Guilt that Cheyenne got to visit their mother every day. Guilt that she'd lost her job when even two jobs wouldn't pay the bills. Guilt that her younger sister was the only one pulling her weight around here.

The strongest emotion was always guilt, and Cheyenne had it in spades. The guilt was followed closely by anger. Hadley deserved more than this broken family and a pathetic sister who couldn't even keep a steady job. Cheyenne had worked at Food Land since she was sixteen, and she'd worked her way up to manager. Not even that could save her when the store closed its doors.

Not that managing a grocery store was her dream, but what did dreams matter when Mom had needed help raising two daughters? Money had been tight since before the stroke. It just hit a new level of danger after.

Hadley secured her hair into a high ponytail and let her thin arms flop to her sides. "Cheer up, buttercup. I can wake up early every now and then if I have a good reason."

Cheyenne forced a smile. "Look at you. My little girl is growing up."

Hadley rolled her eyes. "Stop it. I am a mature woman. I can be responsible."

Hadley was barely nineteen, and while she usually made good decisions, there were many mature situations Cheyenne didn't want her sister to have to face.

Cheyenne had lost count of the decisions she'd had to make since their mom had a massive stroke two months ago. Most of those decisions involved either their mom's healthcare or how to keep the sagging roof over their heads.

"You have time for breakfast?" Cheyenne asked.

"Sure. Can you make me a fried egg? I just need to put my makeup on."

"Fried egg, coming up."

At least Hadley was resilient. They'd both struggled to come to grips with the aftermath of their mom's stroke, but Hadley hadn't complained once about the new responsibilities. She hadn't even told Cheyenne she'd dropped out of college until after it was done.

There it was again. The guilt. The anger.

Cheyenne headed to the kitchen where the light buzzed and flickered before steadying when she turned it on. She opened the fridge and groaned. The shelves were almost bare, but at least there was an egg carton. She picked it up and flipped open the top. One egg. Thank goodness

Hadley hadn't asked for two. Or toast to go with it. There wasn't a stitch of bread in this place.

Once she had the egg frying in a hot pan, Cheyenne scanned the kitchen, then the living room. She needed to sell something, but they were running out of things that had any value. She'd sold the couch to an old woman last week, and if she got rid of the recliner, there would literally be nowhere to sit in the living room. Did they really need to sit? They weren't home that much, and keeping the lights on was more important.

Hadley bounced into the kitchen whistling an old country song. Their mom had raised them on Tim McGraw and George Strait, and there was something comforting about those old tunes. Cheyenne always scanned the radio stations, hoping to hear one for just those few minutes of happiness.

Hadley's straight ponytail swished from side to side as she pulled a plate from the cabinet. "What are you up to today?"

"Mom has an appointment with Dr. Krenshaw this morning. Then I'm headed to the library to apply for more jobs. If you can wait for me to take a quick shower, we can ride together."

"Nah. I don't want you to have to leave Mom to take me to work. I'll drive myself."

Cheyenne looked up from the sizzling egg in the skillet. Could they sell one of the cars? Right now, it would be easy to get by with one, since they didn't have to work around two work schedules.

But selling a car meant taking something else away from Hadley. She was the one with a job, and she worked hard. She deserved her own car.

Cheyenne slid the spatula beneath the egg.

"You're huffing again. Stop it," Hadley said.

"I'm not huffing. I'm just thinking."

Hadley leaned back against the counter and crossed her arms over her chest. "You huff when you think. You always look angry. You're going to need Botox soon, and we don't have the money for that."

Cheyenne lifted her head. "Hadley—"

Hadley held up a hand. "Stop. It was a joke. Lighten up."

"How can you joke about this? We literally have no money. Like, none. We can't afford a Coke, much less Botox."

The real kicker? Cheyenne hated that she always looked angry. She wasn't angry. She was worried sick that she'd lose everything while trying to keep their heads above water. There was a really good chance they'd be sharing a can of pork and beans for dinner if she didn't get a job soon.

Cheyenne brushed a hand over her forehead and hair. "I'm sorry. I don't mean to unload on you."

"How's the job hunt going?" Hadley asked quietly.

"No luck yet."

"Where have you applied?"

Cheyenne huffed. "The better question is where have I not applied."

"There's not much in Bear Cliff," Hadley pointed out. "You should apply all over. You could get a job as a celebrity's assistant or at a luxury resort in Tahiti."

Cheyenne snuck a glance at her sister. "I've applied to some out of the area, but nothing quite so glamorous."

Hadley punched Cheyenne's shoulder. "Dude. You are so getting out of here. I can totally handle things." Hadley gasped. "You could be a flight attendant. I've always thought that would be so much fun."

"Are you really okay with that?" Cheyenne asked tentatively. "If I could get a job paying more, I could send money for you and Mom."

"I'm definitely okay with it." Hadley bounced and clapped. "You're gonna have so much fun!"

"Work is never fun."

"But you need to live a little. What are you doing here, besides worrying and sitting at Mom's bedside? I can spend time with her, and we can video chat with you. People do that now. It's the twenty-first century."

Maybe things would be easier for Hadley if Cheyenne wasn't walking around with a cloud over her head like Eeyore.

"We'll see. I haven't gotten a single interview yet."

"It only takes one," Hadley said cheerily.

"My resume is pathetic. It's not even half a page long."

"Don't you know that employers only look at a resume for an average of thirteen seconds? That's long enough to read the whole thing in your case!"

Cheyenne threw her head back and groaned. "Stop it."

"And you have managerial experience! Employers like leaders."

"Managing a grocery store doesn't translate well into anything else."

Hadley clamped her hand over Cheyenne's mouth. "Shhh. You're spiraling."

Hadley slowly removed her hand and stepped back. Cheyenne huffed a deep sigh.

"Feel better?" Hadley asked.

Cheyenne plated the fried egg and handed it to her sister. "How are you so optimistic all the time?"

Hadley shrugged and stabbed her fork into the runny center of the egg. "It's a gift from Mom. I'll start sending you motivational texts."

"Please don't." Cheyenne was plenty motivated. The threat of hunger or not being able to pay the electricity bill was enough to keep her trudging forward through anything. She'd already lost her apartment, and she wasn't about to lose her mom's house too.

Hadley swirled the egg on her fork in the runny yellow on the plate and stuffed it in her mouth. She mumbled around the food she chewed, "I've got to get on the road."

"Drive safe." Cheyenne checked her watch. "Mom's appointment is at 8:00. I'll let you know if Dr. Krenshaw says anything important."

"Thanks. Love you." Hadley kissed Cheyenne's cheek, leaving a smear of egg where her lips touched.

"Love you too."

Hadley was out the door before Cheyenne finished washing the skillet. She had just enough time to shower and eat a bowl of oatmeal. Thankfully, she was in the mood for maple and brown sugar because that was the only thing in the pantry.

Cheyenne walked into Hidden Ridge Rehab ten minutes before her mother's appointment. She waved at the nurse behind the desk, Clara, and adjusted her purse on her shoulder.

"Cheyenne," a sweet voice called from behind her.

Her feet stopped, but she waited an extra beat to turn and face the music. "Good morning, Rhonda."

Cheyenne forced a smile. Rhonda was a good woman. Her job just always came with bad news.

Rhonda was in her late fifties, but she could have passed for mid-forties. With smooth skin and glossy hair, she was the poised and pristine face of Hidden Ridge Rehab.

"Come on in," Rhonda said, gesturing to the open door of her office.

"Can I come back in half an hour?" Cheyenne didn't want to miss the visit with Dr. Krenshaw.

"I'll make this quick," Rhonda said as she stalked back into her office, not even looking to see if Cheyenne would follow.

Cheyenne looked down the hallway and hoped Dr. Krenshaw would be running late. Ducking into the office, Cheyenne closed the door behind her.

Rhonda steepled her hands on her desk. "Dr. Krenshaw ordered another six weeks of occupational therapy and physical therapy for your mother. Unfortunately, the additional therapy can't be approved until there is proof of payment or the claim has been submitted to the insurance company."

"What? Why would they do that?" Cheyenne asked quickly. "The doctor ordered it."

"Your mom has been in our therapy programs here for two months, and you haven't made many payments. If we see a lack of payment, we can deny a renewal."

Cheyenne gripped the armrests on the chair. "She's getting Medicare. It just hasn't come through yet."

"I'm aware of that, but we can't keep treating without payment on the account."

"What does this mean?"

"It means she won't be here much longer if she isn't approved for a therapy program. By an insurance company or by proof of payment. The rehabilitation center is–"

"Won't be here much longer? You mean you'll kick her out?" Cheyenne asked. Her pitch was rising, and her ears were burning hot.

"Yes, if her therapy orders aren't renewed and accepted, she'll be discharged."

The air left Cheyenne's lungs in a whoosh, as if she'd been kicked in the chest. "Where will she go?"

"She should be approved for a long-term care facility or home health care. Has her disability claim been approved?" Rhonda asked.

"No, and I've called about it numerous times. No one is in a hurry to get it approved." Cheyenne didn't even want to think about what would happen if her mom's disability was denied. There'd be no Medicare and no possibility of her mom ever having an income. No help paying for the bills or prescriptions. They could appeal, but that was another hurry up and wait scenario. Her mom needed approval now.

"Don't worry just yet. I'm going to contact Medicare this morning to find out why they haven't approved her yet. I'll send a copy of today's medical record as well."

Cheyenne scooted to the edge of her seat. "Today's? Has Dr. Krenshaw already come by?"

"Yes, she made her rounds at about 7:00," Rhonda said.

Cheyenne frowned again and remembered Hadley's joke about Botox. Botox! Her mom couldn't roll over on her own, much less be discharged home, and Hadley was joking about wrinkle repairs. The whole idea was so ridiculous that Cheyenne stifled a laugh.

Yet, she'd missed her mom's doctor appointment this morning, and nothing was actually funny about it.

"Are you okay?" Rhonda asked softly.

"Not even close," Cheyenne said. She was close to locking herself in a closet and screaming until her throat was sore, but "okay" was lightyears away.

"I'll come find you today after I speak with Medicare."

Cheyenne said a soft, "Thanks," before ducking out of the office. One hand fisted tightly around her purse strap and the other at her side. Now that she wasn't running to get to her mom's room before the doctor arrived, she walked a lap around the first floor of the facility.

Adrenaline was still pumping in her veins, but less urgently, when she slipped into her mom's quiet room. Hadley's paintings decorated the walls, and a misshapen clay bowl Cheyenne had made in high school sat on the bedside table.

Her mother had always clung to anything that was beautiful.

Apparently, that also included Cheyenne's dad–another injustice she didn't want to think about today. She'd never even met the man, but she knew his face well and hated it anyway. Football star Jerry Keeton had turned more than his fair share of heads, and even in his fifties, the man had a face made for TV.

Too bad fame and a handsome smile didn't make him a good father. There was no denying the resemblance in Cheyenne's features, but if her mom's words hadn't convinced him, dimples and a pointed chin wouldn't either.

Whatever. Cheyenne didn't need him. She needed to be here for her mom–the one who'd never complained about raising her kids alone.

She smiled at her mom as she closed the door behind her. Her mother had been beautiful too. Now her tawny hair was pulled into a low ponytail that hung over one shoulder and fell over the white bedsheets. Her once bright eyes were dull, and her collarbones jutted out beneath the top of her nightgown.

It was the lack of expression that always hit Cheyenne hardest. Her mother had been a joyful woman, even though she'd had few things to smile about. She'd kept a smile on her face through the darkest times.

Hadley was right. She'd inherited that blissful optimism from their mother, and sometimes, jealousy reared its ugly head. What Cheyenne wouldn't give to go through life without the worry that was giving her premature wrinkles.

"Baby," her mother murmured.

"Hey, Mom. You look nice." Cheyenne put her purse on the shelf by the door. "I'm sorry I missed Dr. Krenshaw."

"It's okay. How are my flowers?" her mom asked. She spoke slowly and carefully, but most of the time, it was understandable.

"Good as always," Cheyenne lied.

Their mother had always called Cheyenne and Hadley her flowers. When she was a child, she'd loved the nickname. Now, it reminded her of all the good they'd lost since Mom had the stroke.

"Hadley is working a lot, but she said she was coming by today."

"She did. She was here when the doctor came," her mom said. Her eyes darted to a handpicked pink flower in a short vase. Hadley had probably picked it off the side of the road.

She was like their mom–always stopping to smell the roses.

"Good. I thought the appointment was at 8:00."

Cheyenne had barely sat down before her phone rang. The number was out of area. Probably spam, but what if it was a job offer? It was a long shot, but the hope of hearing from anyone about an opening had her answering the call.

"Hello."

"Hi, is this Cheyenne Keeton?" the woman asked.

Oh no. The woman sounded like a bill collector. Way too peppy. Cheyenne gave her mom a tight smile and answered, "Yes, it is."

"I'm Jaden from Lang Corp. I'm calling about the PR position you applied for last week. I'd like to set up an interview."

Cheyenne's mouth went dry, and her mind was inconveniently blank. "Um, yes." She had no idea what Lang Corp. was or anything about PR. "Can I get your address?"

"Sure, it's 551 South Crest Boulevard."

Cheyenne reached for a pen on the bedside table and scribbled the address on her hand. "And the city?"

"Chicago," Jaden said.

Cheyenne almost dropped the pen. "Illinois?"

Jaden giggled. "Yes, that's the one. Are you available today at noon?"

Cheyenne twirled the pen between her fingers. The first bite she got on a job and it was hundreds of miles away from Bear Cliff, Tennessee. "Well, I—"

"Is the address on your resume current? We can set up a video call."

Cheyenne's shoulders sank in relief. "Yes. That would be great."

"Your application says you're willing to relocate. Is that still true?"

"Yes. Definitely."

Thankfully, she'd had the talk with Hadley this morning about leaving Bear Cliff if necessary, but the fear of leaving her sister to handle everything here gripped her throat.

"Great. Can you be on a video call at noon today?" Jaden asked.

"Oh, um. Yes. Noon would be great. That's Central Time, right?"

"Yes, Central. Is the email address on your resume current? I'll send you the link where you can enter the call."

"Yes. Thank you." Cheyenne bit her lips. Would it be rude to ask for a job description too? She couldn't remember the job she'd applied for to save her life. She'd sent dozens of applications just this week.

Jaden hummed for a second on the line and then announced, "Done. You should have an email from me. I look forward to seeing you in a few hours."

"Thank you. I look forward to seeing you too."

Cheyenne ended the call and released a long breath. "It was a call about a job," she told her mom.

"Good. What job?" Cheyenne's mom asked quietly.

"It's a public relations position. I'm not even really sure what that is," Cheyenne added. She still hadn't caught her breath from the phone call. She had an interview in four hours, and though she was woefully unprepared, she *had* to get the job.

At this point, she'd dig ditches on the sides of the road if it meant she got a paycheck that would help keep her sister fed and her mom here where she could get the care she needed.

Chapter Two

Cheyenne

Cheyenne raised her shoulders as she stepped up to the front desk at Hidden Ridge Rehab. "Sadie, I need a favor."

Sadie looked up from her computer and adjusted her glasses. "Hey! I didn't see you come in."

Cheyenne tilted her head back and forth. "Rhonda caught me."

Sadie grimaced. "I bet that wasn't a fun conversation. Any luck on the job front?"

In the two months since Cheyenne's mom was admitted to the rehab center, Sadie had become a friend. Not like one of those friends from work you only hung out with while you were both on the clock. Sadie had helped

Cheyenne through the toughest time in her life, and kindness like that left a mark. They talked almost every day now.

"Um, that's what the favor is about. I have a video interview in fifteen minutes."

"What do you need?"

That was another reason Sadie was the best kind of friend: she never hesitated to offer help.

"Can I use your laptop? And is there a private place I can use for half an hour?"

Sadie stood and smoothed her navy blouse. "Come on."

As soon as Sadie stepped from behind the desk, Cheyenne wrapped her up in a hug. "Thank you. Thank you."

"Don't mention it. You're getting that job." Sadie stepped back at arm's length and gave Cheyenne a once-over. "Are you wearing that?"

Cheyenne looked down at her T-shirt and gasped. "Jose's Cantina! I can't wear this for an interview!" She pulled on the bottom of the shirt, displaying the armadillo next to a margarita glass.

"Don't blow a fuse. You can wear mine for the interview," Sadie said.

The navy blouse she wore with a gray pencil skirt paired perfectly with her dark hair and olive complexion. She tied the outfit into a perfect bow with her dark-rimmed glasses and high ponytail.

"Thank you," Cheyenne said again.

Sadie held up her hand. "Don't get mushy."

"I'm not getting mushy."

"You totally are, and we don't have time for tears."

Cheyenne adopted her signature frown. "I don't cry. I'm made of stone."

Cheyenne wasn't a crier, but the idea of letting out the stress and anger sounded nice right about now. Sadie was right. She didn't have time for tears. This was the best, and only, chance she'd had at getting a job since she was laid off a month ago.

Sadie gently bumped Cheyenne's chin with her fist. "That's my girl. Now follow me."

Sadie turned and stuck her head into an office and said, "I'm taking a break. Cover the front."

Cheyenne wanted that kind of confidence. Sadie was the receptionist, but she dressed and held her chin high like she was the head honcho.

After following Sadie into a stall in the bathroom, Cheyenne looked around.

"Don't just stand there. Get your shirt off," Sadie said.

Cheyenne lifted her shirt over her head and accepted the thin blouse from her friend. "Glad I wore a bra that doesn't show."

Sadie laughed. "Me too. We're not the same size."

Cheyenne took deep, calming breaths as she buttoned the shirt up the front. "I've never met anyone who would literally give me the shirt off her back before."

"No. No. Don't get mushy, remember?" Sadie tugged the T-shirt over her head and started fixing Cheyenne's hair. "You look great. What kind of job is it?"

"Um. Public Relations?"

Sadie halted. "What's with the question? I asked *you* a question. You're supposed to say the answer."

"I don't know anything about the job. I applied to so many that I can't keep them straight."

Sadie mumbled something. "Okay. Then go into that interview with a smile. It's hard not to like someone when they're smiling."

"Smile. I can do that."

Sadie tilted her head. "Can you? I haven't seen you smile in weeks."

Cheyenne's shoulders sank, and she looked at the tile floor.

"Nope. Not doing that. Let's get you set up. There's an empty office down the hall, and you can use my laptop."

"I owe you so much," Cheyenne said as Sadie stalked out of the bathroom.

"We're not keeping score. Walk fast."

The office Sadie led Cheyenne to was bare, except for a desk chair. A window looked out over the parking lot.

"Oh, I'll be right back," Sadie said before running out of the room.

In the office alone, Cheyenne wrapped her arms around her middle. Was this going to work? Having Sadie on her side gave her hope.

Sadie ran in with a laptop under one arm and a small, square stand under the other. "This is your desk."

"It's perfect," Cheyenne said. The laptop was almost twice the size of the top of the stand.

"It's the table the candy bowl sits on in the break room."

"Will it be missed?"

Sadie plopped the laptop on the table and started unraveling a charging cable. "Nope. I left the candy. No one cares about the table."

"Thank you. Thank you," Cheyenne chanted.

"You said that already." Sadie winked. "You're always welcome. Now, what's our time?"

"Starts in three minutes."

"Perfect. Get into that virtual waiting room and remember that I said you're gonna get that job. Say it in my voice too," Sadie demanded.

"Okay. Okay." Cheyenne smoothed the borrowed blouse. "Here goes nothing."

Sadie wrapped her arms around Cheyenne and squeezed. "You've got this."

No, what Cheyenne had was a mound of debt and nothing to eat. What she wanted was this job. Or any job.

Why did it have to be a job outside of Bear Cliff? The thought of leaving Mom, Hadley, and Sadie was enough to have her stomach clenching.

Sadie stopped at the door. "I'll be praying."

Cheyenne felt the weight of those words on her shoulders. Praying had never solved her problems before, but Sadie always seemed so sure praying was the answer to any problem. Maybe Cheyenne was just out of practice. She hadn't been to church in a few years, and her praying knees were a little rusty. "Thanks."

Sadie walked out, and Cheyenne sat in front of the laptop. She logged into her inbox and clicked the link from Lang Corporation. She made it into the virtual waiting room without any hiccups. She'd only been on a video call like this once, and it was when her mom's doctor had consulted with a doctor in New York after the stroke.

The image of a well-dressed woman with black hair filled the screen. She couldn't have been much older than Cheyenne. "Hi. I'm Jaden."

"Hey, Jaden." Cheyenne remembered to smile, but the expression was forced.

"It was nice talking to you earlier. I have your resume here, and Mr. Lang wanted me to ask you a few questions before he meets with you."

"Sure." Cheyenne relaxed a bit. Jaden was nice, and Mr. Lang sounded like some intimidating big shot.

Cheyenne's cheeks twitched from smiling, but she held the expression while Jaden asked about her hometown, the grocery store she'd managed, and her family. Cheyenne opened up about her mother's condition. How was it so easy to confide in a woman she'd just met? Actually, was it called "meeting" if you only saw each other over a computer screen?

"Wow. It sounds like things are hard for you," Jaden said with a hint of sympathy.

"Mostly because I knew nothing about strokes or any of this until a couple of months ago. Now, it consumes my life."

That and the mound of bills waiting for her in the mailbox every day.

"That must be tough. I see why you could use this job. You didn't mention your dad. Where is he?"

Great. The subject she hated. "He's not around."

"I'm sorry to hear that." Jaden looked at something over her camera. "Give me a moment, and I'll get Mr. Lang on the video for you."

"Thank you, Jaden. It's been nice talking to you." It had. All of the nervousness from earlier was gone.

"You too."

The screen went black, except for a circular photo with the Lang Corporation logo, and Cheyenne rested back in her seat. Maybe this would work out. Jaden had said that she didn't have specific numbers for the salary, but Mr. Lang would go over that in the interview. However, Jaden had hinted that it would be a considerable help to her mother's situation.

Suddenly, the screen changed, and a dark-haired man wearing a gray suit appeared. The scene that had been behind Jaden had changed to a cream wall with dark shelves supporting trophies, plaques, and photos.

"Cheyenne Keeton. I'm David Lang."

The nervousness was back, and not even his friendly tone could chase it away. "Hi, Mr. Lang. It's a pleasure to meet you."

"It's a pleasure to meet you as well. You can call me David. Jaden told me a little bit about you. She said your mom is having a hard time."

"Yes, she had a stroke, and she's still in a rehab facility." Well, she was for now. Hopefully, Rhonda would have good news later.

He clasped his hands on the desk in front of him. "I'm sorry to hear that. What happened at the grocery store where you were working? It looks like you had a considerable history there."

"Yes, but the store closed."

"That's always tough. Part of what I do is help struggling businesses keep their doors open."

"Really? That's nice." Why couldn't this guy have set his sights on Food Land in rural Tennessee six months ago?

David narrowed his eyes as he studied her resume. "Cheyenne Keeton. You ever heard of Jerry Keeton?"

Cheyenne had reached up to brush her hair behind her ear, but her entire body froze at the mention of her dad's name. "What?" The word was more of a monotone exhale.

"Jerry Keeton, the famous quarterback." David stood and reached for a frame on the shelf behind him. "This guy."

In the photo, Jerry Keeton had his arm draped over David's shoulders. Both men wore the easy smile of the rich and famous.

Yes, too-wealthy-to-care had its own smile.

"I met him a few years ago. Great guy," David said.

Cheyenne couldn't breathe, but she managed to squeak out, "Um, okay."

"I'm a professional sports agent. I negotiate multi-million dollar contracts for players."

Sports. David Lang, who she'd virtually met less than five minutes ago, was talking about her estranged dad. Of all the ways a job interview could blow up in her face, this was the most unexpected.

She clasped her hands in her lap, hard enough to make her knuckles turn white. "Oh. That's nice." Cheyenne kept the twitchy smile on her face, but everything inside her was steaming like the Tennessee pavement in July.

Her slimy dad had been enough to ruin sports for her even in middle school. Athletes were all the same. Well, male athletes. They took what they wanted, got everything else for free, and left everyone else behind. Even children.

Cheyenne vividly remembered her mom crying while watching the Superbowl the year the Patriots won. Yet, her mom had watched the whole thing, pining after the man who'd rejected her after he'd supposedly promised her forever.

She'd never know the truth about what happened between her parents, but Mom had always told her the same story. Jerry Keeton had been at the top of his game when he met her mom, and he'd promised her she could go with him when he got traded.

Then he left without a backward glance.

When she'd contacted him through his agent to let him know she was pregnant, she'd gotten a template letter with a small check.

No, thank you. Cheyenne wasn't the kind to fall head over heels for a man who would leave her.

She didn't need a man. She needed money.

"The position you applied for has been filled, but I have another job offer I'd like to extend to you."

Cheyenne couldn't breathe. What did she want—a job, or to get as far away from this man and the memory of her dad as possible?

Once again, she was completely unprepared for whatever was coming next.

"Are you familiar with Ridge Cooper?" David asked.

Cheyenne pulled at every part of her brain, seeking any recollection of the name. "I'm sorry, but I don't know him."

"I'm sending you an email. Check it."

Cheyenne clicked away from the video screen, and, sure enough, there was an email waiting for her. The body was empty, but there was a file attached.

"This is a comprehensive bio on Ridge Cooper."

Cheyenne opened the file and clicked. A photo of a handsome man filled the screen. He looked to be in his early thirties with broad shoulders and a charming smile.

She clicked to the next photo and gasped. It was a typical sports television type image. The man was wearing a football jersey and only visible from the chest up. His dark hair was cut shorter in this photo, and he wasn't smiling. "He's a football player?"

"Used to be," David said.

Cheyenne tried to swallow, but her mouth was dry. "Used to be?"

"He was a first round draft pick out of college, but he was cut from the NFL after his assault charge."

Cheyenne clicked back to the first photo and stared wide-eyed at Ridge Cooper. "Assault," she whispered.

"Second degree assault. The man he attacked is all but brain dead now."

Cheyenne gasped. She knew the kind of man who would do that to someone. Cheyenne had an absent father, but Hadley's father had beat the life out of both of them before he left.

Cheyenne knew which one was worse.

"Why are you telling me this?" Cheyenne asked.

"Because Ridge Cooper hasn't served a fair amount of time for his crimes."

"For what he did to that man, or what he did to you?" she asked.

David smiled. "Both. He basically took a man's life and got a slap on the wrist. Now, he's hiding out in the backwoods of Wyoming while he sabotages my business. I own several hotels across the country. As I mentioned, I take struggling properties and turn them into luxury accommodations."

Cheyenne minimized the photo of Ridge Cooper and gave David her attention. All the talk about NFL athletes was making her sick to her stomach. "What does that have to do with this man?"

"Lang Corp. was all set to acquire the Palms Resort in Destin, Florida at the beginning of this year. It was an acquisition that would have made me millions in its first year alone."

Cheyenne's head was spinning at the mention of millions of dollars. "And it didn't go through?" she asked.

"It didn't. This man stole my investors and purchased the property."

"So he took it from you, in a sense?"

"Yes, he took millions of dollars from me, but he didn't stop there. I've had two other contracts fall through, and now I have confirmation that Ridge Cooper is the one behind it. I've worked hard for every dollar I've made. I won't let anyone take it away from me."

Oh, Cheyenne didn't doubt him. The fire in his eyes when he talked about losing hotels made her want to hide in the closet.

Cheyenne squeezed her hands in her lap. "What does all this have to do with me? What does it mean?"

"It means someone has made an enemy of me, and you can help me set the record straight. I want to send him a message," David said.

Was this business or personal? Either way, it didn't sound anything like the job she'd been hoping to get when she applied.

"What kind of message? And what does this have to do with me?"

David leaned back, relaxing an inch. "I want to know what he's up to. Why is he meddling in my business? Why is he hiding? I think you could help me with that."

Cheyenne shook her head. "Um, no. I don't think so. I don't know him, and I don't want to." The more David talked, the more she was certain she didn't want to get mixed up with Ridge Cooper. He was a criminal!

"You haven't let me finish, Miss Keeton." David picked up the frame with the photo of her father and set it back on the shelf.

"He deserves punishment. He basically took a man's life and got a few months in jail. Now he's interfering with my business deals. I take the purchase of a property very seriously. I hire locals, I pay them well, and I give back to the communities. Ridge Cooper is buying these properties to spite me. He doesn't care about the people who lose their jobs."

Cheyenne looked around the empty office. If Sadie was praying, she needed to pray harder.

"I need someone who can get close to Ridge Cooper. Someone he will trust," David said.

Cheyenne shook her head. "That's not me."

"But you just opened up to Jaden and then me about your mom's health."

"I was just having a conversation," Cheyenne said.

"And you trusted me enough to confide in me."

She was beginning to think that was a mistake but kept her mouth shut.

"You and I can help each other. I feel terrible about your mother's condition. I do. If you help me, I'd be happy to pay for any of her medical bills."

Cheyenne laughed. "You have no idea how expensive her treatment is."

"I can guess. Listen, I heard you talking to Jaden. You were sweet and friendly. I don't need someone like you to do this job. I need *you*."

"He has a criminal history. He assaulted someone. It would be crazy to knowingly try to get close to him."

"I can assure you, he won't hurt you. Plus, there are dozens of other workers there. You won't be alone with him."

"You said it was in the middle of nowhere."

"It's a dude ranch, so there are always cowboys and guests around. There's a wedding venue. Lots of people around."

Cheyenne studied the keyboard. "If you know where he is and what he's doing, why do you need me?"

"You'll get close to him and find out what he's really up to."

Shaking her head, she blew out a long breath, still unsure it was safe to knowingly get close to a man who'd been charged with assault.

"He's the head of a new program, and they're looking for someone to be his business partner, in a sense." David shuffled through a few papers in front of him. "The job title is assistant manager."

"I'm from Tennessee. I don't know anything about Wyoming or dude ranches."

David leaned forward and clasped his hands on the desk in front of him. "You don't have to. If you get this job as the assistant manager and do what I ask, your mother's bills are paid. I'll pay you another fifty thousand dollars a month on top of that."

Cheyenne gasped, resulting in a coughing fit. She sputtered and inhaled for half a minute before she could catch her breath again.

"Miss Keeton, I like you. You're a genuinely good person, and I know it probably bothers you to see a monster like Ridge Cooper get away with the closest thing to murder. Three months in jail is hardly retribution for stealing a man's life. He's out for himself, and he doesn't care who he steps on along the way."

Good grief, was this man listening to her thoughts? She'd just been thinking the same thing.

Ridge Cooper sounded like a monster.

And he was an overpaid athlete. She despised him sight unseen.

"Only someone like you can do this job," David said softly.

She swallowed, making sure the coughing fit was over. "What exactly do you want me to do?"

"Study him. Find out what makes him tick. What are his weaknesses, his vices? What does he love most? What is he hiding at that ranch? Basically, I want you to be his assistant, make him trust you, and tell me everything you find out about him."

Cheyenne rested her forehead in her hand. Did he say fifty thousand dollars?

"I'll send you everything you need, including the link to the job application at Wolf Creek Ranch. Once you get the job, I'll pay for your move."

"Can I have some time to think about it?" Cheyenne asked.

"I'll give you two days. In the meantime, I need you to apply for the job now."

"What if I don't get the job?"

David smiled as if he knew a secret. "Don't worry. You will."

Chapter Three

Ridge

The old hinges on the barn door creaked as Ridge opened it. The room he'd been hoping to make into an office was full of sagging cardboard boxes.

"Colt, I thought you cleaned this room out," Ridge shouted over his shoulder.

"No, I cleaned the one on the other side."

Ridge stalked across the barn to the room Colt was pointing to and flung the door open. Sure enough, the room that would soon be used to store tack was spotless.

That meant the desk Ridge had ordered was being delivered this afternoon and the "office" hadn't seen the light of day in thirty years.

"Change of plans, fellas. We're all cleaning this room today." Ridge shoved his thumb at the office.

Colt grabbed the hand truck, and Blake jumped on as the two-wheeled mover passed. Colt huffed as the hand truck jerked under the weight, then laughed like a kid as Blake balanced on the short ledge.

Blake's new puppy, Angel, barked and ran around the hand truck. The German shepherd followed Blake everywhere.

"Please stay seated until the ride has completely stopped," Colt said.

Ridge grabbed a second hand truck. "We have five hours until they're scheduled to deliver the desk. We need as much of this cleaned out as possible."

"Got it, boss," Colt said as he dumped Blake onto the floor, sending a cloud of dirt into the air.

Blake coughed and clutched at his throat. "I can't breathe!"

Angel licked at Blake's face.

Ridge propped his hands on his hips. "We're going to need more help."

"I can call Remi!" Colt shouted.

Ridge shook his head as he picked up the first box. "Remi has a full schedule today with the kids."

"Everly is getting ready for a rehearsal dinner tonight. What about Lincoln?" Blake asked.

Colt was already pecking at his phone. "I'll call him."

Ridge picked up another box, and the bottom fell out, sending old papers shooting out of the bottom like a waterfall.

Ridge closed his eyes and tried not to breathe in too much of the dirt in the air. He'd been moving boxes and old equipment out of the barn for five days all while working a full-time schedule at the ranch and moving into a new house.

The room was silent, until Colt finally spoke up. "I say we leave that for Linc to clean up."

Ridge grabbed the industrial-size trash can out of the corner of the room and pulled it over to the mess. "Just get back to work."

"Somebody is about to lose it," Colt whispered in a sing-song voice.

Ridge ignored his friend and hefted the papers and folders into the trash. Angel barked at the mess on the floor and the trash can as Ridge dumped the papers in. He wasn't about to lose anything, especially not his temper. There was one thing he had a good check on, and it was his attitude.

Mr. Chambers had said the barn on the western ridge needed some work. He hadn't mentioned that it was falling apart and full of junk from the 1950s.

It didn't matter. Ridge had a home base for the Wolf Creek Youth Learning Program, and that was his top priority. Spring was already here, and the clock was ticking on his few weeks of moderate Wyoming weather.

This program was the first thing he'd cared about enough to pursue since leaving the NFL. He'd taken the jobs no one else at the ranch wanted just to stay away from the guests. Taking on this program meant putting himself and his name out there again, and nothing else had been worth that risk until now.

"You think this place will be ready in two weeks?" Blake asked.

Ridge huffed and stacked another box onto the hand truck. "Don't have much choice. The kids will be here, ready or not. Plus, I don't start anything I don't plan to finish."

"What about the cabins? When are they supposed to be ready?" Colt asked.

Ridge held the tower of boxes and leaned the hand truck back. "Middle of June. Why?"

Colt scratched the back of his neck. "Who do I need to talk to about getting one of those? Linc isn't a bad roommate, but he snores. And he's grumpy. And he doesn't like it when I sing in the shower."

"You can move in with me," Ridge said as he wheeled the boxes toward the door.

"Really?" Colt shouted.

Ridge shrugged and stopped in the doorway. "I don't need that big house to myself, and Blake is about to become a family man."

Ridge and Blake had been best friends on the road with the NFL and roommates since they moved to Wyoming, but Blake was marrying Ridge's sister soon, and that meant he had way too many square feet for just himself.

Ridge tossed the boxes into the dumpster right outside the barn and went back for another load.

"Oh yeah, you'll love it there," Blake said as he shoved Colt's shoulder. "It's even sweeter, since Ridge bought it to mess with David's head."

Ridge had made a bold move buying the house David Lang had owned in Blackwater, but Ridge's sister, Everly, had loved the place so much. It was just another perk that it was a slap in David's face.

"You're asking for trouble, man," Colt said.

Ridge propped an arm on the stack of boxes. "He doesn't even know."

Blake threw his head back, laughing as he wheeled a load out of the room. "That's even better! He's really going to have a hissy fit when he finds out."

Ridge shrugged. "He should've known better than to harass my sister. He just needs a reminder that he isn't in charge of everything like he thinks."

"But you got a new house out of it. How cool is that?" Colt asked as he stacked a box on the hand truck.

"I also got a few hotels. Just to sweeten the deal."

After David slapped Everly to the ground, Ridge should've gotten an award for not leveling the guy. Since one of the Blackwater police officers was at the wedding where it all happened, Ridge had let the higher-ups handle it.

Well, Blake had gotten to David first, and while that punch probably stung, it wasn't enough justice in Ridge's opinion.

Still, he'd wanted to give David a taste of his own medicine. Ridge would do anything to protect his sister, and David had come too close when Ridge's vision had turned red that day.

If he couldn't lay hands on the woman beater, he'd take David for all he was worth, starting by buying up the hotels he wanted.

Colt's mouth dropped open. "No way."

Ridge nodded. "There's remodeled lodging in Destin, Florida and Asheville, North Carolina. Coming soon to Freedom, Colorado."

David liked to buy properties and hike up the prices. Granted, he added things like spas, but there were plenty of luxury hotels in hot travel destinations. Ridge wanted to see more affordable, family-oriented accommodations. He'd traveled all over the States with his family, and he'd been working at the Wolf Creek Ranch for over five years. Seeing the families have fun here reinforced his goals to help make those kinds of memories accessible. He knew what middle-class parents and their kids were looking for in a vacation, and he was putting it all into action.

"How do you have time to do all that?" Colt hefted a box onto the hand trucks. "I saw your truck here at sunrise this morning."

"I pay people to manage everything." What was the point of having money if he kept it all to himself?

Ridge's phone buzzed in his shirt pocket, and he pulled it out to see Jordan's name. "Speak of the devil."

Ridge answered the phone and moved to the side as Colt went to dump the boxes. "Hello."

"How's the weather?" Jordan asked.

"Couldn't be better. You should come visit."

"Nah. I'll stay warm in Tampa. I'm more of a beach kind of guy. I just sent you some contracts on Freedom. For the love of all things good, please check your email."

"I don't know why you're already griping at me. I haven't even done anything yet."

"Are you kidding me? I have to hold your hand through every email thread," Jordan all but shouted.

Ridge chuckled as he stepped outside the barn. The sun was shining in Wyoming, and the snow had melted a few weeks ago. "Lighten up. I was joking. Yes, I'll check my email, but it'll be later tonight. I'm working right now."

"You know, you could get so much more accomplished during the day if you just sat behind a desk and told people what to do. You're always working, but you're never doing any work besides farm stuff."

"It's not a farm. We don't raise any animals for profit, and we don't grow any produce. How many times do I have to explain this to you?"

Jordan sighed. "At least a dozen more. Please look at the contracts tonight. This is going to be huge."

"You mean affordable, right?" Ridge asked.

"Of course. When I say huge, I mean good for our mission. I heard back from Pete O'Rourke this morning, and he's on board with the management. He's a local guy, and he keeps an eye on the properties himself."

Ridge walked around just outside the barn and watched Colt and Blake fill the dumpster with the mess they hauled out of the office. "Perfect. I'll look over everything tonight."

Jordan was unusually quiet.

"What's on your mind?" Ridge asked.

"What do you think he'll do this time? We need to be proactive," Jordan said.

Ridge's neck heated at the thought of David. "I'm not worried about David. You shouldn't be either. I have no respect for a man who lays a hand on a woman, and he should've thought twice before messing with my family. He spent half an hour in a Blackwater jail cell before he bonded out. He hit my sister. Do you hear me?"

"Okay. Okay," Jordan said. "No need to get riled up."

Ridge sighed. "Sorry." And he'd had such a good handle on the frustration this morning.

"I know what he did to Everly. It makes me want to rearrange his face too. No one deserves that."

The low rumble of an engine drew Ridge's attention, and he squinted to see who was coming. Ava's car crested the hill, billowing dust behind it. They needed rain in a bad way.

"Let me let you go. My boss is here."

Jordan laughed. "Your boss? I still think it's funny that you're a multi-millionaire digging ditches and repairing fences."

"I don't mind it. And Ava's better than any other boss I've had."

Ridge was way down the chain of command at the ranch. Ava and her grandpa owned the place, Ava's husband was the foreman, and pretty much everyone else on the payroll was above Ridge in rank. That was his choice, and he wanted to stay at the bottom. Something had to keep him grounded, and it wasn't piles of money.

"I'll call you tonight to make sure you did your homework," Jordan said.

"Thanks, man." Ridge ended the call just as Ava parked next to the dumpster.

"To what do I owe this visit?" Ridge asked.

Ava brushed her dark hair over her shoulder and smiled. "I have good news."

Ridge got back to work tossing boxes into the dumpster with Blake and Colt. "Great. Lay it on me."

"She said yes!" Ava squealed.

"Who said yes to what?" Colt asked.

"The woman I interviewed. She'll be here on Monday," Ava said as she bent to pet Angel.

Ridge tossed another box and dusted off his hands. "She doesn't have a place to stay yet. Unless she can find something in town, and Everly struck out for months looking for a place around here."

"I told her we'd put her up at the Kellerman Hotel until the cabins are ready."

"That might be a month or more," Ridge said.

"It's fine. We'll take care of her. She was super sweet. She's definitely the one. You should have been on the interview call with me."

Ridge shook his head. "I'll let you make the important decisions. I trust you."

Who he didn't trust was a stranger who was willing to pack up and move across the country for a mediocre job in northern Wyoming. Wolf Creek Ranch was perfect for a week-long getaway, but most of the men who worked the ranch were here because they didn't have a single soul in their lives who cared about them.

Loners. It was a solitary life working dawn to dusk on the ranch. Thankfully, that was exactly what Ridge had been looking for when he left the NFL. He went from penthouse suites to mucking stalls, and the change suited him.

"What kind of experience does she have again?" Ridge asked.

"She managed a grocery store for five years. She's worked at the same place since she was sixteen, and she'd still be working there if the store hadn't closed. Did you look at her resume? I emailed it to you."

"Ridge doesn't read his emails," Blake said.

"I opened it. I just didn't look closely." That was the truth. He'd read the name, and that was about it. Cheyenne Keeton.

Ridge narrowed his eyes at Ava. "So she knows nothing about working on a ranch, and she's never worked with kids?"

Ava stopped petting Angel and stood, propping her hands on her hips. "I thought you said you trusted me to hire the right person."

She'd gotten him there, and she was right about one thing: he should have been in on the interview. "I just need this to work. It's important."

"I know that," Ava assured. She pulled her phone from her back pocket. "Here she is."

She held up her phone to show a photo of a smiling woman with long, blonde hair. The woman had wide brown eyes and dimples, and she couldn't have been over twenty-five.

So this was Cheyenne Keeton. It was just his luck that the new assistant manager was insanely gorgeous. This was never going to work.

Instead of complaining that his new co-worker was going to be a constant distraction, Ridge said, "She looks young."

"Twenty-seven. Not too young to get this program off the ground. She's passionate about what we're doing here, and she's excited. We need someone just as determined as you are about this. You're not the only one who wants this to be a success."

"I know that." Ridge studied the photo for another second. Cheyenne Keeton. She had a familiar face, but he couldn't piece together how he might know her. She probably looked similar to a female sports reporter or something.

Ava pocketed her phone and started walking backward toward her car. "You're going to love her."

Ridge shook his head and grabbed another box. He might do a lot of things, but loving was far from possible.

Chapter Four

Cheyenne

Cheyenne rummaged in her suitcase. Where was her hair dryer? Everything she owned was crammed into the three suitcases she'd brought, and she hadn't had time to unpack. She was still groggy from the drive.

Twenty-four hours of driving had been enough time to really make her freak out over this whole situation. Packing up her things, leaving her mom and sister, and driving across the country all in one weekend.

What kind of hotel didn't provide a hair dryer? Apparently, the Kellerman Hotel in Blackwater, Wyoming. She needed to leave in twenty minutes, and her hair was soaking wet.

Her phone rang, and she looked up from the suitcase. Following the ringing into the bathroom, she cringed when she saw the name on the screen.

"Hello."

"You ready?" David asked.

No, she wasn't ready. She hadn't had a first day at a new job in eleven years, and the stakes were much higher this time. Her mom's bills could be paid. They could afford an amazing long-term care facility for her. Cheyenne wouldn't have to worry about her sister going hungry. Hadley could even go back to college.

No pressure.

"I'm supposed to be there at 7:00."

"Remember, get on his good side and this'll be a breeze."

Cheyenne clinched her jaw. Befriend the violent ex-football playing behemoth and stab him in the back. Easy-peasy.

"Got it."

David had been right when he'd predicted she would get the assistant manager job at the ranch. Why was it so easy to get a job on the other side of the country but not in her hometown? The injustice had her gripping the phone tighter. If the job at the ranch paid more, she could have just told David to pack sand.

Well, it would be great, except the working with a cocky jock part. She didn't need a real-life visual of her selfish dad.

"Report to Jaden every afternoon, and she'll be sending your next check a week from today."

"Okay." She couldn't find the will to thank him, and she'd rather talk to Jaden any day. Hopefully, she wouldn't have to interact with David much, if she kept her word to check in with Jaden every evening.

"We'll talk soon," David said before a quick good-bye.

Maybe Cheyenne's luck wouldn't be so good.

She set the phone to the side and moved to the next suitcase in search of her hair dryer. She found it and rushed to the bathroom to finish getting ready. She was applying the new mascara she'd bought at a drugstore on the trip from Tennessee when her phone rang again. This time, it was a video call.

"Hey!" Cheyenne said as the image of Hadley filled the screen.

"Hey, sis. I'm here with Mom." Hadley turned the phone to show their mom reclining in the bed.

"Hey, Mom. How are things going this morning?" Cheyenne wanted this to be a normal and casual new thing between them, but nervousness and longing for her family had her throat tightening.

Her mom weakly responded, "Good."

"Show us your hotel room," Hadley said excitedly.

"I'll make this really quick. I have to leave in just a few minutes for my first day on the job." She flipped the camera and showed her mom and sister her unmade bed, the suitcases lying open on the floor, and the tiny bathroom.

"So cute!" Hadley squealed. "Was that a painting of a wild horse? And I love the rough wood furniture!"

Cheyenne forced a smile. Her sister would have been the better choice to manage a youth learning program in Wyoming. She was great with kids, and she knew at least a little bit about everything. Cheyenne had spent the last week studying every resource she could find about horses and Wyoming.

How had she gotten the job? She had no training. Better yet, how had David known she would get the job?

"It's definitely cute, and I'll give you the whole tour later. I really have to go. I love y'all." Cheyenne waved at the screen.

"Our little cowgirl is riding away," Hadley said. "Bye, sis. Call me later!"

Hadley turned around to where their mom was tugging on her sleeve. Hadley leaned in to listen. When she raised her head, her usual bright smile was subdued. "Mom says to remind you who you are and whose you are."

Cheyenne tugged her smile wider, trying to hide the rush of emotions at hearing Mom's old saying. "And return with honor. Thanks. I will."

When they ended the call, Cheyenne finished getting ready and left the room a mess. She darted down the stairs and waved at the receptionist at the exit.

Apparently, a Wyoming spring was nothing like a Tennessee spring. She'd been wearing shorts and T-shirts for weeks in the South, but Wyoming hadn't gotten the memo about the season change.

In the car, she checked the GPS and added the ranch address. If the ETA was accurate, she'd make it to her first day of work ten minutes early. She kept the radio off so she wouldn't miss a direction from the navigation system, and she replayed the call with her mom and sister. She already missed them so much.

But hearing her mom bring up that old saying warmed her heart and chilled it at the same time. Cheyenne hadn't heard the words since well before the stroke, but what used to be a comfort was now a reminder that no matter how she came home, there wouldn't be any honor.

Cheyenne knew who she was. She was a woman who was determined to help her family, and she was willing to do anything to make it happen. That's what she needed to focus on today.

She knew whose she was, too. Cheyenne's heart belonged to her mom and sister.

She was also lying and essentially spying on her new employer, but that wasn't important. Was it?

Unless she couldn't do it. What if she couldn't do it? What if Ridge hurt her or threatened her? What if he found out and lost his temper?

Cheyenne had read every article on the internet about Ridge Cooper. Half of them were praising his ability to hold onto a catch and quick thinking on the field, the other half claimed he should have rotted in prison.

She took a deep breath just as the navigational voice said, "Turn left in eight hundred feet."

Following the signs for Wolf Creek Ranch, she slowed and rumbled up the gravel path. This was the ranch? It looked nothing like the website photos. All she could see were towering trees on both sides of the road.

Finally, the forest opened, revealing the gently rolling hills and valleys. Barns and cabins dotted the nearest rise with a two-story house at the center. Pastures stretched on for miles, and there were people everywhere.

She slowed the car as she neared the house, following the signs for the check-in office where Ava said Ridge would be waiting for her this morning. Kids played as parents shooed them out of the way as Cheyenne parked in front of the office.

This wasn't the Monday morning greeting she'd gotten when she worked at the grocery store. Everyone smiled and laughed like the beginning of the work week didn't exist.

Stepping out of the car, Cheyenne smoothed her shirt. Ava had recommended light long sleeves and jeans for working on the ranch, and Cheyenne had chosen a cream knit sweater she'd owned since high school. The wool itched, but at least it was familiar, unlike everything else in Blackwater.

Two cowboys stood on the porch beside the check-in office, and the louder of the two called out as she ascended the first step.

"Good morning. Can I help you find what you're looking for?"

Cheyenne looked around, hoping to see Ridge Cooper appear out of nowhere and make this search easier. "I'm looking for Ridge Cooper."

The two men glanced at each other, passing silent words between them. "What are you looking for Ridge for?" the other man asked.

Wow. Talk about a one-eighty. The friendly demeanor was gone, replaced by wariness.

"Um, I'm the new assistant manager for the Youth Learning Program. I was told he'd be meeting me here this morning."

The louder man nodded. "Oh! Ava told me about you." He stuck out his hand and his easy smile returned. "I'm Brett. Nice to meet you."

Cheyenne took his hand. "I'm Cheyenne. Nice to meet you too."

The other more cautious man extended his hand next. "Lincoln."

Cheyenne shook his hand, but the skepticism in his gaze didn't falter. "Nice to meet you."

When Lincoln released her hand, it was sweating, and she discreetly wiped it on her jeans. *Note to self: Be on your guard around Lincoln.*

What if Ridge was as wary of her as Lincoln? Did she look guilty? Sweat broke out on her brow, despite the cool morning air.

Brett waved her toward the check-in office. "Come on. I'll introduce you to everyone."

Great. She was meeting lots of people, and she had to fool them all. No pressure.

What would Hadley do? Hadley made friends with everyone she met. Cheyenne, on the other hand, didn't have that overly friendly demeanor, and it showed in her single-digit list of friends.

Hadley would smile. Cheyenne could do that. She stretched her lips until her cheeks tingled and followed Brett into the office.

The inside was quiet compared to the bustle outside. The walls were dark wood, and framed prints of horses hung on the walls.

A young woman with long, strawberry-blonde hair who was leaning her elbows on the desk straightened at their entrance. "Morning. Welcome to Wolf Creek Ranch. You checking in?" she asked sweetly.

Brett leaned an elbow on the desk. "This here's Cheyenne. She's the new girl that'll be working with Ridge."

The young woman's smile faltered a fraction. "Oh. It's nice to meet you. I'm Bethany. I'm always at the desk here if you need me."

An older woman with graying hair strolled into the small check-in area from a connecting room. "Hello! Morning, handsome." She winked at Brett and turned her attention to Cheyenne. "Morning! You checking in?"

Cheyenne's cheeks trembled from smiling so much. "I'm Cheyenne. It's my first day."

"She's working with Ridge on the Youth Learning Program," Brett said as he jerked a thumb toward her.

The woman's eyes widened, and she gasped. "A new girl for Ridge! Oh, it's so nice to meet you. I'm Stella."

Cheyenne took Stella's hand, and the woman grasped it with both of hers, shaking furiously.

"What about me?" Brett asked.

"You're going to love Ridge *and Brett*," Stella said. She leaned in and covered one side of her mouth to whisper, "You'll definitely have something nice to look at."

Cheyenne laughed–a true laugh–at Stella's bold words. "I believe that."

It was true. No one could deny that Ridge Cooper was unfairly handsome. Cheyenne had pulled up the photo David had sent her of Ridge more times than she'd like to admit. She wasn't gawking. She'd simply hoped to desensitize herself to his attractiveness.

She would never fall for an athlete the way her mother had, especially not one with a capacity for extreme violence. She'd alternated looking at the photo with reading articles about his assault charge. The truth of the handsome jock was written in red. She couldn't get close to him. Distance would keep her safe and get her through this job.

"I just messaged Ridge. He's on his way," Brett said.

Ava Ford appeared from the hallway leading farther back into the building. Her long, dark hair was swept into a ponytail that hung in loose waves over her shoulder. As soon as she caught sight of Cheyenne, her eyes widened, and she opened her arms. "Cheyenne! It's so nice to finally meet you in person."

Ava came in for a full-on hug, and Cheyenne took a deep breath. The overly-welcoming greeting was more than she was used to, even in the Deep South.

"It's nice to meet you too." Cheyenne hugged Ava and stepped back, putting her hands in the front pockets of her jeans. Hopefully, Ava would be the only person she had to hug today. At least they'd chatted face-to-face during the video interview.

"Come on back, and you can get started on the paperwork." Ava led the way toward an office in the back where she gestured for Cheyenne to sit in one of the chairs in front of the desk.

"There's not much. You should be able to get it all finished before Ridge gets here." She slid a few papers in front of Cheyenne and noted where she should sign. Once the paperwork was completed, Ava filed it away and jerked her head toward the door. "Let me show you the ranch map. It might help if you get lost."

Cheyenne stood but halted immediately. "Lost? Is that a possibility?"

Ava laughed. "Hopefully not! Plus, you'll be with Ridge most of the time, and he'll take care of you."

Lovely. She'd willingly entered into a business deal where she was to be babysat by someone she disliked.

Ava fanned her arms in front of the map that covered two-thirds of the wall. "This is Wolf Creek Ranch."

Cheyenne gasped and cleared her throat. "That's huge."

"There are trails that give access to some of it, but most is wild. You'll get to see a lot of it working with the kids. Ridge has big plans."

Big plans, huh. Cheyenne had big plans of her own, and none of them included letting a violent man cart her off into the wilderness.

Ava explained every corner of the ranch, going on and on about specific places as if she could see the landscape in her mind. The excited description had Cheyenne hanging on Ava's every word, until a few hard knocks drew their attention to the doorway of the office.

Cheyenne felt the blood drain from her face, leaving her dizzy and her vision blurry. She'd prepared for this moment for over a week, but no amount of anticipation could curb her body's natural reaction to seeing Ridge Cooper in person.

He was bigger than the photos let on. His shoulders were as broad as the doorway, and a thick beard covered the details of his jaw and chin. The red shirt he wore had a smear of what looked like dark mud across his abdomen.

If she hadn't been wary of him before, she was now, especially with his dark eyes focused intently on her.

But her instinctual reaction was conflicted. The looming, dangerous man before her was undeniably gorgeous, and a tingling sensation raced down her spine. His attractiveness only fueled her resolve to do what she came here to do and get out before Ridge Cooper could change her heart.

Chapter Five

Ridge

The wonder that had been in Cheyenne's eyes as she listened to Ava talk about the ranch died as soon as she faced Ridge. He'd waited a few extra seconds before announcing his arrival, and he'd learned one thing: Cheyenne could put up walls faster than anyone he'd ever met.

It was fair. He had walls, too, and secrets to protect inside. Until he figured out why Cheyenne's demeanor had changed so quickly, she wouldn't be seeing any of his good side.

Two could play this game.

Ridge extended a hand. "I'm Ridge."

Cheyenne eyed his hand before meeting his gaze and grinning. "I'm Cheyenne. Nice to finally meet you."

Her grip was firm–too firm to be friendly. He could crush every bone in her hand if he wanted, but this wasn't a sparring match. If they were going to work together, he needed things to get off on the right foot.

When her power play was over, her hand relaxed. Now that was better. It wasn't that he thought the fairer sex should be dainty. He'd just spent too many years negotiating and fighting to prove his worth. He left all that behind when he moved to Blackwater.

One thing he loved about Wolf Creek Ranch was that he didn't have to prove himself to anyone.

Cheyenne narrowed her eyes at him and tightened that fake grin. *She* had something to prove.

"I thought we were meeting at the check-in office at seven." Cheyenne looked down at her watch. "It's almost eight."

Great. Someone thought he needed another boss. Ridge sized her up. Her light hair was braided along her hairline and continued behind her ear where the rest was pulled into a low ponytail that hung over one shoulder. A fancy hairstyle for ranch work. And her light sweater? It'd be ruined before lunch. When his gaze hit her shoes, he stifled a chuckle. Tennis shoes wouldn't last out here. Not with the day he had planned for them.

"Sorry I'm late." He contemplated explaining about the sick horse this morning, but he didn't owe this woman an explanation. "I assume Ava got your paperwork sorted out."

Cheyenne glanced at Ava, and her smile turned genuine. Apparently, her distaste didn't extend to everyone here.

"She did. She was just showing me around." Cheyenne pointed to the map on the wall.

Ava stepped up and rested her hands on Cheyenne's shoulders. "I told her you'd give her the real tour. You're the expert."

Cheyenne's eyes widened as she turned back to him. "Expert?"

"Ava hasn't been here long. I've been working here for almost six years, and I've seen a lot of the place. I'd be happy to show you."

Cheyenne's placating grin was back, and she looked him up and down. "Oh."

Oh? What did that mean? Why wasn't there a feature for this on Google Translate? And what was with her scrutinizing gaze? If she was waiting for him to slip up, she could get in line. He might not be the king of the end zone anymore, but he knew his way around the ranch.

Ridge clapped his hands and jerked his thumb toward the door behind him. "You ready to get started?"

Cheyenne glanced back toward Ava as if waiting for an out.

When she turned back to Ridge, he focused on keeping his expression neutral. *Sorry, princess. You're stuck with me.*

Cheyenne pushed her shoulders back and lifted her chin. "As ready as I'll ever be."

"You're going to have so much fun today. Just wait till you see the western ridge. That's where your office is set up. You'll love it!" Ava gushed.

Ridge stifled a laugh. Cheyenne might be expecting a nice office, but she was about to get a rude awakening.

Ridge gestured for Cheyenne to lead the way, but she stopped in the doorway of the office.

"I don't know where I'm going."

Ridge took a deep breath and led the way down the hall back to the check-in office. His parents had always taught him to let a woman lead. Too bad they hadn't met Cheyenne Keeton. Having her behind him felt like turning his back to a predator. It was definitely in his best interest to keep her in his sights.

When they reached the check-in office, Stella was busy helping a customer in the gift shop, and there was a chance he and Cheyenne would make it out without drawing attention.

"Ridge!"

Nope. There were very few times he'd been able to sneak past Bethany without getting caught, and he'd used up all of his luck when he made it past her earlier.

"Sorry I didn't get to say hi a minute ago." Bethany leaned her elbows on the desk. "I had a couple checking in. You coming to the trivia game tomorrow night?" she asked. Loudly. Everything about Bethany was loud.

"Not this time," Ridge said. That was his answer every time. He really needed a new way to decline her invitations because she never let it go on his first try.

"Come on," Bethany drawled. "You never show up for the fun stuff around here."

Ridge cut his eyes to Cheyenne, who waited with her arms crossed over her chest. The real grin was back, and why did she look like she'd just won some unspoken challenge?

"I'm a little busy. I'm trying to get the youth program ready for summer," Ridge said.

"That'll be fun!" Bethany said. "Can I come see what you're working on?"

Ridge looked around. Where was Stella? The older woman had a sense about these things and usually rescued him from Bethany's overly-friendly come-ons.

Cheyenne took one step forward and lowered her clasped hands. She tilted her head slightly. "We really need to get going. Maybe Ridge could show you around some other time."

Bethany frowned and waited an extra second before replying. "Okay."

He didn't need Google Translate for this one. It was not okay.

"Right. Cheyenne and I are headed to Grady's. I'll see you later." Ridge grabbed his hat from the hook and opened the door. This time, when he waved his hand for Cheyenne to step out first, she didn't protest.

As soon as Ridge closed the door, Cheyenne giggled. "Your girlfriend?"

Ridge donned his hat and headed for his truck. "Not my girlfriend."

The crunch of gravel marked Cheyenne's footsteps behind him. She was definitely keeping up.

"An admirer?"

Ridge opened the passenger door of his truck and jerked his head toward the seat. He wasn't about to discuss his dating life–or lack thereof–with his new business partner.

Cheyenne stopped and eyed the truck but didn't get in.

"Everything okay?" Ridge asked.

Scanning the parking area, Cheyenne turned her head one way, then the other. "I can follow you in my car."

Ridge narrowed his eyes at her. Was she nervous?

"You can do that, but I don't mind driving. I can point out some places in town, since you're new here."

When she didn't move to get in the truck, Ridge stepped away from the open door and started walking around to the driver's side. "It's up to you."

By the time he'd made it to his seat, Cheyenne was buckling her seatbelt in the passenger side. Whatever issue she'd had about riding with him had passed, but was her distrust the same for everyone she'd just met, or was it only him?

"What's Grady's?" Cheyenne asked as she tucked her purse in the seat beside her.

"Grady's Feed and Seed. You'll need to know where it is, in case you need to pick something up for the ranch. I expect you'll be seeing a lot of the place."

"What would I need at a feed and seed store?"

Ridge glanced over at her. "You ever been to one?"

She chuckled. "No. I've never been on a ranch before."

Finally, some blatant honesty. "I hope everyone gave you a good welcome this morning."

Cheyenne clicked her tongue behind her teeth. "I'm pretty sure I got off on the wrong foot with Bethany."

"Yep. You're not going to be buddy-buddy with her for sure."

Cheyenne gasped. "I wasn't that bad."

Ridge shrugged. "She's young, and I tread lightly around her because I have to work with her. First impressions mean a lot."

Sighing softly, Cheyenne's shoulders sank. "I wasn't trying to be rude. We really were heading out."

"I get it, but Bethany won't."

Cheyenne let her head roll back against the seat. "I'm sorry. I'm just nervous. I've had one other first day on the job before today, and bagging groceries isn't as stressful as this."

"Nothing about today should be stressful."

Whipping her head to face him, she huffed. "How could it not be?"

"If you're worried about not knowing what goes on at a ranch, don't. Ava liked you because you seemed eager to learn and you'd had the same job for over ten years. That shows loyalty and dedication. You didn't get the job because you were a ranch expert."

When Cheyenne didn't respond, Ridge looked at her. Her brows were furrowed like she didn't understand what he'd just said.

"This ranch is important to Ava, and she hires people based on integrity, not experience," Ridge said.

Cheyenne turned to look out the window and didn't speak for the next few miles. Good. He'd talked more in the last fifteen minutes than in the entire last week. Maybe he needed practice talking to people other than his friend Blake before the kids arrived for the summer programs.

Maybe he wanted Cheyenne to keep talking so he could figure her out. She'd thrown him for a loop this morning, and his days of quietly working alone were over.

He glanced over at her again. She wasn't your average beautiful woman. Her bottom teeth were slightly crooked, her frown was definitely her default expression, and the snarky look in her eyes when she grinned warned him to tread carefully. Even the dimples on her cheeks that should've been cute only showed up when she was giving him that mocking grin.

Still, he couldn't stop looking over at her. There was no doubt she was beautiful, but he hadn't expected the push and pull going on in his head this morning. Something about the sadness in her eyes made his chest ache.

When they pulled into town, Ridge slowed at an intersection. "You miss home?"

Cheyenne turned to look at him then, and he knew the answer before she spoke.

"I've never been away from home," she whispered.

Man, what would that be like? He'd spent more time away from home than actually home when he was young. His parents had traveled with him to football camps across the country, dragging his younger sister along with them. Everly had never complained, but he'd definitely stolen any real sense of home from her.

"If it makes you feel any better, I didn't have a home."

Cheyenne narrowed her eyes at him.

"Really. I think Blackwater is the first place I've felt settled."

Cheyenne shifted in her seat. "Why didn't you have a home?"

Well, that little share backfired. He wasn't about to tell her his life story. "My family has always moved around a lot. We had a house, but we weren't there a lot."

"Why were you gone so much?" she asked.

Ridge gripped the steering wheel, twisting it in his hands. He wasn't going to let his beautiful new assistant make him sweat. "We just had a lot of extracurricular activities going on."

He cut a glance to her and caught her smiling. He could actually see her teeth this time, and what was happening to his chest? His lungs were tight, and a wave of heat washed over his skin.

He was getting sick. There wasn't another explanation. He wasn't rattled by Cheyenne.

Maybe if he said it enough times, he'd believe it.

It was that smile. She was so pretty when she smiled.

Snap out of it!

Ridge pointed to the restaurant on the corner. "That's The Basket Case. They have the best onion rings. That's the bank and the post office. Sticky Sweets Bakery is down that way."

"I saw it this morning. I'm staying at the Kellerman Hotel," Cheyenne said.

"They have a really good bacon, egg, and cheese breakfast sandwich."

"I feel like I have my own personal tour guide."

Ridge kept going, pointing out things and places in town Cheyenne might need to know, until they pulled up at Grady's Feed and Seed. "This is the place you need to remember. Grady's has almost everything you'll need, and if they don't have it, they'll get it for you."

"Grady's," Cheyenne repeated. "Got it."

Ridge jogged around the truck to open the door for her, but she beat him to it, hopping out before he had a chance to show his chivalry. He'd try again next time.

Cheyenne looked all around the entrance and parking area. She stopped in front of a solar-powered snail statue and pointed at it. "Grady sells lawn decor?"

Ridge held the door open for her to enter. "Grady sells everything."

Cheyenne chuckled and strolled ahead of him into the store. Ridge followed at a safe distance, but she hadn't gone far into the store before she stepped to the side, clearly waiting for him to lead.

"What are we here to get?" she asked.

Ridge opened his mouth just as Grady's gruff voice shouted behind him.

"Well, look what the cat dragged in." Grady was in his early seventies and hefty, but the extra weight didn't slow him down. He gave Ridge a welcoming handshake before giving Cheyenne his full attention. "I don't think I've met your friend."

"This is Cheyenne. Today's her first day. She's helping with the youth program at the ranch."

"You don't say! I'm Grady, and it's a pleasure to meet you. Is Ridge treating you good? You let me know if I need to whap him."

Cheyenne's cheeks splotched light pink as she shook Grady's hand. "It's nice to meet you too, and he's been okay so far." She cut a glance at Ridge, and the pink darkened.

Ridge couldn't stop looking at the uneven color of her cheeks. Something was definitely wrong. He'd seen beautiful women before. Why was Cheyenne any different?

It was the mystery. It had to be. He didn't know anything about her, and the allure would fade once they started seeing each other every day.

But when Cheyenne smiled, Ridge knew it was all wishful thinking.

"Ridge!"

Turning slowly, he fortified himself for what was coming. "Hey, bud. What are you doing here? Shouldn't you be at school?"

Hudson bounced on the balls of his feet and shook his head. "Nope. School got out last week. Grady said I could help out here this summer."

In recent years, Ridge's biggest fan was the fifteen-year-old whose dad worked at Grady's. The kid always wanted to talk sports, and Ridge liked it, as long as no one else was around because Hudson was notorious for slipping into things like "Back when you were with the Colts," or any number of things he didn't want Cheyenne to know just yet.

Hudson's eyes widened and his whole body stilled when he caught sight of Cheyenne. "Hey."

Hey? That was all? The kid talked Ridge's ears off on a regular basis, and Cheyenne got "Hey."

"Hi, I'm Cheyenne."

Hudson stared at Cheyenne. He didn't hold out a hand to shake. He didn't introduce himself. Nothing. Just stared at her. Ridge had been caught in a similar trance a few times in his teens, but the boy's reaction was comical.

"Hudson!" Grady said.

The kid jerked out of his daydream. "Sir?"

"I know you're not finished stocking the dog food."

Hudson snapped his fingers as if remembering his purpose. "Right. I was just taking a... a bathroom break."

Grady jerked his head toward the back of the store. "Then head on that way and get back to work."

"Right. See you." Hudson waved, but the motion was awkward.

Ridge chuckled as Hudson strolled off. "I think you have an admirer."

"I think *you* have an admirer," Cheyenne said. "What did you do to become his hero?"

Grady laughed, but the laugh turned into a cough. The old man beat his chest a few times.

Ridge shrugged. "I guess he wants to dig ditches when he grows up."

"What brings you in?" Grady asked once he gathered his wits.

"I need metal bins for storing horse feed," Ridge said. He turned to Cheyenne and gave her a once-over. "She needs boots and a hat."

Cheyenne opened her mouth to protest, but Grady spoke up first.

"Oh, for sure. Those shoes won't last long on the ranch. Let me show you which boots you'll need," Grady said as he pointed toward the clothing side of the store.

Cheyenne followed Grady but looked back at Ridge over her shoulder. That one look had his skin heating again.

When she turned away, Ridge took off his cowboy hat and rubbed the back of his neck before putting it back on. He definitely needed a few minutes away from Cheyenne.

Chapter Six

Cheyenne

Who did this guy think he was telling her she needed boots and a hat? Her shoes were fine. They were fairly new. She'd bought them a little over a year ago, and they were her favorites.

Grady stopped in front of a wall of boots and shoe boxes. "Now, I personally prefer these, but most of the ladies go for this one." He picked up a brown boot and tapped the bottom. "They say they're more comfortable than the others."

"Good to know. Thank you." Cheyenne picked up the first boot Grady had pointed out and checked the price tag. Whoa. That was way more than she'd ever paid for a pair of shoes.

"Don't let the tag get you. These will last many years." Grady leaned in, and the smell of chewing tobacco wafted around her. "Here's my first piece of advice: take care of your feet. You can thank me later."

Cheyenne eyed the boot Grady still held. He turned it sole up so she could see the tag. It wasn't much more than the other, and something about this man made her want to trust him. Her mom's parents, the only grandparents Cheyenne had ever known, died when she was young, but she imagined Grady to be a stereotypical grandpa. She didn't get the sense that he was trying to push her to buy the more expensive ones because it would line his pockets.

Plus, she had the money to afford a nice pair of boots now. Not that she hoped to be using them for the next ten years. Her time at Wolf Creek Ranch was limited to how fast she could find out whatever David wanted to know about Ridge.

"Okay, I'll take those."

"What size you wear, miss?"

It had been a while since she'd bought a new pair of shoes, and she'd never owned work boots. "Let me try a seven, please."

Grady pushed boxes around on the higher shelf until he found the one he needed. She sat on the small stool Grady pulled over for her and tried on the boot.

"You need about this much extra room in boots like these." He held his fingers about an inch apart. "In the winter, you'll need room for sock layers."

Cheyenne whistled. "Layers of socks? How cold does it get here?"

Grady's hearty laugh had her smiling. "You haven't seen winter until you've lived through one in Wyoming."

Cheyenne pulled off the boot and put it in the box. "You're probably right. We get snow in Tennessee but not tons."

"I expect I'll see you back in here in a few months for a full winter wardrobe then. And Ridge said you need a hat. Come right this way, and we'll get that picked out for you."

She didn't plan to be here when winter rolled around, but Grady didn't need to know that little fact.

Cheyenne followed Grady through the store. He slowed every ten feet to say hello to someone, and he knew everyone by name. Blackwater couldn't be much bigger than Bear Cliff, but she definitely didn't know every face she saw at the store back home.

Grady gestured to the wall of hats, all in shades of brown, gray, and tan. "Here you go. This side is ladies'. This one's popular." He picked up a tan hat with a simple braided band. The brim turned up a little on the sides.

"I like it," Cheyenne said as she took it from him. She rested it on her head and looked up at Grady.

"That one's a little big." He picked up another and checked the size. "Try this one."

The second one fit better, and she took it off and turned it in her hands. "I'm not really a hat person."

"You'll want to be. The hat isn't for looks. It keeps the sun out of your eyes and shades your face."

Cheyenne rubbed her thumb over the braided band. "I never thought of that. I guess I'll take this one."

"You see anything else you need?" Grady asked. "If you think of something, have Ridge send me a text, and I'll make sure we have it."

"That's sweet of you," Cheyenne said as she followed Grady back toward the front of the store.

"Oh, it's what I love. The folks around here need things, and I want to make it easy for our ranchers to do their jobs."

"Can I tell you a secret?" Cheyenne whispered.

Grady turned back to her but kept walking. "Anytime."

"I don't know what ranchers do," she said quietly.

Grady let out his boisterous laugh again, and Cheyenne laughed too. She wiped her eyes and looked up to see Ridge walking toward them. The joyous sound died in her throat, and she lifted her chin.

Cheyenne grinned as indecision swirled in her middle. Ridge had been fairly nice to her so far, and he'd been kind to Grady and the young boy. If he kept this up, she was going to have a hard time remembering he was a criminal. She'd read some articles about the man Ridge Cooper assaulted. The guy was a shell of his former self. He'd never work, get married, have a family, or see any of the world outside of that long-term care facility.

She'd just remember those articles and the photos whenever she felt soft around Ridge.

"You find everything you needed?" Ridge asked.

"I did. Boots and a hat." Cheyenne held up the items and looked at his empty hands. "I thought you were getting something here too."

Ridge pointed a thumb over his shoulder. "Already loaded up. Let's pay for those and get back to the ranch."

Grady slapped a hand on Ridge's shoulder. "I told her you'd let me know if she needed anything else. You take care of this young lady."

Ridge turned to her with a scrutinizing gaze. His mouth quirked up slightly on one side as if Grady's demand amused him. "I'll do that."

They said their good-byes to Grady and headed to the checkout. A gray-haired woman was running the register, and she chatted with Ridge like she'd known him her whole life. Cheyenne gave a quick "Hello" followed by a smile when she was introduced. She'd officially met half the town this morning, and she didn't remember a single name except Grady's.

Ridge paid for the boots and hat while talking to the woman, not even giving Cheyenne an opportunity to protest without interrupting the conversation. Heat flooded her chest and neck. She'd intended to pay for those things herself, and this guy had the nerve to shut her out without a word.

This forwardness was exactly why she didn't like men like Ridge. They did what they wanted and didn't ask anyone else for input. She finally had the money to buy what she wanted, and the blasted man had taken that small joy away from her.

They didn't speak until they were back in Ridge's truck, and Cheyenne's temper was near boiling.

Ridge shifted into reverse and backed out of the parking space. "You want to grab lunch at Sticky Sweets? Or we can go back to the ranch and eat in the dining hall. Lunch is free for ranch workers."

"Either is fine," Cheyenne said. Though the dining hall sounded like a bustling place, she'd seen Sticky Sweets this morning. It would be much smaller and quieter.

"Let's go to the bakery. I think you've met enough new faces for one day, and if we go to the dining hall, all the other ranch workers are going to want to meet you."

Cheyenne wanted to be irritated that he'd implied that she couldn't handle meeting the others at the ranch, but he was right. She just wanted a simple lunch and some peace and quiet. She hadn't found out anything interesting about Ridge yet, and Jaden was expecting a check-in later this evening.

Five minutes later, Ridge practically jogged around the truck to get to her side. She jumped out and met him at the front of the truck. He'd been showing off his chivalry all morning, and she hadn't decided what to think of it yet. Even in the South, opening car doors for women seemed to be a thing of the past, but Ridge was either trying to hold onto it or put on a show for her.

When he saw she'd opened her own door without any mishap, he changed direction and held the door to the bakery open for her. Well played.

As she stepped in, the noise inside hit her like a brick wall. She'd mistakenly assumed the small eatery would be quiet, but the place was bustling.

On the one hand, she wouldn't have to make too much conversation with Ridge. On the other hand, she wouldn't be uncovering any of his secrets.

Cheyenne leaned closer to Ridge to be heard above the noise. The musty smell of hay filled her senses. Maybe it would help divert her attention, since Ridge didn't smell like a Hollister model. "What did you say was good here?"

"The breakfast sandwich."

"But it's lunch," Cheyenne said.

Ridge shrugged. "Tracy serves breakfast all day, and I don't think I've tried anything else here."

Cheyenne glanced up at him. He was a good eight or nine inches taller than her, and being eye-level with his biceps was making her sweat. "So, you're a creature of habit?"

He looked down at her with a slight frown. "I guess so. That's a good thing."

Cheyenne held up her hands. "I didn't say it was a bad thing."

"Your tone said it was."

Cheyenne huffed and crossed her arms over her chest. "My tone said it was an observation."

Ridge was eyeing her like she was a spy trying to sneak into an enemy's camp. Well, that wouldn't be far from the truth, but she pushed that thought aside.

"I may be a creature of habit, but there's nothing wrong with finding something you like and sticking with it. It goes hand-in-hand with loyalty and determination."

Cheyenne opened her mouth to ask if that was how he made it all the way to the NFL but clamped her jaw shut at the last minute. She wasn't supposed to know anything about him, but she'd been studying his background for weeks. In some ways, that was an advantage, but a small slip-up like that would get her cover blown in a heartbeat.

They stepped up to the counter where a young, smiling girl took their orders. Well, she smiled when she was drooling over Ridge and didn't spare an extra second of her attention for Cheyenne.

Then Ridge paid again. Ugh. What was with this guy? This was the furthest thing from a date, and he was still throwing his money around. It was money she wasn't supposed to know he had. NFL superstar quarterback Ridge Cooper had a net worth that was more than she would ever even touch in her entire life.

Cheyenne picked a table in the far back, and Ridge waited at the counter for their food. As soon as she sat down, she pulled her phone from her pocket. She hadn't known what to expect, but the lack of messages had her breathing easier. Maybe David wouldn't be too harsh on her. If he was going to give her some slack, she might be able to build Ridge's trust and really get to know him without stressing about it.

She slipped her phone back into her pocket and picked up a napkin on the table, tearing the thin paper into strips. Ridge chatted with an older woman at the counter. The genuine smile on his face said he wasn't just holding the conversation because some woman had cornered him. And the way the woman looked up at him with bright eyes said she had no idea he'd been imprisoned for second-degree assault.

Did the people here really not know about his past? It had been all over the internet at the time, or at least, that's what her search led her to believe. America's football star fell from grace in a split second, and from the comments she'd read, most people had strong opinions about him one way or the other.

When the older woman behind the counter handed Ridge their food, the smile remained on his face as he turned to walk back toward their table. Cheyenne gathered the ripped pieces of napkin on the table into a ball. He had an innocent face, she'd give him that.

Ridge put the food and drinks on the table and returned the tray to the shelf by the trash cans. Cheyenne scoffed. What a golden boy. He probably stopped to help old ladies cross the street and carry their groceries. He said hello to everyone with a suave tip of his hat. He asked about sick family members and kids who were graduating high school. Just listening to him chat with people in town today had her rolling her eyes.

Ridge Cooper was not a Goody-Two-Shoes.

He sat down in the seat across from her, hung his hat on the back of the empty chair beside him, and rested his elbows on the table, threading his fingers together. "I'd like to say grace. Is it okay with you if I say it out loud?"

Cheyenne felt like the breath had been knocked out of her lungs. She stared at him for a moment, waiting for him to finish with, "Just kidding," or something equally immature.

When he didn't retract his comment, she cleared her throat and clasped her hands. "Sure."

Ridge bowed his head and thanked the Lord for the food. Cheyenne barely heard his words over the roaring in her ears. When Ridge's deep, "Amen," pulled her from her spinning thoughts, she looked around the bakery. Heat flared over her chest and neck.

Ridge dug into his sandwich like he hadn't eaten in weeks, and Cheyenne watched him. She'd been raised in church, but regular attendance had taken a backseat when she started working full time. In fact, she couldn't remember the last time she'd prayed over a meal.

Her breaths were coming faster now, and each was more difficult than the one before.

When Ridge looked up at her, his brows furrowed as he chewed. "Are you okay?"

Air. She needed air. Why did he have to pretend to care if she was okay or not? Why did he have to thank God for his meal? He could buy a million meals like this one without thinking twice!

"I'm fine. I'm just going to run to the restroom." Cheyenne stood and scanned the room. *Please let there be a clear sign so I don't have to speak to anyone right now.* Her fingers tingled, and her vision blurred. She'd stood too quickly.

Ridge pointed to the register. "It's past the line and down the hallway. On the right."

"Thanks," Cheyenne said in a short breath. She strode across the room without taking her eyes off the hallway Ridge had pointed out.

When she turned the corner, Cheyenne leaned her back against the wall. There wasn't any chance Ridge was actually a good guy, right? No way he'd had some kind of momentary lapse in sanity, then reverted back to a stand-up, law abiding citizen.

No. She wasn't supposed to ruin a good man's life. He was violent, dangerous, and crazy. He'd beat a man half to death.

Cheyenne had about three minutes to get herself together and get back to lunch with the confusing man she was supposed to hate.

Chapter Seven

Ridge

Ridge kept quiet on the drive back to the ranch. Whatever had spooked Cheyenne had her walls back up.

It had to be the prayer, but that wasn't something he planned on changing. He'd just thank the Lord for his food in silence if it bothered her. He had too much to be thankful for to stop counting his blessings.

He drove slowly past the main house, keeping an eye out for the guests walking in the paths.

"My car is parked here," Cheyenne said as she pointed out the window.

"I can drive you back to it this afternoon if you want. The path out to the barn is washed out in a few places. We're getting a delivery of riprap to fill the holes in tomorrow."

Cheyenne craned her neck to watch her car as they passed. "Okay."

Ridge drove toward the barn but turned off on a side path. "This is where the new cabins will be. I think Ava said you'd be moving in here when they're finished."

Cheyenne leaned close to the window as they approached, and Ridge stopped the truck at the first cabin. The walls were up and the windows and roof were on, but that was all. Trailers with equipment and material were parked in the stirred-up dirt, and a few workers milled around.

"Can I see the inside?" she asked.

"Sure." Ridge got out and started toward Cheyenne's side of the truck, but she was out before he got there.

She could be determined to sidestep his chivalry, but it wouldn't stop him from trying.

Cheyenne followed him into the first cabin. The floors were bare, and sawdust covered every surface. Cheyenne turned in the small room, studying everything from the floors to the ceilings.

"This is… nice."

Ridge leaned a shoulder against the wall. "Nice as in good or nice as a substitute for your criticism?"

Cheyenne glared at him. "Nice as in good. I didn't expect to get housing here. I was surprised when Ava offered it."

"The town is full of tourists, and most housing is already taken as rentals for either travelers or seasonal ranch hands. With the way this part of the state is booming, Ava knew we needed to get ahead of the game."

Cheyenne's ire relaxed. "That's still really nice of her."

Ridge bit his tongue. It had been his idea to add the cabins, and he'd insisted on paying for the construction. If he was going to invest in something besides the hotels he snatched from David, he wanted his money to go toward the ranch.

The youth program was his idea too, but it wasn't in his name. Mr. Chambers had offered to lease the land to Ridge, but business was safer if it wasn't in his name and tied in any way to his past.

Ridge waited by the door as Cheyenne peeked into the other rooms. When she came back into the main room, he asked, "What did you think?"

Cheyenne stuck her hands in her back pockets. "It's really nice."

"It's small," Ridge said.

"I don't need much. Small is good."

Ridge adjusted his hat on his head. He still hadn't figured out why she was willing to uproot her life in Tennessee to move to Wyoming. Wranglers did it all the time, but it usually meant they didn't have anyone in their life to tie them to one place. They moved with the need for work. Ridge had his reasons for coming to the ranch, and the need to know Cheyenne's reasons itched at him.

"You ready to get to the barn?" he asked.

"Yes, let's go."

They didn't speak on the short drive. Was this what it was going to be like working with Cheyenne? He hadn't decided if the silence was awkward or just casual.

He pulled up at the old barn and held out his hands. "Here it is. Your new office."

"New?" Cheyenne said with a chuckle. "New in the beginning of the twentieth century?"

"New to you. Definitely not new. This is our temporary home base. We're planning to build a new barn with dedicated offices after this first year. Until then, this is what you get."

They both got out, and Ridge pointed out things in the area. "That's the arena. We'll use that area for riding lessons. That shed is for supplies. The small one on the other side of the barn is the feed shed."

"So, there are real horses here?" Cheyenne asked.

Ridge chewed his lip to hide his grin. "Yeah. We'll have horses. They're still at the main barn for now, but we'll move them over later this week."

Ava had told him more than once that the lack of applicants for the assistant manager position had her worried, but had she really not had any applicants with equine experience? Not that Cheyenne would be teaching the riding lessons. That would be Ridge, and it was hard to believe he hadn't been on a horse before coming to the ranch. He'd learned everything he needed to know in the years since.

Still, Cheyenne would be his helper, and it would be best if she knew a little about what she was doing. Thankfully, Ava had assured him Cheyenne could handle the registration and communication with the parents. That was the part he really didn't want to get into.

They stepped into the barn, and Ridge gestured toward the office. "This will be your space. I have a second desk set up in here, in case

I need to take care of anything during the day, but for the most part, I'll stay out of your way."

Cheyenne stepped inside and gaped. "This is an office?"

Boards filled with feed schedules, vet records, feed inventory, and dietary guidelines for the horses filled one wall. The other was a white board with the schedule of deliveries on one side and the class schedule on the other. The picture windows had distorted glass, and the filing cabinet he'd cleaned out yesterday was the only thing in the room besides the main desk and smaller area he'd set up for himself.

"It's the best we have right now. The desk is new, and so is the laptop. You have a Wi-Fi hotspot, but if you need a phone line for anything, you'll need to use Ava's office."

Cheyenne kicked her foot over the ground and dust billowed. "Is this dirt?"

"Yep. You're lucky to have electricity."

She looked up at him with wide eyes. "Okay then." Looking around, she wrung her hands. "My last office wasn't much more than a broom closet. I wasn't expecting to even get one here."

"It's a good thing your expectations were low. The nicer part of the ranch is back over the hill."

Cheyenne studied the room from top to bottom, turning in all directions. "It's fine."

He pointed toward the desk. "Let me show you the programs we'll be using. Ava said she'd be sending a detailed job description. We can work our way through that list to get you up to speed before the kids get here next week."

"Right." She made her way around the desk and turned on the laptop. "She sent me a list after the interview. I asked some questions, and she pointed me in the direction of places online so I could get familiar with some of the things we'll be doing."

Ridge stood behind Cheyenne where she sat at the desk. Had she really been trying to prepare for the job? For the sake of the program, he hoped so. They still had a lot of work to do to get things ready for the opening, and they'd be spending half that time training her for what was coming.

Leaning one arm on the back of the chair, Ridge pointed to the screen with the other. "This is the program we're using. Ava has everything up-to-date. It's separated by week, and the groups are under each tab." He used the wireless mouse to click through the options. "Each participant will have paperwork to file, and there's a place to attach the completed forms here."

He clicked through a few more tabs with explanations, and Cheyenne stayed silent. When he turned his head to ask if she was listening, her rigid posture had him backing up. She was still as stone with her arms tucked in close to her sides, and her shoulders up close to her ears.

"Are you okay?" he asked, careful not to scare her more.

She nodded emphatically and looked up at him. "Yeah. I'm fine."

Google Translate, what does it mean when a woman says she's "fine"? Cheyenne was a liar, and he needed to know what had her so timid.

He was leaning close to her–close enough to see the tense muscles of her jaw.

Ridge stood and took a step back. "You should get an email notification whenever someone registers online. If you want to log into your email, I'll show you what to enter into the program when we get new registrations."

"What if someone calls?" Cheyenne asked.

"Those calls still go to Ava's office. We're hoping to get the internet and a landline out here in a couple of weeks."

"Wow. Okay." Cheyenne busied herself with logging into the email Ava had set up for her.

Careful not to get too close, Ridge went over the registrations with her and each part of the waivers. They'd just pulled up the list of job duties Ava had sent when Brett knocked on the open doorway of the office.

"Hey, boss," Brett said before he became completely transfixed with the woman in the room.

Here it was. Brett couldn't pass up a chance to flirt with a woman. He was Ridge's complete opposite when it came to interacting with women.

"Good to see you again, Cheyenne." Brett smiled and winked as he extended his hand to her.

"You already met Brett?" Ridge asked.

Cheyenne smiled up at him. "We met this morning when I was looking for you."

Ridge couldn't help it. He watched Cheyenne's hand as it grasped Brett's. Definitely no power-play squeeze going on. Why did she act differently around Brett than she had when Ridge had been introduced to her earlier today?

Brett shot Ridge a mischievous grin.

"You settling in okay?" Brett asked Cheyenne. "If you need someone to help you move in, I'm your man."

Cheyenne rested back in her chair. "Thanks, but I'm staying at the Kellerman Hotel for now."

"Why don't I give you my phone number so–"

"Brett, those boards aren't going to replace themselves," Ridge said, quickly interrupting Brett's obvious come-on.

Brett's shoulders sank. "But I was just–"

"You were just getting to work." Ridge jerked his head toward the door.

Sulking, Brett turned but stopped with a hand on the doorframe. "If you need me, I'll be out here. Working hard. It's hot. I may take my shirt off."

"Brett!" Ridge growled.

"Sorry. I'm going." Brett jogged off chuckling.

Ridge rubbed the back of his neck. Brett was great to have around when you needed a hand, but Ridge should have known Cheyenne would be a distraction.

"Let me know if he bothers you," Ridge said. He kept his distance and leaned against the filing cabinet.

Cheyenne had already turned back to the computer, but a playful smile lingered on her face. "I think he's harmless. I've been pretty good at deciphering the difference over the years."

The difference between dangerous and harmless? That's a crucial difference for women—one he hadn't been willing to risk when the question had risen for his sister, and he'd been right. He would have spent years in prison instead of months if it meant Everly was safe.

"Brett is a good man, but if his flirting makes you uncomfortable, don't hesitate to tell me."

Cheyenne looked up at him then, and she frowned, creating two small lines between her brows. "Is there something I should know about him?"

"No. He really is good." Great. Now she would think he was throwing his own friends under the bus. "I don't want you or any woman to feel uncomfortable here."

Cheyenne looked him up and down. "Is there anyone else here I should be afraid of?"

What was that look? Was she implying *he* was a threat to her?

Never. He would never hurt a woman.

"No. I trust the men who work here."

She gave him a look he couldn't quite decipher. "Enough to believe them over a woman who made a harassment claim against them?"

"No. Of course not." Ridge pushed off the filing cabinet and straightened his shoulders.

What was she getting at? Why was she trying to trick him into slipping up? "If you don't feel comfortable coming to me, you can always contact Ava."

Cheyenne nodded and turned her attention back to the computer. "Good. Thanks."

Ridge's breaths came shallow, and his skin heated. Why did things feel unsettled between them? Why had she tensed when he'd been standing beside her but was completely at ease when Brett came around the desk to shake her hand?

It was day one, and she had Ridge overthinking, and overthinking wasn't Ridge's M.O. So why did it bother him that Cheyenne had some silent grudge against him?

"You got everything covered here?" he asked.

"I'm checking the emails. There are quite a few messages here. One is from Ava with some pretty detailed instructions."

"Good. I need to help Brett with these boards. You can get started reading those, and I'll be out here if you need me."

Cheyenne didn't even look up from the screen. "Thanks. I think I've got it."

Ridge turned, leaving Cheyenne in the office. He could take a hint. She didn't want to be around him, and he could handle that arrangement.

Chapter Eight

Cheyenne

Cheyenne propped her elbows on the desk and rested her head in her hands. What was she doing? She was doing a great job of pushing Ridge away and not so great of a job getting to know him like she was supposed to do.

Focus. You can do this. So what if he's scary? That self-defense class from the YMCA might come in handy.

She needed to push her personal biases aside and do what she was here to do. David seemed to think Cheyenne would be able to get Ridge to open up, but she was seriously doubting her ability to do that at all.

Cheyenne lifted her head. Two more unread emails sat in her inbox. Another registration, which she'd learned to input and account for in the database, and an email from Ava.

Ava was quickly becoming Cheyenne's hero. The woman seemed to have her hand in everything at the ranch, and she did it all like it was as easy as walking. Little mishaps and last-minute changes didn't rattle her. She adapted and improvised until the problem was solved. If Ava was the successful woman Cheyenne wanted to be, she had a long row to hoe.

Cheyenne clicked the email from Ava and scanned the message. Instructions on how to clock in and clock out, the dining hall menu for the rest of the month, and the contact for the company delivering the fill dirt and riprap to repair the path to the barn tomorrow.

If you get caught up in the office, Ridge will need your help with other things. He can show you how to do anything, and he's a really great guy. I'm telling you this in case he's been quiet today. He likes to keep to himself, but don't confuse his silence for rudeness. This program is important to him, and I know you're going to be a good teammate for him.

Teammate. Ridge felt more like an opponent than a teammate.

And that was her fault. She rested her head in her hands again. It was her first day, and she'd completely messed up the one relationship she was supposed to carefully cultivate.

Cheyenne closed everything and shut down the laptop. It was time to face the music, or, in this case, the scary but gentle giant she was supposed to befriend.

She'd started off the morning accusing him of being late, snapping at Bethany, and basically calling him sexist. Maybe he would agree to start over. She needed to find out if his boy scout act was real or a put on because the things she'd read and the things she'd seen from him didn't match up.

She stepped into the open area of the barn. Ridge and Brett were at the other end tearing out rotted boards on the farthest stall. Half of the wall was new and straight. To her surprise, Brett did have his shirt on.

"Anything I can do to help?" she asked, shoving her hands in her back pockets.

Ridge looked over his shoulder. Sweat beaded on his neck, and he'd rolled his sleeves up to the elbows. "There's a magnet in the tack room across from the office. You could grab it and pick up the loose nails. Most of them are still in the old boards, but we need to get them all up before the kids get here."

"Magnet. Got it."

She strode to the other end of the barn and peeked into the room across from the office. She'd read about tack and storage in the blogs she'd studied, but this was her first time seeing one in person. It was organized in the same way as most of the photos.

"If I were a magnet, where would I be?" Propped up against the wall beside the door was a metal rod with a thick magnet on the bottom. She grabbed it and headed back out to where Ridge and Brett were working.

After running it back and forth over the area, she had a handful of old, rusty nails. "Where do you want these?"

Ridge looked over his shoulder. "You can put them in the cupholder in my truck."

Cheyenne did as she was told and returned to where Ridge and Brett were working. "Anything else I can do?"

Ridge lifted his hat and wiped his arm over his brow. He looked around for a few seconds. "Do you think you could load these old boards into the bed of my truck? I'm going to burn them later."

She looked at the pile of broken pieces of wood. "Sure."

"Gloves are in the tack room."

Cheyenne jogged back to the tack room and found the gloves. She slid them on as she approached the pile. The pieces were broken and fairly light, and she fell into the monotony of doing the same motion over and over. Soon, she'd forgotten all about Ridge and her purpose.

Brett chatted the entire time they worked, and Cheyenne listened, in case he mentioned something about Ridge. Brett asked her a few questions, and she told him the truth about everything. She needed to be open if she ever expected Ridge to do the same for her.

Soon, her shoulder was aching from tossing the boards, and a sticky sweat dripped down her back. It wasn't terribly hard work, but she'd been at it for an hour, and the guys hadn't stopped throwing boards on the pile she'd been trying to dwindle.

Finally, Brett stood and checked his watch. "I told Jess I'd help her with her last lesson. I'll be back tomorrow to fill in the trail."

Ridge jammed the prying end of a hammer behind a board and pulled it off. "Thanks, man. Take it easy."

Brett stepped up to Cheyenne and winked at her. "It was nice to meet you. Can I get your number so I–"

"Bye, Brett!" Ridge shouted over his shoulder.

Brett leaned toward Cheyenne and whispered, "I'll see you tomorrow."

She grinned and waved at Brett. He really was a nice guy. She wasn't getting any creepy vibes from him.

She was watching Brett walk to his truck when Ridge cleared his throat. She jerked her attention back to him and stifled her smile. Brett was good-looking. He was friendly and always smiling. Unfortunately, Ridge had a rugged handsome look that Cheyenne hadn't been able to ignore.

"You going to keep studying Brett's jeans or get to work?"

A giggle bubbled up Cheyenne's throat. "Sorry. He's nice."

Ridge huffed and kept working.

Picking up a board, Cheyenne asked, "So, what does Brett do around the ranch?"

Ridge cut a glance to her before turning back to his work. "He and his sister, Jess, manage the main stables. He's also in charge of the rodeos on Friday nights."

"Rodeos? Here?" she asked.

"Yeah. It's the kids. Remi and Jess get them acquainted with the horses during the week, and they get to show their parents what they've been learning on Friday night. Brett and Colt usually do some calf roping too."

Cheyenne rested her gloved hands on her hips and took a breather. "That sounds like fun. What did you do at the ranch before you started helping with this program?"

He was silent, and her palms itched in the gloves as she waited.

"I was just a ranch hand. I did the hard jobs no one else wanted to do."

Cheyenne watched him, searching for any lie tells, but she wasn't sure if he was lying, being vague, or telling the truth.

"I thought you'd been here a while. Shouldn't you have moved up in the ranks?"

Ridge shook his head slightly but didn't look up at her. "I don't care about moving up, and I don't mind the work."

She was supposed to be finding out what Ridge *did* care about, and now she knew what he *didn't* care about. Her sleuthing skills were terrible. Nancy Drew would hang her head in shame.

Cheyenne shifted her weight from one side to the other. The new boots were unforgiving, and they were rubbing her heels in all the wrong places. "You like being a cowboy?"

Ridge looked over his shoulder before turning back around without answering.

Why was he so difficult to talk to? Couldn't he make it a little easier to get to know him? She opened her mouth to spit a snappy comment when he spoke.

"I like it enough." He stood and wiped his arm over the side of his face. "We need to spread hay in the stalls." He pointed with the handle of the hammer to a wheelbarrow just inside the barn.

Cheyenne tugged off the gloves. "Okay. Show me what to do."

Ridge held out a hand toward her. "Leave those on."

"They're a little too big."

"They're better than nothing. I'll pick up a smaller pair for you tomorrow."

She stuffed her hands back into the hot gloves. "Whatever you say."

They spent the next half hour spreading hay on the floor of the stalls. Ridge spoke to give instructions but didn't say anything else. He hadn't said anything earlier when Brett had basically talked to himself while they worked. Brett hadn't seemed irritated by Ridge's silence.

Cheyenne, however, was irritated, and she gave up asking questions once it was clear Ridge wasn't going to give her more than short answers.

Ridge's phone rang, and he pulled off a glove to answer it. "Hello."

Cheyenne kept working but listened intently. Unfortunately, Ridge's side of the conversation consisted of, "Yeah." She chuckled as he disconnected the call without even saying "Bye."

"Jameson needs me to meet him at the front office. It's close to quitting time, so I'll take you back to your car."

Cheyenne removed her gloves and pulled her phone from the back pocket of her jeans. "It's 4:30."

"I don't know how long this meeting with Jameson will take. He's the foreman, and he didn't say what he needed. I don't want to leave you over here alone without a way to get back to your car."

Cheyenne sighed. She was tired, and she didn't have the energy to argue with Ridge's logic. "Okay. Let me get my purse."

By the time she met Ridge back outside the barn, he'd put away everything and leaned on the passenger side of the truck, waiting on her.

"You win," she said as she walked up.

Ridge quirked a brow. "What do you mean?"

"You've been trying to open the door for me all day."

Ridge opened the truck door and gestured for her to get in. "You didn't make it easy."

She rolled her eyes, but her mouth stretched into a grin. She climbed into the seat and turned back to him. "You don't have to open my door for me. I'd actually appreciate it if you didn't."

Ridge narrowed his eyes. One hand rested on the truck and the other gripped the open door. "Why?"

"Because it's out of your way, and now I know you're willing to do it. I appreciate it, but I want to pull my own weight around here."

Ridge nodded and said, "Okay," before closing the door. He walked around and got in on the driver's side. He started the truck and looked at her. He didn't shift into gear. He just looked at her until her skin heated.

Why did she feel so scrutinized when he looked at her? It was like he could see her duplicity, her malicious intent.

She was supposed to betray him. What if he knew?

"You ready to quit yet?" he asked.

Cheyenne kept her gaze locked with his. "Not even close."

Seemingly satisfied with her answer, he shifted into gear and started toward the main house.

"How long are you going to be out here working today?" she asked.

He kept his attention on the bumpy path ahead. "Until I feel like going home."

"Do you live on the ranch?"

Ridge just shook his head.

"Why not? Some of the ranch hands do, don't they?"

"They do. I don't," was Ridge's short answer.

"Why not? You seem to like it here."

"I do. Housing is hard to find around here, and the other guys need it more than I do."

"Will you live in the new cabins when they're finished?" she asked.

"No."

His one-word answer hurt her more than it should. She'd really messed up her first impression today. It shouldn't feel personal when he snubbed her questions, but it did.

Ridge parked beside Cheyenne's car at the main house and killed the engine. "Don't forget your shoes." He pointed with his thumb to the back seat.

"And my hat." She reached into the back seat for the items. "I didn't even wear it today."

"We didn't work outside, but we will soon. You'll want to bring it every day or leave it here."

Cheyenne put her hand on the door handle and stopped. Ridge wasn't trying to beat her to the door this time.

"Cheyenne?"

She turned back to him. "Yes."

The defeated look on his face had her tightening her grip on the door.

"Want to start over tomorrow?" he asked.

Relief had her gasping in a deep breath, and moisture filled her eyes. "I'd love that."

Ridge took off his hat and tossed it on the dash before running a hand through his hair. "You did good today."

Cheyenne chuckled. "I'm not the grammar police, but I think you mean to say I did well."

"No. I meant what I said. You were good to everyone."

"Except Bethany," Cheyenne added. She looked up at the door of the check-in office. "Should I go apologize to her now?"

"That's up to you, but don't expect her to have an instant change of heart. She's not going to be as eager for a do-over as I am."

"Thanks for everything today. I know I wasn't the best, but I'll be better tomorrow."

Ridge grinned at her, and that heart-stopping expression should have been illegal. He was even better looking with messy hair after a day of work.

"Meet you here at seven in the morning?" he asked.

"Sounds good."

Ridge turned to get out and stopped short. "I'll be on time tomorrow. Promise."

Cheyenne laughed. "And I'll be on my best behavior."

"Deal."

They got out, and Ridge waved as they went their separate ways.

Cheyenne watched him walk into the check-in office and decided it probably wasn't a good idea to walk in with Ridge when she went to apologize to Bethany. She'd get here early in the morning to talk to her.

Tossing her hat, shoes, and purse into her car, Cheyenne exhaled a long sigh of relief when she sat in the driver's seat. She'd made it through her first day, and she wouldn't call it a complete loss.

Her hands shook as she raised them to take the wheel. Now came the hard part. She was supposed to call Jaden and give a report every night, but her instincts told her to hold onto every little detail she found out about Ridge.

Her mom needed the money. Hadley needed the money. Those were the reasons she'd agreed to help David.

But an equally strong part of her heart said it was wrong, and she would regret turning her back on Ridge Cooper.

Chapter Nine

Ridge

Don't turn around. Don't turn around.

Ridge turned around just as Cheyenne got into her car. His impulse control was slipping today. At least she'd agreed to the do-over. He'd fortify his defenses before morning. Cheyenne had taken up too much of his headspace today, which probably meant he hadn't been busy enough.

At least, he hoped that was the problem.

Ridge stepped into the check-in office, and Bethany squealed before he closed the door behind him.

"Ridge! It's good to see you!"

What was she going on about? She'd seen him this morning. Instead of reminding her about that less-than-friendly run-in with Cheyenne, he hung his hat on the hook by the door and forced a grin. "It's good to see you too."

Bethany pranced around the desk to meet him. "Want to go to the fire pit tonight? I get off work in twenty minutes."

Ridge took a step back and to the side. "I've still got a lot of work to do before I call it a day."

Bethany rolled her eyes, but her playful smile didn't falter. "Like what?"

"I'm headed to meet with Jameson now."

"Then you'll be done?" she asked.

Good grief. He was going to have to spell it out for her before she got the message. "I have a lot to do before the program starts next week. I won't be sitting around a fire pit for a while."

Bethany's shoulders sank. "Right. Well, let me know when you're free. We could go somewhere besides the ranch."

"Ridge!" Stella shouted as she burst into the room with her arms wide. "How was the new girl's first day?"

Ridge opened his arms for Stella's full-on hug. She was probably in her sixties, and while her greetings were always touchy, he was glad he didn't have to worry about letting her down easily.

Bethany, on the other hand, was going to have to be beat off with a stick–something he hadn't needed to do since coming to the ranch. Keeping a good distance from the guests lessened his chances of getting recognized and also cut down on female attention.

"She managed okay," Ridge said.

Stella pulled back and huffed an exaggerated sigh. "Use your words, stud. What do you think about her?"

Bethany's glare rivaled some of the looks he'd gotten from coaches right before they fell into a screaming fit and turned red-faced. This was dangerous territory. If Stella's prying question had made him itchy, Bethany's simmering anger at the mention of Cheyenne might set the place on fire.

Ridge shifted his weight toward Stella, eager to put distance between Bethany and himself. "She handled the work well enough today. Aside from that, I don't think much about her."

Lie. That was a lie. He'd been thinking about Cheyenne all day. It was stupid. He shouldn't care so much about her, but the blasted woman was a mystery.

Stella's grin widened. "Are you sure? Ava showed me her picture. She's a looker."

A looker? Ridge barely stifled a chuckle at Stella's outdated slang, but she had a point. Cheyenne was a knockout, and her willingness to work today made him more attracted to her.

But his focus was the program, and his attraction would fade after they worked together for a while. At least, that's what he hoped.

"She is attractive."

He didn't dare look at Bethany.

"Tell me more. Spill the beans," Stella said as she shoved his arm. "I'm not getting any younger, and someone around here should be getting some action."

Bethany gasped. "Stella!"

"Oh, you know I don't mean it in a dirty way. I just mean you younger folks should be flirting and dating and telling me about it after. Throw me a bone or something."

Stella and her husband used to visit the ranch every year, and when her husband died, she came back to stay for good. Ridge didn't have a clue what it was like to lose someone like that, but Stella wasn't the kind to wallow in grief. She kept everyone at the ranch on their toes and was always urging someone to get out and live life to the fullest.

If Ridge survived this conversation with red-faced Bethany and intrusive Stella, he deserved an award.

Please, Lord. Save me from this conversation. "I don't know much about her yet, but why don't you ask her to have lunch with you one day? I don't think she's met too many people here yet."

"Well, she was pretty snippy to me this morning. Who does she think she is coming in and acting like she owns the place?" Bethany said.

"She was probably overwhelmed. Ava had her signing papers for a while, and it's not easy starting a new job," Ridge said, unsure why he was rushing to her defense.

"I'm sure she didn't mean to be rude," Stella said. "Lincoln is stern like that, and he's just a big ol' teddy bear on the inside."

Stern was a mild description of Lincoln. Ridge liked working with him because he got straight to the job, but the guy had a few tells. Ridge would bet his first million that Lincoln had spent time in prison.

"Oh, I'll be asking her to lunch," Stella said. "I'll find out all about her and get back to you." She nudged Ridge with her elbow and gave him an exaggerated wink.

"Could you maybe not–"

"I won't," Stella said with a raised hand. "Your secrets are safe with me."

"Why don't you want anyone knowing you were a football star?" Bethany asked.

"Because it's the past." That was partly true, but he hadn't seen the need to give Bethany the whole story yet. She hadn't proven trustworthy enough either. She could find out for herself, but she likely wouldn't take the time to search.

"Oh," Bethany drawled. "I bet you were a player. You know, in more ways than one." She smirked at her play on words.

"Not exactly," Ridge huffed.

The whole idea that players were constant partiers was all smoke and mirrors. Sure, some fell off the wagon and into the party lifestyle, but the ones who made it past the first season took care of their health and didn't have time to recover from a hangover when practice started early.

That lifestyle didn't appeal to Ridge anyway. What kind of man would willingly want his judgment to be impaired? He wasn't controlling of many things, but control of his mind and body was a must.

"What do you mean a player? Ridge is a good man," Stella said.

"I know that, but most guys like to party," Bethany said with a shrug.

Stella patted the side of Ridge's arm and smiled. "You need to find a good woman and think about settling down. I just know you're going to do a great job with this youth program, but wouldn't you like to have kids of your own?"

Nope. He wasn't giving an honest answer to that one. Stella meant well, but his indecision about having a family and kids was more complicated than a simple yes or no.

He wanted a family–badly. But he wasn't sure he could trust anyone enough to spend the rest of his life with her. So many players in the NFL got married when they thought it sounded like fun and split up just as fast. Add kids into the mix, and it always ended nasty.

His own parents were a model couple. They were unwaveringly supportive, loving, and kind. Sure, they had their occasional disagreement, but he hadn't met another couple who lived up to that level of commitment.

Ridge would be better off steering clear, just to be on the safe side.

"Maybe one day," Ridge said before pointing at the hallway behind the women. "Jameson is expecting me."

"Oh, go, go," Stella said, waving him on by. "I'll let you know what I find out about Cheyenne."

"Thanks, but that's not necessary. She was kind of quiet today, so she might be shy or something."

Cheyenne was far from shy, but maybe he could steer Stella away from running the new girl off.

Stella clicked her tongue behind her teeth. "Shy won't last long around here."

Ridge shook his head. Who was he kidding? Stella would dig her claws in and hang on whenever she got her paws on Cheyenne.

"Bye. See you tomorrow," Bethany said with all of her usual pep. Her irritation hadn't lasted long.

Ridge slipped down the hallway and knocked on the doorframe of the foreman's office. "Knock, knock."

Jameson looked up from his computer for a second before turning back to it. "Hey, man. How many hours can you realistically put in for the ranch next week? I'm working on the schedule."

"The kids are here from nine till four Monday through Friday. I was planning to be here around five to get things ready and stay until suppertime. It shouldn't take me long to get everything set up, so I'm hoping to spare an hour in the morning and an hour or two in the evening for whatever else you need."

Jameson nodded and typed something in. "I'll mark you for nine hours a day for the program and three for the ranch. Sound good?"

"You got it." Now there would be no spare time to sit around thinking about Cheyenne.

Jameson stood and walked around his desk. "Now, I have something cool to show you." He rolled out a blueprint on a long table under the window and placed a rock on both ends. "We got the updated design on the new barn."

Ridge rested a hand on the end of the table and studied the drawing. "If you'd told me eight years ago I'd one day be geeked up to build a barn, I would have called you nuts."

"Look at you now," Jameson said as he shoved Ridge's shoulder.

Ridge shook his head. "What were the changes again?"

Jameson pointed to the print. "We moved this wall back to make room for a bigger horse shower. Jess said she wished the one at the main barn was bigger, so we're going to have to grant that wish soon. Then we added extra room for supply lockers on this side, moved the wash station to the other side, expanded the office, and added a closet in it."

Ridge calculated the dimensions in his head. "What's the upcharge? That's an extra forty square feet."

"Not much." Jameson slid a paper over the prints with the new quote.

Ridge stood and clapped a hand on Jameson's back. "Sounds good. Let's do it."

"You sure about this?" Jameson asked.

"Of course I'm sure. Why wouldn't I be?"

Jameson looked out the window at the expanse of the ranch. "Nothing is keeping you here."

"I'm not being held hostage. I want this." Ridge pointed to the blueprints.

"Got it. Just wanted to make sure you know. Mr. Chambers is thrilled about the new program, and we know you're the best man for the job."

Ridge huffed. "I have no experience with kids."

Of all the things that went into starting this program, his lack of experience with kids was the one thing that gave him pause. Cheyenne didn't have experience either, which only added to Ridge's concerns.

"You'll do fine. The kids will be excited to be here, and you have a lot to teach them." Jameson leaned his back against the wall and crossed his arms over his chest. "How did Cheyenne do today?"

Back to Cheyenne. "She made it. We'll see if she shows up tomorrow."

Jameson chuckled. "That bad?"

"It's just an adjustment. I wish she'd started earlier so she could get used to the ranch before the kids get here."

Jameson shook his head. "We didn't have many applicants."

"I know, and I hope Ava is right about Cheyenne. The biggest strike against her is that she's too much like me."

Ava shouted from her office across the hallway, "She's going to be great! Trust me!"

Jameson pushed off the wall and stepped back behind his desk. "Ava is right. That's not a bad thing that Cheyenne is like you. If you're talking about determination, that's what we need."

"I hope you're right."

Ridge's phone dinged in his pocket, and he pulled it out to see Blake's name on the screen.

Blake: Everly is making dinner tonight. She wants to grill you about the new woman.

Ridge groaned. Did the people around here not have anything better to talk about than

Cheyenne? "I have to head out. I'm late for another interrogation."

Chapter Ten

Cheyenne

Cheyenne grunted as she dragged a bag of horse feed from the bed of Jess's truck into the wheelbarrow. No one talked about how heavy everything was at a ranch, and despite Jess's small stature, the woman didn't have a problem throwing her weight around.

Cheyenne's first days at the ranch consisted of gasping for air, groaning, and achy muscles. And sleep. Lots of sleep. She'd almost slept through her alarm this morning.

The rumble of a truck echoed through the barn, and Cheyenne lifted the wheelbarrow. Ridge was back from picking up the lumber they'd be using to build the raised beds, and she wasn't sure if she wanted to cheer or cry. He'd either be helping her unload the feed or he'd have something else to add to the long list of things that needed to be done.

A sharp prick stuck into her neck, and she dropped the handles. Grunting, she clawed at the collar of her shirt.

"Is it the hay?" Jess asked.

Cheyenne had been relieved to work with Jess today. The barn manager was straight to the point about everything, and Cheyenne was able to relax when Ridge wasn't around. Her thoughts on him were still scrambled, and the more time she spent with him, the more she wanted to know. Too bad he was being tight-lipped.

Or maybe that was a good thing. She didn't have anything incriminating to share with Jaden yet.

Cheyenne scratched her neck, but the annoying pricking didn't let up. "Does it do this to you?"

Jess shrugged. "You get used to it. Just try not to let it ruin your day."

Cheyenne groaned. "I'm going to invest in a bodysuit so the hay can't get under my clothes."

Jess let out a bubbly laugh. "Good luck with that. Wait till it gets in your boots!"

"What are you two laughing about?"

Cheyenne quieted at Ridge's words. She'd seen him driving up, but she hadn't heard him walking in. "Hay."

"Hey," Ridge replied.

Cheyenne shook her head and chuckled again. "No, we were talking about hay."

Jess jerked her head toward Cheyenne. "Your girl here has an itch she can't scratch."

Cheyenne glared at Jess. Now Ridge was going to think she was a complainer. "I'm fine. I just didn't realize I would be medicating with antihistamines every night after work."

"Welcome to the first year on a ranch," Ridge said.

Cheyenne gasped. "A year?"

No, she was not going to let that crippling fact beat her today, but good grief did she want to sit down and throw a hissy fit. The itching hadn't stopped since spreading the hay yesterday, muscles she didn't even know she had ached, and the over-the-counter medication was making her tired all the time.

Ridge squinted. She could see pity coming from a mile away, and she did not want him feeling sorry for her.

"Um, how long have you been out here without your long-sleeve shirt on?"

Cheyenne frowned at him. "Since right before lunch. Why?" She'd gotten hot in her long sleeves when they were putting the fire pit together, and she'd conveniently worn a tank top underneath her sweater.

Ridge pointed to her shoulder, and she turned to look. Her skin was the color of a ripe tomato.

"Are you kidding me? I was out there for maybe two hours. I've been working inside the barn since."

Jess sucked in air through her teeth. "You can still get burnt when it doesn't feel hot out."

Ridge jerked his head toward the office. "There's a bottle of burn relief in the bottom drawer of my desk."

Cheyenne reached for the next feed bag. "I'll get it after we finish unloading the truck." She ignored the telltale wobble in her voice that said she was about to lose it.

Just as she grabbed the bag, Ridge placed his hand over hers, stilling her in an instant. His hand was almost twice the size of hers, and his hard chest pressed against her shoulder.

Her heart pounded in her chest. If she looked up, she'd be nose-to-nose with Ridge.

"I'll finish this. Please put something on that sunburn before it starts hurting."

Cheyenne stared at his hand on top of hers. Why did he have to care about her sunburn? Why was he offering to do the job she'd started?

Why did he have to be nice?

"There are only a couple of bags left. Take care of that sunburn, and we'll call it a day." Ridge's soft words were close to her ear, but she didn't dare turn to him.

Instead, she slid her hand from beneath his and whispered a soft, "Okay" as she headed toward the office. She kept her chin up, determined to chase away the defeat that had her chest tightening.

She found the gel right where Ridge had said it would be and squirted it into her hand. The slimy glob filled her palm. Sighing, she unscrewed the cap to pour some back into the bottle. A quick assessment said only her shoulders, arms, and chest were scorched. She didn't need to bathe in the stuff.

Once she'd slathered the gel on her skin, she headed out to the toilet building. It was basically an outhouse, but she refused to call it that. Jess said they'd put in the small tank in the eighties when they'd used this part of the ranch for the injured horses while they were in therapy. They'd had a therapist on staff back then, and even a chiropractor. Cheyenne had never heard of a horse chiropractor until today, and the silly thought chased away some of her frustration.

She stepped into the small bathroom, washed the gel from her hands, and checked her reflection in the mirror. Okay, maybe Ridge had cause for concern. Her shoulders were fire-engine red.

Her phone dinged, and she pulled it out to see a text from Sadie. Cheyenne had only been in Wyoming a few days, and she was already missing her friend.

Sadie: Praying your first few days have been great. Send pics when you get a chance.

Cheyenne smiled. It was just like Sadie to send encouraging messages.

Cheyenne took one look around the bathroom stall. She'd hidden away long enough, and she hadn't taken one single photo of the ranch since she'd arrived.

When she stepped outside, Ridge was walking out of the barn carrying a square bale of hay on one shoulder. How did he do that, and how did he make it look so easy?

Without thinking, Cheyenne raised her phone and snapped a photo of Ridge. He hadn't noticed her yet, and his determined stance and serious expression were straight out of an ad for Wrangler jeans.

She understood the appeal, really. Ridge was insanely attractive, and his brooding persona only added to the allure. But she couldn't forget what had happened to her mom, and Cheyenne wasn't going to let a pretty face break her heart.

Instead of sending the photo to Sadie, Cheyenne turned to the east and snapped a scene of the hills leading to the main house. She sent the photo with a short message.

Cheyenne: It's beautiful here. Keep the prayers coming.

Slipping the phone back into her pocket, she met Ridge at the supply shed. They'd been stocking the barn and shed all day, and the dimly lit building was getting crowded. Especially when Ridge was around. He tended to take up a lot of space in any room.

"What can I do to help?" she asked.

Ridge turned around and wiped the sweat from his brow. "I think we're done for the day. You can clock out when you're ready."

Cheyenne leaned against the doorframe and crossed her arms over her chest. "And when will you be clocking out?"

Ridge shrugged and continued working. "I don't know. Why?"

"Just wondering. I'm starting to think you actually do live here. You're here when I get here in the mornings–early, I might add–and you never leave at five."

He looked over his shoulder and smirked at her. "I leave when I get tired of working."

"So you like to work ten-hour days?" she asked.

Ridge turned around and gave her his full attention. His gaze swept down her body and then up. "Why are you worried about it?"

Why *was* she worried about it? She didn't have the slightest clue, but she wanted to know what made him work this hard from dawn to dusk. Seeing him break his back every day was humbling, and her respect for him was growing despite her better judgment. "I could help you. Just tell me what I can do."

Ridge stared at her, causing her skin to heat from her head to her toes.

No, it wasn't the sunburn.

After one too many seconds of silence, Ridge cleared his throat. "I'm just not ready to go home yet. When I am, I'll quit for the day." He turned back to the shelves filled with horse medication and ointments.

Cheyenne pushed off the doorframe and stepped closer to him. "Are you homeless?"

Ridge chuckled. "What? No."

"You sure?"

"I'm sure. Actually, one of the wranglers here is moving in with me soon."

"Which one?" she asked.

"Colt."

"I haven't met him. Is he real?"

Ridge turned to her, and a half-smile played on his lips. "He's real."

She forced herself to breathe, and the musty air wasn't doing anything to calm her racing heart. "So, until he moves in, you're lonely?"

"I didn't say I was lonely!"

Cheyenne held up her hands and laughed. "Easy, player. I was joking."

Ridge halted and stared at her. Why was he looking at her like that? What had she said?

Player. That wasn't a slip, was it? It didn't mean football player. It was just a generic nickname.

Cheyenne backed toward the shed door. She had to get out before he questioned her, but the heel of her boot caught on something, and her body tipped back. Her eyes widened, and her stomach flipped, preparing to hit the ground hard.

Her body jerked to a stop as his arms wrapped around her. Suspended a foot above the dirt-covered floor, she stared up at Ridge. Even in the dim light, she didn't miss the way his gaze dropped to her mouth before returning to her eyes.

"Are you okay?" his deep voice rumbled, and she was close enough to feel the vibrations of his words.

"Yeah." The word was barely a whisper. She was stuck in a trance with Ridge so close.

Suddenly, he cleared his throat and broke the stare that had her in a daze. In one sweeping motion, she was back on her feet. Ridge released his tight embrace, and his hands moved to her arms, barely touching her sunburned skin. The gentle touch was a contradiction from the violence she'd been led to expect.

And the fear she'd been walking around with lately? It was nowhere to be found. Instead, a comforting peace settled around her.

Cheyenne took a deep breath and broke the trance. "Okay, you're not lonely, and you don't need help. I get it. Thanks for saving me. I'll see you in the morning."

She'd barely made it out the door before Ridge's heavy footfalls were chasing after her.

"Cheyenne."

The bright sunshine was a contrast to the dimly lit shed, and when she turned, there was no mistaking the expression on his face.

Desire.

She swallowed hard and prayed he wouldn't come past the doorway. Prayed he wouldn't question her about the slipup. Prayed he wouldn't say anything to tear down the walls she was building to keep him at a safe distance. Prayed he hadn't picked up on the racing of her heart.

Her prayers were answered, but only in part.

"Thanks for offering to help," he said.

Offering to help wasn't a big deal. Cheyenne inhaled a deep breath and smiled. "No problem."

"And be careful."

That she would. "I will. Thanks."

She turned and walked back to the barn, consciously trying not to run. She needed to get out of here.

In the office, she grabbed her purse and hung her hat on the hook before heading out to her car. When the rumble of the engine covered her voice, she said, "Why does he have to be so nice? Why does he have to care?" She let her head fall until her forehead rested on the steering wheel. "Why does he have to be so good-looking?"

She raised her head, flung the gear into reverse, and backed away from the barn. Ridge Cooper was messing with her head. It was the care about her sunburn, and the concern about her lifting heavy things, and the asking if she remembered to eat lunch. Why did he care?

With the windows down, she drove slowly over the newly repaired path back toward the main house. The closer she got to the bustling center of the ranch, the more she wanted to turn around. Despite the tiring work, she was enjoying her days here. Guests strolled along the side paths, and wranglers laughed with groups beneath the shade of the trees. No wonder the same people came back year after year.

In just a few weeks, Cheyenne would have her own place at the ranch. The little cabin Ridge had showed her hadn't left her thoughts for long. It was perfect.

And yet, she'd have to move in, spy on her boss, and get out of Dodge before he came after her. The thought made her sick to her stomach.

She drove slowly through the streets of Blackwater. Just as she approached the hotel, she spotted Sticky Sweets and made a quick decision to stop for a bite. Ridge said the dining hall was open to all ranch employees, but she hadn't worked up the courage to eat a meal there yet.

Inside the bakery, the warm smell of baking bread and spices greeted her along with the older lady at the register.

"Hi there! What can I get for you?"

Cheyenne looked up at the menu on the wall behind the counter. "Can I get the breakfast sandwich, please?"

"Bacon or sausage?"

"Bacon."

"Drink of choice?"

Cheyenne looked at the refrigerator case by the counter. "I'll have a bottle of water."

The woman rang up the sale and gave Cheyenne the total. "Did I see you in here with Ridge the other day?"

Cheyenne grinned at the woman she'd watched Ridge talk to when he brought her here. "You did. I just started working with him at the ranch."

"Tracy," the woman said as she extended a hand.

"Cheyenne. It's good to meet you." She shook Tracy's hand and pulled her wallet out of her purse.

"We're all so excited about the new program he's starting for the kids. Bless that man, he's a hard worker."

If Cheyenne hadn't gotten the impression Tracy was a fan of Ridge before, she knew it for certain now. "Do you know him well?"

"Sure. Everyone knows him," Tracy said. "He goes to church with my daughter and her family, and he comes in on Sunday mornings about once a month to get cinnamon rolls for the kids in Sunday School.

Cheyenne smiled, but her chest grew tighter. She handed over the payment for her food. "That's so sweet."

"Sure is. I'll have this order out to you in a jiffy. Grab a bottle of water there and find a seat."

The bakery wasn't as busy now as it had been when Ridge brought her during the lunch rush. Five of the tables were taken, and she found an empty two-seater table near the back wall. Her phone rang as soon as she sat down. She pulled it out of her pocket and answered the call from her sister.

"Hello."

"How was the job today?" Hadley asked in her usual peppy tone.

"It's been good."

There was silence on the line. Then Hadley sighed. "Please tell me more. I need to live vicariously through you."

"You should be the one here. You'd love it, and you'd be so much better at this than I am."

"No way. You're going to rock this. It's going to be fun! Enjoy it!"

Fun? Cheyenne couldn't see any fun in her future. In fact, a dark cloud was hovering over her wherever she went.

"The ranch is beautiful. The weather is nice, and I got a nasty sunburn today."

"Did you ride a horse?" Hadley asked.

"Not yet, but I'm assuming I'll have to eventually."

Hadley squealed. "That's going to be so awesome. Tell me more."

Cheyenne bit the inside of her cheek. There were so many good things she could say about the ranch. The people were great, the Big Horn Mountains and the valleys were huge and breathtaking, Ridge had been good to her and taught her so many things already.

Tracy appeared at the table and handed Cheyenne a plate with an enormous breakfast sandwich on top. "Enjoy. Let me know if you need anything else."

"Who was that?" Hadley asked.

Cheyenne smiled up at Tracy and said, "Thank you." She'd thought Tracy would call her name to come pick up the order at the counter when it was ready, but apparently, they had table service at Sticky Sweets when it wasn't busy. "I'm at a bakery."

"You're eating dinner at a bakery?"

"It's right across from my hotel, and I've heard they have a good breakfast sandwich."

"You're eating breakfast for dinner? You hate breakfast for dinner," Hadley said. "Who are you, and what have you done with my sister?"

Cheyenne stared at the sandwich. It did look good. "Trying something new isn't bad."

"No, but it's not like you. I'm glad you're stepping out though. You need something different."

"Why? What's wrong with the way things are?" Cheyenne asked. Her life was fine. It was working, and why would she rock the boat?

"You've never been one to go after your dreams or chase happiness. It's okay to do that. Things have been hard lately, and I worry about you."

"I'm fine. I promise. I worry about *you*. I hate that I left you to handle things there on your own."

Hadley scoffed. "Everything is fine here. Seriously, it's cool. And it's okay for you to enjoy this new opportunity."

Guilt. Again. The job at the ranch was something Hadley would love, and she'd thrive here. Cheyenne was here to be devious and betray her boss.

"How is Mom?" Cheyenne asked.

"She's good. She got the approval for the move to the new facility today."

Finally, some good news. The first thing Cheyenne had done when she got the check from Lang Corp. was submit an application at the best long-term care facility in east Tennessee. "That's great!"

"And Sadie wanted me to tell you she misses you, but she's so happy you got the job."

"It's all thanks to her. Did she tell you she let me borrow her shirt and laptop for the interview?"

Hadley laughed, and the joyous sound eased the tension in Cheyenne's shoulders. "No, but that sounds like her. We were lucky to have her around through all this with Mom."

"That's the truth." Cheyenne hadn't been praying for a friend at the time, but she'd been thanking the Lord for sending Sadie ever since the interview.

A muffled voice came over the line from Hadley's side of the call. "I've got to get back to work. Talk to you soon, sis."

"Love you."

"Love you, too."

Cheyenne put the phone down and picked up the sandwich. As soon as the first bite was in her mouth, she knew why Ridge was stuck on this one menu option. Toasted bread, crispy bacon, and a perfectly cooked fried egg. She wanted to savor every bite. The ham sandwich she'd brought for lunch was long gone and looking pathetic compared to this masterpiece.

Her phone on the table rang, and Jaden's name lit up on the screen. Cheyenne wiped her mouth with a napkin and picked up the phone. "Hello."

"Hey, Cheyenne. Is this a good time?"

Cheyenne looked up to see Tracy wiping a table nearby. Tracy clearly trusted Ridge, and the man Cheyenne had seen these last few days validated that kindness the woman had shown him. If she hadn't seen all the evidence, it would be easy to believe Ridge was the great guy Tracy liked.

Which side of him was the true Ridge?

"I'm actually having dinner at a little bakery right now. Can I call you back in fifteen minutes?"

"Sure," Jaden said.

When Cheyenne ended the call, she stared at the phone. What was she going to tell Jaden?

Chapter Eleven

Cheyenne

Cheyenne parked next to Ridge's truck outside the south barn. The faint light of dawn was just beginning to color the sky over the towering eastern mountains, but she'd passed a handful of wranglers milling about at the main barn and dining hall on her way in. Grabbing her purse and her pullover for later, she breathed in the still of the morning before stepping into the barn.

Things were quiet inside, but Ridge was no doubt well into whatever project he'd started. She'd been getting to work earlier each day, but she still hadn't beat him to the office.

She peeked into a few of the stalls before shouting, "Ridge?"

"Tack room!" he yelled from the other side of the barn.

Cheyenne put her things in the office and made her way to the tack room. Ridge was doing something with a saddle. Was he buffing it? Waxing it? Who knew? She leaned against the doorframe and crossed her arms over her chest.

When Ridge looked up from his task, a small smile lifted his mouth at the ends. "Morning. You're early."

"So are you. I just haven't figured out how early. Do you sleep in the hay loft?"

Ridge stood and wiped his hands on the rag from his back pocket. "I sleep in a bed–my bed–just like everyone else."

"I stopped by Sticky Sweets last night. Tracy kept going on and on about how much she adores you. And you're telling me the Blackwater famous Ridge Cooper puts his pants on one leg at a time like everyone else?"

He took a step toward her, and his gaze swept down her body and back up. It was quick, but with her focus all on the grinning man in front of her, she couldn't have missed it.

Good. It helped to know she wasn't the only one affected.

"Give Tracy a week, and she'll be singing your praises too."

"I tried the breakfast sandwich," Cheyenne said.

Ridge's brows rose. "And?"

"And you were right. It was delicious. Tracy deserves an award."

Ridge's gaze slipped to her mouth before he cleared his throat and turned back to the saddle resting on a metal bar. "What brings you in so early?"

"Well, I have a lot to learn before next week, so I might as well get in as many hours as I can."

Ridge looked over his shoulder. "We're bringing the horses over today."

"Really?" Her voice was too high, but she didn't care. She'd been promised horses, and she hadn't seen one up close yet.

"Really. And I think we should have a crash course day so you can get up to speed on what we'll be doing with the kids and how to take care of them."

"The kids or the horses?" she asked.

"The horses. I'm hoping you already know something about taking care of kids."

Cheyenne grimaced. "Unfortunately, I don't, but I'm a fast learner."

"Maybe we both need a crash course on kids from Remi."

"Who's Remi?" Cheyenne asked.

"She's the kids' activities coordinator here."

"Oh, then we definitely need to talk to her," Cheyenne said.

Ridge jerked his chin toward the office. "If you want to check your emails right quick, I should be finished with this in about fifteen minutes. Then we can go to the main barn to get the horses."

Excitement like she hadn't experienced in years bubbled in her middle. "Okay. Come get me when you're ready."

Three online registrations waited for her, and she replied to an email from Ava. Fifteen minutes later, as promised, Ridge stood in the office doorway.

"You ready?"

"Yep." She jumped up and followed him to his truck.

Morning light covered the hilltops in waves, and the birds were chirping in the trees. It had been a long time since she'd been up before dawn.

"Is it always so beautiful in the mornings?" she asked.

Ridge started toward the passenger side but changed direction at the last minute. "Um, no. Sometimes, everything is covered in snow and the cold wind cuts you from the inside out every time you breathe."

Cheyenne frowned and got in on the passenger side. "That doesn't sound good."

Ridge got in on the other side and started the truck. "Nope. The winter is brutal, and most of the ranch closes down. Some of the wranglers move to Texas, and some work other seasonal jobs up north."

"More north than here?" she asked. "Who would want to go where it's even colder?"

Ridge shrugged as he steered the truck toward the path. "Some work in gold mines, some are arctic fishermen, some train sled dogs."

Cheyenne shook her head. "You couldn't pay me to do any of those things."

Ridge snuck a side glance at her. "But you could be paid to work here."

"Well, yeah. It's practically summer." Cheyenne gestured to the grass and trees out the window.

"You know we'll probably take a few months off in the winter, right? Just preparing you for that."

"Ava told me."

At the time, it had sounded like the perfect scenario. She'd thought her job for David would be over by then, but now, she was wondering what would happen here when she was gone. Not that the ranch couldn't survive without her, but she was definitely getting attached to this place, the job, and the people here. They were some of the nicest and most welcoming people she'd ever met, and instead of betraying them, she wanted to call them friends.

That was a problem, and she wasn't sure how to slow things down.

***

Cheyenne brushed a hand down Butterscotch's mane. She'd just spent the last forty-five minutes getting the crash course on all things horse grooming, and Butterscotch sure looked pleased with the attention.

"You're a sweet girl," Cheyenne whispered.

Ridge stepped around Butterscotch and held out his fisted hand to Cheyenne. "She's one of the calmest horses we've had in a while. Jess thought she'd be perfect for the inexperienced kids."

Cheyenne took one of the treats from Ridge and held it out to Butterscotch who quickly grabbed it up. "And me. I'm inexperienced too."

"You'll learn quickly. Weren't you telling me that this morning?"

"Yeah, but some people spend their whole lives with horses. I bet they know a lot more than I ever will."

Ridge led Butterscotch out of the barn. "Maybe, but don't sell yourself short. You'll do fine, and there are lots of people here who can answer your questions if you have any."

Cheyenne fell into step beside Ridge as they headed toward the pasture west of the barn. "Did you always want to work with horses and kids?" she asked.

Instead of answering, Ridge opened the gate and led Butterscotch through. Once the horse was happily grazing, he stepped out of the gate, locked it, and joined Cheyenne where she stood by a fence post. They watched Butterscotch in silence for a moment, and Cheyenne was sure he'd forgotten her question.

"I had no intention of doing any of this. It's just where I landed. The horses are great because the trust you build with them is mutual. You respect them, and you earn their respect." He glanced at her, then back to the pasture. "Horses aren't as deceiving as people."

Cheyenne released a shaky breath. He knew. He had to know her secret. Why wasn't he angry? The hair on the back of her neck stood on end, and she reached out a hand to grab the metal on the gate to regain her balance.

"As for kids, they're just easier to be around. They're deceptive, sure, but their motives are usually harmless. Like, they'll try to sneak an extra snack or get out of helping clean up. That's a lot different than most adults who sometimes do harmful things on purpose."

Oh no, she couldn't breathe, couldn't see her hand a foot from her face. He was talking about her–doing harmful things on purpose. Wasn't he? She was here to trick and manipulate with the intention of allowing David to get the justice he thought Ridge deserved.

And none of it made her feel good. In fact, her heart was dark and ugly. She could feel it pulsing poison into her veins, killing the goodness she'd once had.

But her mom needed help. She needed the money David had offered. Why did the job have to cost her the ruin of her soul?

Cheyenne took a few steps away from the fence. "I need to check some emails. I'll catch up with you later."

If Ridge said anything about her hasty retreat, she didn't hear it. The pounding of her heart or the thudding of her footfalls as she jogged toward the barn might have drowned out the sounds around her.

When she was safely back in the office, she closed the door and leaned her head back against it. Ridge said those things because he knew, right? Or was he just prepared to be betrayed? What kind of life was that?

She'd barely regained her resting heart rate when a light knock sounded on the door behind her. She whirled around and threw the door open.

Ridge stood a few steps back from the office door. "You okay?"

She brushed a hand over her hair, taming the strands that had come loose from her ponytail in her mad dash back to the barn. "Yeah. Yes. I'm fine. I'm fine."

"You're lying. What's going on?"

Cheyenne's lungs constricted. This was it. She'd been caught.

"No. I'm not." She managed to say the words without faltering, but it was clear she was lying. But what choice did she have? She could confess it all right now and get fired before her job even started.

Ridge lowered his head, then looked up again. "Okay." With that one word, he walked away.

Cheyenne gasped for breath. She was lying, and he knew it. She was doing everything to keep him from trusting her when she was supposed to be doing the opposite.

Closing herself back in the office, she paced and prayed. Well, she called it praying, but her silent requests were convoluted and muddy. What did she even want? Was God playing a part in this at all? Was she here to learn a lesson or cement her role in Ridge's downfall?

Eventually, she sat down in front of the laptop and worked through a few emails. Ridge hadn't come back to the office yet, and the way she'd rushed off was weighing on her more and more.

Finally, she pushed out of the seat and went looking for him. She didn't find him in the barn or the feed shed. His truck was still parked outside the barn, but there wasn't any sign of him. She walked around the barn and spotted him next to the fence. He pulled a hose and let it hang over the side of the horse trough. Butterscotch nudged his side, and he stood to give the horse his attention.

She took a deep breath and started toward the pasture. Ridge spotted her when she was about ten yards away and pulled the hose from the trough.

Ridge stepped out of the gate, locked it behind him, and rested his back against the first fence post. The guarded stance with his arms crossed over his chest was more than she deserved. If he knew the whole truth, he'd run her out of Wyoming.

Before she'd made it all the way to him, Ridge pushed off the fence post he'd been leaning on and inhaled a deep breath. "You ready for lunch?"

Cheyenne didn't move. Was he taunting her? Was this a test, and what would it take to pass?

"Sure." The word was barely a whisper. Fear had her muscles seizing.

Ridge turned to walk back to the barn. "You haven't been eating at the dining hall," he said.

Cheyenne turned to follow him, keeping a good distance between them. "I bring my lunch." The words were still shaky, but she grabbed on to the change of subject like a life preserver.

"Sandwich every day," Ridge said.

"Yeah."

"You know the food at the dining hall is really good. Vera is the head cook, and everything she makes is delicious."

Cheyenne took another deep, steadying breath. "I've learned to trust your recommendations when it comes to food."

"Did you bring your lunch today?" he asked.

"I did. Sandwich as always."

They walked into the barn and headed for the office. Cheyenne pulled her lunchbox from the bottom drawer of her desk, and Ridge did the same, setting the brown paper sack on his desk.

"You brought your lunch today too?"

"Yep. If you're missing out on the good food at the dining hall, then maybe I should too."

Cheyenne rolled her eyes. "That's ridiculous. Go eat the good food."

"Not unless you do."

They sat locked in a staring match for a moment before Cheyenne broke her gaze. "It's not about the food. I'm just not ready to meet a bunch of people at once. It's–"

"Overwhelming?" Ridge asked.

"Yeah. I've met a few other people here, and they've all been great. I want to ease into it."

"I moved here a few years ago, and it took me months to meet everyone."

Ridge unwrapped his sandwich, removed his hat, and bowed his head in prayer. Cheyenne bowed her own head and said a silent prayer. She thanked God for the food, for the new job, and for watching over her.

Then she prayed for guidance. She could really use a clear sign right about now because she had no idea what she was doing.

They lifted their heads and took the first bites of their sandwiches at the same time.

"What's yours?" Ridge asked.

"Banana and mayonnaise," Cheyenne said, holding up the sandwich to show the inside at the corner she'd just bitten into.

Ridge stared at the sandwich. "You're kidding."

"Nope. It's good."

"It sounds disgusting."

"Okay, enough about the sandwich that I happen to like. How's yours?"

"Ham, turkey, cheese, mayo, and pepper." He held up his sandwich. It was twice as thick as Cheyenne's.

"That's a monster," Cheyenne said before taking another bite.

"I have another one too."

Cheyenne's eyes widened. "I bet you spend a fortune on groceries."

Ridge shrugged. "Not really. I eat at the dining hall a lot, and Everly cooks for me about once a week."

"Are you talking about me?"

Cheyenne looked up to see a smiling woman in the office doorway. She had the same dark-blue eyes as Ridge, but her blonde hair was a contrast to Ridge's dark-brown.

"Hey, Ev. I was just telling Cheyenne about how you cook for me."

"I'm Everly." The woman held out her hand over the desk to Cheyenne.

"I'm Cheyenne. So you're Ridge's sister."

"I don't always claim him," Everly said with a wink.

Cheyenne glanced at Ridge, then held up a hand beside her mouth to whisper, "I don't blame you."

Everly chuckled and rested her hands on her hips and turned to Ridge. "I didn't see you at the dining hall, so I came over to check on you."

"I'm fine. Just brought my lunch today." He held up the half-eaten sandwich.

"I hope you have two of those," Everly said.

"I do. Thanks."

Everly looked Cheyenne over. "I know Ridge isn't missing a meal. I actually came over to meet you. I haven't had a chance to get over here this week, and our paths haven't crossed yet."

"It's nice to meet you," Cheyenne said.

"How are you liking it so far? The ranch is beautiful, isn't it?"

Cheyenne sighed. "Gorgeous. Do you live on the ranch?"

"I'm actually living in the main house right now. Blake and I are getting married soon, and then I'll be moving in with him."

"Does he live on the ranch?" Cheyenne asked.

"No. I'm definitely going to miss it here, but Blake's place isn't too far. Plus, we'll get to ride to work together." Everly shrugged, and her smile beamed the whole time she talked about her fiancé.

"That's so sweet."

Everly clasped her hands and grinned. "I've been so excited to meet you. Some of us get together at Stella and Vera's house on Tuesday nights for quilting. We'd love it if you could come."

Cheyenne glanced at Ridge, who seemed unfazed by the idea of a quilting bee. "Well, I don't know anything about sewing or quilting."

"That's okay!" Everly waved a dismissing hand. "I don't either, but I like sitting around and chatting with the girls."

Chatting with the girls? While the idea of making friends sounded amazing, the harsh truth reminded her that her whole reason for being here was to spy. Guilt rolled in her gut at the thought of making friends and then leaving after she did what David had asked.

"Um, I'd like to come, but I don't know what this coming week is going to look like. We might have a lot to do after the kids leave," Cheyenne said.

"I get it. You don't have to RSVP or anything. Just come by Stella and Vera's place after work if you want."

"I don't know where they live."

"I'll show you," Ridge said. "They live in the old foreman's cabin."

Everly held up a finger. "And you're welcome to join in the evening activities here. We have dancing, a fire pit, karaoke, trivia, and lots of other stuff at the dining hall and dance hall."

Cheyenne perked up, unable to temper her excitement. "That sounds like so much fun. I'd love to, but I'm usually exhausted when I leave here in the afternoons."

Everly narrowed her eyes at her brother. "Are you working Cheyenne into the ground?"

Ridge held up his hands and kept chewing the massive bite he'd just put in his mouth.

Cheyenne chuckled. "He's not so bad. I'm just not used to work like this. I managed a grocery store before I came here."

"Everly!" a man yelled from out in the breezeway of the barn.

"I'm in the office!" she yelled back.

Seconds later, a tall man dressed similarly to Ridge and wearing a black cowboy hat walked into the office. He wrapped his arm around Everly and kissed her temple. "I didn't see you at lunch."

Everly jerked her head toward Cheyenne. "I came to introduce myself."

Blake reached out a hand to Cheyenne. "It's good to meet you. Ridge treating you good?"

Cheyenne grinned. Everyone mentioned Ridge's treatment of her, but so far, he'd been a perfect boss. "He's been great. I'm currently experiencing an overload of all things ranch related, but other than that, he's doing a great job."

Blake pointed at Ridge. "Take it easy on her."

Ridge was halfway into his second sandwich, so he gave Blake a thumbs up and continued chewing.

Blake turned back to his fiancée. "I have an afternoon ride later, and I thought we could sneak off to the creek for a minute before I have to leave."

Everly turned to Ridge and Cheyenne. "Gotta run. I'll see you later, Cheyenne. Oh, and I also wanted to invite you to church. I don't know if you've found one here yet, but you're welcome to come with us."

Church. Of course Everly would be a sweet and welcoming Christian. Now Ridge's insistence on blessing his meals seemed genuine.

"I'd love that."

Everly pulled her phone from her pocket. "Can I get your number? I'd love to chat more."

Cheyenne gave her number, and her phone dinged beside her.

"I just sent you a text so you'll have my number too. Call or text me if you ever want to talk. Ridge can give you directions to the church. He might even pick you up if you ask nicely." Everly wiggled her eyebrows.

"Let's go," Blake said.

Everly waved as she walked out. "Bye! It was nice meeting you!"

"You too!" Cheyenne shouted after the two were out of sight. She turned to Ridge, and said, "They were nice."

"Yep. Everly's always been by my side. She's a good sister."

Ridge's ease around Everly was clearly different from the cautiousness she'd observed him use around the guests. He wasn't as overly friendly with them as some of the other wranglers were, and he kept his head down. Was he really hiding as David had suggested?

"And Blake? Do you like him?"

Ridge crumpled the napkin his sandwich had been wrapped in and stuffed it back into the paper sack. "We've worked together for about a decade now. He's my best friend."

Oh no. It was happening. Ridge was letting her in, and now she knew something she was contractually supposed to tell David. Ridge had friends here, and despite knowing he used to be a football star who had a violent criminal offense on his record, they were unashamedly loyal to him.

David had to already know at least that much. Anyone could find out that Ridge had a sister. If Blake had worked with Ridge ten years ago, they'd probably met in the NFL. Did David already know that, or was it the kind of information he was looking to find out?

Chapter Twelve

Ridge

Ridge counted heads one more time. Ten kids. They'd been officially under his supervision for four hours, and his heart rate hadn't dropped below 120 beats per minute.

Ten kids. In his care.

He'd rather face the starting defensive lineup for the Patriots right now. He'd coached kids in football camps before, but this was different.

"Cynthia! Keep your hands out of Heather's plate!" Cheyenne yelled across the picnic table.

Ridge had rocked the teaching part of the day, but handling the kids one-on-one was obviously something he needed to work on. One of the girls had cried to him that a little boy was pulling her hair, and Ridge had been at a loss for words, until Cheyenne showed up and set the kids straight, sending them to opposite sides of the group.

Cheyenne sat down beside him and sighed. "Why can't they keep their hands to themselves?"

Ridge shrugged and grabbed a chip off Cheyenne's plate. He popped it into his mouth just as her eyes narrowed at him.

"You're setting a bad example, Ridge."

"No one ever called me a role model," he said before stealing one more chip and standing. He chucked his trash into the garbage can and replaced the lid. "Listen up! We only have a couple of minutes left for lunch, so eat a few more bites and bring your trash here." He pointed to the covered bin. "Don't forget to replace the lid when you're finished. We don't want any unwelcome visitors."

The little girls gasped. "Like what?" one yelled.

"Bears," Ridge said.

Now the girls were squealing. Ridge looked to Cheyenne for help, but she was slowly shaking her head at him. What? The kids asked him a question, and he answered it.

"Don't worry about the bears," Cheyenne said as she stood to dump her own plate in the trash. "I doubt we'll see any today."

"What about the other days this week?" Cynthia asked. The firm and bossy tone Ridge had come to expect from her was replaced with wariness.

"No bears allowed," Cheyenne said. "Plus, we have bear spray." She pointed to the tiny holster on her belt.

"Do you know how to use that?" Preston asked.

Of all the ten and eleven-year-olds in this group, Preston had the most suspicion. He'd questioned everything Ridge had taught them this morning.

"She does," Ridge said. It might not be the truth, since he'd told Cheyenne to aim and spray, but surely she'd be able to manage that if she actually came in contact with a bear.

"Ahh!"

The scream came from the third picnic table, farthest from the barn, and Ridge was darting past the kids before thinking.

Kaylee was the smallest kid they had this week, and she'd been skittish from the start. Now, she was swatting at her legs and screaming.

"Ants!"

"I've got you," Ridge said, grabbing her upper body and hoisting her away from the ants. When he sat her down in the grass five feet away, Cheyenne was already there to help.

"Hold her up, and I'll get them off," Cheyenne said as she started swiping at Kaylee's legs.

Ridge did as he was told, but Kaylee was still wailing. When all the ants were gone, Cheyenne opened her arms. Ridge passed the girl over, and Cheyenne carried her toward the barn. The ten-year-old wrapped her thin arms and legs around Cheyenne.

Ridge would have gladly carried Kaylee to the barn, but Cheyenne had reached for her and carried the kid more than half her size to the barn without missing a beat.

Ridge had treated the area around the barn for ants just last week, and while he didn't mind ants himself, the number of them he and Cheyenne had just brushed off Kaylee's legs concerned him. He hadn't gotten a good look, but if they were fire ants, the little girl would be in a lot of pain.

The other kids had abandoned their seats at the picnic table and were talking about Kaylee. Even the kids had picked up on the dangerous number of ants.

"Miss Cheyenne is taking care of Kaylee, and we're going to start learning how to care for the horses. After today's lesson, you'll be ready to ride tomorrow."

Preston raised his hand but didn't wait to be called on before he shouted, "I already know how to ride a horse!"

"Of course you do," Ridge said. "You've said that about everything we've learned today." The kid hadn't given him much trouble, but Ridge wasn't buying into the know-it-all attitude.

After wrangling the kids into the barn, Ridge led the golden horse from her stall. The kids gasped in awe, even though horses were a dime a dozen in this part of the state.

Ridge brushed a hand down the horse's mane. "This is Vanilla. She's a palomino. That's what we call a horse with a gold coat and white mane."

"She's beautiful!" shouted Felicia, a little girl with hair the same white-blonde as the horse.

"What did I say we had to remember about horses?" Ridge asked.

"Respect and caution," the kids said in unison.

"Right. First lesson: be careful where you approach. Vanilla here is well-trained, and she's used to being around people. With that said, I could walk behind her like this," Ridge stepped behind Vanilla, dragging his fingertips around the horse's left flank, over her tail, and to her right flank, "but I have to keep my hand on her at all times. That's how she knows where I am. The key is to make her aware of you. If you approach a horse from behind, they may kick first and ask questions later."

Cynthia took a step back, bumping into Preston. "Um, she's really big."

"She's about fourteen hands high," Ridge said.

"What does that mean?" Jared asked.

"You measure the height of a horse in what's called hands. The measurement is from the hoof to the top of the withers." He put his hands on Vanilla to show the slight hump at the base of her neck.

"I knew that," Preston said.

Ridge tried to hide his grin. Preston was one to keep an eye on this week. "I think you should be my volunteer."

Preston's eyes widened, but only for a split second. "Yeah, sure."

"Let's take a water break before we get started," Ridge said.

As soon as the kids were gathered around the locker area where they stored their drinks, Ridge ducked into the office. Kaylee was sitting in Ridge's chair that had been pulled over by Cheyenne's, the little girl's legs had welts on them, and her eyes were red-rimmed.

Cheyenne was on the phone, but she looked up at Ridge with an unreadable expression as he walked in.

The bites must have been worse than he thought. She mouthed, "Her mom," and pointed to the phone.

Ridge craned his neck to see the kids outside, then squatted in front of Kaylee and rested a hand on the side of the chair. "You okay?"

Kaylee shook her head, a tired pout dragging her mouth down. "It hurts. Bad."

"I bet. Fire ants are nasty boogers."

That got him a small chuckle. "You said boogers."

"Well, I figure I can get away with calling names if they bit my friend."

"They started it," Kaylee said with a laugh.

"Did Cheyenne give you anything?" he asked.

"Benadryl. It's what my mom gives me when I get bit."

"You think your mom is coming to get you?"

Kaylee sighed, her shoulders sagging lower. "I want to stay, but it hurts so much."

Ridge leaned a little closer. "That Benadryl might make you sleepy. If everything looks good, and your mom says it's okay, you're welcome to stay. But if you want to go home and sleep it off, you can come back tomorrow when you feel better."

Kaylee nodded, and a fresh tear slid down her cheek. Good grief, these kids had Ridge on a roller coaster today.

Cheyenne put the phone down and walked around the desk to crouch in front of Kaylee. "Your mom is on her way. Ava is coming to get you and take you back to the main house to wait."

Kaylee's lower lip trembled. "Okay."

"Don't worry, sweetie." Cheyenne brushed a hand down Kaylee's hair. "Ava said the two of you could look for something yummy to eat in the dining hall while you wait."

Ridge stood and checked on the kids in the breezeway. The boys were trying to slosh water on the girls from the reusable bottles they'd been given this morning. "I'd better get back out there before the boys run the girls off."

Kaylee looked up at him with the saddest eyes. "Can I come back tomorrow?"

"Sure. As long as you're okay from these bites," Ridge said.

"Promise?" Kaylee asked.

Ridge nodded. "I promise that if your mom is okay with it, you can come back. Trust me, I don't want you to miss out either."

"Okay." Kaylee looked to Cheyenne for a second assurance.

"He's right. We'll be praying you feel better enough to come back tomorrow," Cheyenne said.

Ridge stared at Cheyenne. So she was the praying kind, and his attraction to her ramped up tenfold. Just what he needed: a co-worker who worked hard, cared about kids, always knew what to do, and loved the Lord.

He kept waiting to find out something terrible about her that would lessen the pull he'd felt for her this week, but if anything, it was growing stronger by the minute.

Ridge took a step toward the door. "I'll call to check on you this evening. Get some rest, and we'll see you in the morning."

Cheyenne stood and held out a hand to Kaylee. "Let's go wait for Ava outside. She should be here any second."

Kaylee took Cheyenne's hand, and Ridge turned away. Any concerns he'd harbored about Cheyenne's lack of experience with children had faded. She'd handled the situation with Kaylee like a pro.

Ridge walked over to the group of kids and ruffled Preston's blond hair. "Okay, who's ready to learn how to groom a horse?"

"Me!" Heather shouted with her hand in the air. The boys shouted, "Yeah!" in unison.

Ridge led the kids back over to Vanilla and gestured to a small table where he'd laid out the things they'd need. "We'll start with the pick." Ridge waved Preston over. "I'll need my assistant for this."

Preston stepped up, ready to show off for his friends.

Ridge handed the pick to Preston. "This is for keeping the horse's hooves clean." He leaned over and wrapped an arm around one of Vanilla's legs. The horse pulled it up, showing the bottom to the kids.

Ridge looked at Preston, who held the pick with the pointed end out like a hammer. "I bet you know what to do now, don't you?"

Preston huffed. "Yeah, but you're the teacher." He shoved the pick at Ridge.

With a grin, Ridge took the pick and started digging the dirt out of Vanilla's hoof, talking about the different parts and what to watch for while cleaning.

"Won't they just get dirty again when we ride?" Preston asked.

"Yeah, but you still need to check their hooves regularly. You want to keep an eye out for bacteria or infection." He pointed to a discolored spot on Vanilla's hoof. "We've been treating this spot with some medicine. You'll see the difference when we get to the next hoof."

Ridge looked up to see if Preston and the other kids were listening and saw Cheyenne walking back into the barn. Kaylee must be on her way home.

One of the girls dropped her water bottle, causing Vanilla to turn. The movement wasn't quick, but the horse's backside swung around and bumped Preston off his feet. The kid went down with a flurry of arms waving and landed on his side.

"You okay, bud?" Ridge asked.

Preston's mouth pursed, and his nose crinkled. "Eww!" He lifted his upper body, revealing the mound of horse poop he'd landed in.

The other kids erupted into a laughing fit, and Ridge lifted Preston out of the stinky pile. The kid's cheeks were turning red, and the color could have come from embarrassment or lack of oxygen. Ridge was trying not to breathe too deeply.

Cheyenne was by his side in an instant, reaching for Preston. "Come on, we'll get you some extra clothes."

"From home?" Preston asked.

Cheyenne wrapped an arm around the kid's back, ushering him toward the large opening leading outside. "We have a closet with extra clothes in the kids' activity office."

Ridge had told her about the stash of extra clothes Remi kept, but he'd only mentioned it the one time. Cheyenne hadn't missed a beat today. She'd been quick to take charge, confident, and always running to help when needed.

Ridge had barely earned his wages today, while Cheyenne didn't seem fazed by anything.

Running his hand over Vanilla's withers, Ridge regained his focus. "Looks like I lost my assistant. Who wants to fill in?"

All of the kids looked at each other, but Heather was the one to raise her hand.

"Step right up," Ridge said.

Heather jumped into action with a smile on her face, gripping Ridge's heart in her tiny fingers.

This. The smile on Heather's face was the same excitement that had gotten him through the tough months leading up to now. All the worry and doubt was replaced by that giddy childlike happiness at learning and teaching something new.

During the grooming lesson, Preston and Cheyenne slipped back in, but the boy didn't push his way back to the center of everyone's attention. His ego must have taken a tumble too.

"Okay, guys. That's it for today. Let's get Vanilla back in her stall, and I'll show you how to feed the others."

Heather followed close to him as he led the horse to her stall. The excited girl had definitely made a friend today if Vanilla's nuzzling was any indication. When Heather had to let go of the horse, a sad but content grin stayed on her face.

Ridge closed the door and brushed his hands together. "Great job today. Tomorrow, you'll be grooming in the morning and riding after lunch." He checked his watch. "We can take a short break before we meet up in front of the tack room." He pointed to the tack room, indicating where they should go.

Heather took one step to follow the others, and her hair pulled taut back to the stable door hinge. A sickening rip was followed by a wail. "Oww!"

Ridge was by her in an instant, reaching for the long hair that had wound around and through the old hinge. Heather held her head and squeezed her eyes closed as she screamed.

"Don't move. It's tangled," Ridge said.

Heather began wailing, and tears instantly fell over her cheeks. "It hurts!"

Cheyenne rushed to Heather's side. "Easy now." Holding one hand on the little girl's head, Cheyenne got down on one knee and prompted Heather to sit with a pat on the other. "Let's get you untangled."

Ridge's heart hadn't resumed its normal rhythm, and his hand fisted tight over the stall door. The other kids were either covering their mouths in shock or high-fiving each other because the boys didn't have long hair to get tangled in things.

Cheyenne looked up at him. "Go with the others. I've got this."

"You sure?" He could barely get the words out, and Heather's cries drowned out his question anyway.

"I'm sure."

The determination in Cheyenne's eyes told him to trust her, and he did. Heather was in much better hands with Cheyenne, and the tension in his shoulders eased.

Heather had her face buried in Cheyenne's neck, while her fingers slowly and meticulously pulled each strand from the hinge.

Feeding. That's what he should be doing. Ridge rested his hand on Heather's back and let it slide over to Cheyenne's shoulder. She glanced up at him but continued working her fingers over the hair.

"Thanks. I couldn't do this without you," Ridge said. He didn't wait to see Cheyenne's reaction or hear what she might have to say. He'd sort out everything else he wanted to say to her after the kids went home.

Chapter Thirteen

Cheyenne

The rumble of Ridge's truck startled Cheyenne from the half-sleep state she'd fallen into while logging registrations. She lifted her head from where she'd propped it in her hand. Yep, the drool was confirmation she'd been sleeping on the job.

The clock on the screen read 8:23 PM, and the sun was almost setting outside the ancient office window. Technically, she wasn't on the clock anymore, but everything needed to be perfectly ready for tomorrow morning. After the day they had, anything would be better than this one.

Cheyenne wiped the drool on the leg of her pants and stood. Ridge had left to get ant killer and "a few other things" an hour ago, and while she knew he needed some space, she couldn't leave without making sure he was okay.

It was silly. Of course he was okay. He hadn't fallen into ants or horse poop, and he hadn't gotten a handful of hair yanked out today. Yet, he'd been walking around with a quiet cloud over his head all afternoon, and his brooding had her itching to help.

She couldn't help. What was she even thinking?

Ignoring the screaming voice in her head that said to proceed with caution, she stepped out of the office just as Ridge was walking into the barn. The setting sun behind him cast his face in shadow, but she didn't have to see his features to know his expression.

Just as she'd expected, Ridge walked right past her without glancing her way.

She turned, unfazed by his dismissal. "None of it was your fault."

"Oh, yeah," he shouted over his shoulder. "You sure about that?"

Cheyenne crossed her arms over her chest and straightened her shoulders. "I am."

Ridge stopped his intentional walk and rested his back against the door of Smoky's stall. His chin dropped to his chest. When he took his hat off and hung it on the hook by the stall, Cheyenne had seen enough.

She walked over to stand in front of him and resumed her firm stance. "What's wrong?"

Ridge lifted his head, and his gaze locked with hers. His usually light-blue eyes were darkened in shadow. "Today was a mess."

Cheyenne had to swallow the lump in her throat before answering. "Today wasn't perfect, but days never are."

Ridge huffed. "Fair enough."

Cheyenne let her arms drop to her sides. "Most of the things that happened today couldn't have been prevented. Don't let this ruin what we're building here."

He didn't blink as he repeated, "What *we're* building?"

Cheyenne quickly corrected herself. "Well, not me. You. You've put so much into this program, and you can't let one bad day derail all of your hard work."

"No." Ridge stopped her. The exhaustion she'd seen in his eyes moments before was gone. "You're right. We have been building this. It isn't just me. You were a rockstar today. I couldn't have done it without you."

Oh no. Everything they'd overcome in the last week came rushing back at her. The times he'd helped her carry the heavy load, the times he'd been patient while she learned something new, and the times he'd gone out of his way to do more so she didn't have to were all piling on top of each other, making his kindness impossible to ignore.

Cheyenne covered her mouth with her hand. What was she doing here? She couldn't–wouldn't–betray Ridge to David.

Ridge opened his arms, and she closed the distance between them. Burying her face in his chest, she let the tension of the day melt away in his arms. He smelled like hay and horses, but the scent was as comforting as a warm blanket. How had he known she'd needed comforting too?

His hand brushed over her hair and down her back. "Why are you still here?" he whispered low, though only the horses were around to hear.

Cheyenne felt a tear slide down her cheek. She missed home, but she wanted to be here. She wanted the comfort of Ridge's arms, but she knew the fallout of the things she'd done would tear him away from her. "I didn't want to leave until I knew you were okay."

Ridge's arms tightened around her, and she discreetly wiped the stray tear onto his shirt. This stolen moment was all she would ever have of him. He would hate her when he found out what she'd done.

A few seconds later, Ridge gently lifted her chin with a finger. She had to look straight up at him, and the last rays of sunlight that shone into the barn were dim on his cheek.

"I'm okay. I promise. Thanks to you."

"I didn't do anything," she whispered.

"You saved me today," he said, staring at her as if the words were true and he dared her to contradict him.

"Maybe we just make a good team," she said.

Ridge's gaze slipped down to her lips, and there was a split second when she wanted to reach up and pull him down to her, sealing her mouth to his like a branding iron.

Because one kiss from Ridge would leave a mark on her heart. She knew it to be as true as the sun rising in the east and setting in the west.

Instead of kissing her, he lifted his hand and wiped her wet cheek. "You need to get some rest. We have ten tiny tornadoes coming back tomorrow."

"I'd say the same is true for you. Today wasn't that bad, and all the kids are fine. For some reason, they all want to come back tomorrow."

Ridge chuckled and let his hands slide from her back to her hips before falling to his sides. "I know why the boys will be back."

Cheyenne rolled her eyes. "Because Preston is going to try to ride off into the sunset on one of the horses?" she asked.

"No, I caught them talking about you during a water break. They all share a crush on you."

Cheyenne covered her mouth, but the laugh came out like a snort. "Are you serious?"

"Yep. I took the liberty of telling them you have a type, and they're about a foot and a half too short." Ridge's joking smile settled into a knowing grin. "And the girls will be back because they trust you'll be close by if they need you."

Cheyenne bit her lips between her teeth. Hearing Ridge's compliments boosted her will to make this work. Despite the issues they'd run into today, the girls had completely trusted her to take care of them when they were scared or hurt, and their confidence had built her own.

Clearing her throat, Cheyenne asked, "What can I do to help?"

Ridge shook his head. "Nothing. Go home and rest. I'm unloading these last few things and I'll be headed out too."

"Promise?" she asked.

"Promise."

She took a step back but didn't turn just yet. "Good night."

Ridge opened his mouth as if he were about to say something, then he closed it like he'd changed his mind. "Good night. See you in the morning."

He was smiling now. She could leave knowing he was looking forward to tomorrow.

Why did she still want to stay?

The sun had fully set on her way back to the hotel, and the night sky was inky black. Thousands of tiny stars dotted the sky, and she wanted to pull over and stare at them. There were stars over Tennessee too, but she hadn't taken the time to notice them in years. After admiring the beauty of the ranch, she wanted more of the wide-open spaces and uninhibited night skies.

Her good mood took a turn for the worse when she parked at the hotel and her phone started ringing. It was Jaden. It had to be.

She didn't pull out the phone until she was safely locked in her room. Too bad she couldn't lock out the impending call. Jaden hadn't been pushy in her calls. She'd been satisfied just hearing about the regular tasks they'd done each day to get ready for the start of the program, but at some point, David was going to get irritated that Cheyenne hadn't produced any helpful information.

Cheyenne sat on the bed and called Jaden back.

Jaden's greeting was a hoarse whisper. "Hello."

"Hey. I'm sorry it's so late. Today was the first day with the kids."

"It's okay. I've been home sick all day, so I slept through our usual call time."

"I'm sorry. I hope you get to feeling better soon," Cheyenne said.

As much as she was coming to distrust David, her interactions with Jaden were completely cordial. Cheyenne had even gotten into a couple of side conversations with David's assistant during their daily calls.

When she'd first accepted the job from David, Cheyenne had been completely sold on Ridge's character. David painted him as a monster–a villain. And Cheyenne had bought into the injustice.

Now that she'd met and worked with Ridge Cooper, the real man was rewriting everything she thought she knew, and that included her first impression of David and his intentions.

"Thanks. How was your day?" Jaden asked.

The completely normal question sounded harmless. What David's assistant was really asking was "Have you found any incriminating evidence David can use to ruin Ridge's life?"

Cheyenne knew what David wanted from her. She could tell Jaden right now that sabotaging Ridge's youth learning program would crush him.

But she couldn't say the words. In fact, she pushed all thoughts about anything she knew about Ridge into the recesses of her mind.

"It was fine. The kids came today, and they had fun. One little girl fell into an ant bed, and she's allergic, so her mom had to come get her. One little boy fell in horse poop." Cheyenne chuckled as she remembered the look on Preston's face when he'd lifted himself out of the pile. "And one of the girls got her hair caught in a hinge. I think she lost a chunk of hair when she tried to pull it out."

"Goodness. What a day." Jaden yawned. "Sounds crazy."

"It was, but for the most part, things went well."

A text came through on Cheyenne's phone, and she checked it.

Hadley: How's it going? Mom is good. Call me when you can. I want to know how it went with the kids.

Right on time, there was her reminder. She'd taken the job from David because her mom needed help, and she'd needed it fast. Today was her mom's second day at the new facility, and Hadley was already gushing about the place. All of that could be taken away if Cheyenne didn't come through with her end of the bargain.

The guilt tore at her insides. She couldn't throw Ridge into David's waiting trap, but she couldn't let the opportunity for better care for her mom slip through her fingers.

Cheyenne's hands started to sweat. She'd signed a non-disclosure agreement and a contract saying she'd produce any and all information she obtained about Ridge Cooper. In the event she became unable to continue, she would owe the complete balance paid to her back to David Lang.

A wave of nausea crept up her throat. The new facility was expensive, and he'd already paid thousands of dollars in outstanding hospital bills.

Her mom's words rang in her memory. "Remember who you are and whose you are, and return with honor."

Cheyenne had considered herself a loyal person at one point, but all that integrity went out the window when she met David. Who was she now? She was a sell-out. If she was right about David's plans, she might as well be a hired assassin. David would destroy everything Ridge loved and not think twice.

She didn't know who she belonged to either. Her loyalties were split, and her chances of returning with honor were diminishing by the day.

"Anything else new?" Jaden asked.

Other than the constant doubt and remorse? No.

"Not really."

It was much easier to lie to Jaden than it was to David or Ridge. In truth, she knew almost everything Ridge loved. He had family and friends here, and the people at Wolf Creek Ranch were important to him.

"Actually, I forgot to mention that I met Ridge's sister, Everly. I met her last week, but she came by again today to see the kids."

"I know Everly–quite well, actually," Jaden said.

Cheyenne cleared her throat. That was news. "You do?"

"She used to be engaged to David. They dated for five years."

"What?" Cheyenne spat. "No way. Everly is marrying Blake."

There were so many things she wanted to say, but everything she thought she knew was getting twisted in her head.

"Yeah. David and Everly had a rocky ending. I think that's when things started going downhill between him and Ridge too."

"So David knows Ridge well? They were almost family."

"Yep. Things have changed a lot in the last year. David doesn't like change. Once he sets his mind to something, he likes to see it through. When things fell apart with Everly, other parts of his carefully constructed life started to slip too."

"I know someone else who likes to see things through," Cheyenne said.

Jaden coughed. "Maybe that's why David has such a hard time with what Ridge is doing. They're both so determined, and neither likes to lose."

"Ridge hasn't mentioned the hotels to me at all. I wouldn't know he owned a hotel or anything at all if you and David hadn't told me."

"If I had my guess, I bet few people know. Ridge is very private, and he makes decisions on his own."

"Does David really think Ridge is going to open up to me about his secret wealth and tell me his plans?" She'd only been here a week, but not one thing Ridge had said or done would lead her to believe he was a multi-millionaire. "I'm not sure that'll ever happen."

"Maybe he will. Everly is sweet and trusting. Too trusting, if you ask me," Jaden said.

"I'm still trying to process this big reveal you just laid on me. I can't imagine Everly with anyone except Blake. They seem perfect for each other."

"And they are. I think David knows that, but he would never admit it. Everly was the kind of woman he wanted, but they had very different ideas about what marriage should be like."

"I can imagine." Everly seemed so down-to-earth, and David struck her as a shrewd businessman.

Jaden fell into a coughing fit. "Sorry. This is the most I've talked all day."

"I'll let you go. I hope you feel better soon."

"Thanks. Bye."

Cheyenne cradled the phone in her hands. "Everly and David? Really?" The pairing was wrong on so many levels.

If Everly was with David for years, he should know everything about Ridge. Why did he need her to do the snooping?

Finding out about Everly's former engagement had Cheyenne questioning everything. Where were the loyalty lines drawn, and whose side was she really on?

Chapter Fourteen

Ridge

Ridge walked into the kitchen and inhaled a deep breath. He'd been helping Colt move his things in all morning, and whatever Everly was cooking had his mouth watering.

"Is it ready yet?" Ridge asked as he leaned around his sister to get a look at whatever smelled delicious on the stove.

"Yep. Blake and Colt should be back any second." She handed Ridge a paper plate. "You can be first."

"I think the cook should get to eat first," Ridge said as he laid his plate to the side.

"Thanks, but I'll wait for Blake to get back." She propped her elbows on the counter, completely at home in Ridge's new house. "What do you think of the place so far?"

Ridge sat on a barstool. "I haven't been home a lot. You're the first one to cook in the kitchen."

"I cooked a lot of meals here. This isn't my first rodeo."

When David cheated on Everly, her sheltered reality fell into a million pieces. David was manipulative enough to kick her out of the house she'd been fixing up for months, but not before telling her she could stay if she would take him back.

Thankfully, she hadn't loved the house enough to sacrifice her integrity. He slept well at night knowing his sister hadn't married a cheater.

"I'm glad you did all this work. It made moving in a breeze," Ridge said.

Everly looked around the kitchen she'd decorated and smiled. "It was fun."

"You miss it?" Ridge asked.

"Not in the way you'd think. I liked the idea of starting something new, but a house isn't anything if the right person isn't there. If David hadn't been caught cheating on me, I might have married him, and no house could have made me happy with a husband who couldn't stay faithful."

"Amen. And now you get to live at the ranch."

Everly's smile broadened. "And I got to live with you and Blake. Thanks for taking me in, by the way."

"You're my sister. You always have a home with me."

Everly reached across the counter and patted his arm. "I know. What about you? Do you miss living with Blake?"

"Not really."

Everly scoffed. "He's your best friend!"

"I know, but now it's time for the two of you to finally get to be together. I was getting tired of Blake's silent pining over you."

Everly laughed. "He wasn't pining."

"So bad. He's been hung up on you since he first saw you."

Everly opened her mouth to say something just as Blake and Colt burst through the front door.

"And that's all, folks," Colt shouted. "All my stuff is officially here."

"Good, lunch is ready," Everly said. She turned around to grab two plates and handed one to Blake and Colt.

Colt went straight for the food, and Blake stopped to give Everly a quick kiss.

"Dude, please stop smooching in front of me," Colt said.

"How old are you?" Everly asked.

Blake slapped Colt on the back. "He's just pouting because he's not getting smooches from Remi."

Colt threw a heaping spoonful of seasoned meat onto his plate. "It's not just Remi. There are no kisses at all." He laid the spoon down and huffed. "Who am I kidding? Remi is the problem."

Ridge stood with his plate in hand and walked around the counter to make his own tacos. "I don't blame her. You're ugly."

"What? I'm not ugly!" Colt shouted.

"You're a man, and that means you're ugly by default," Ridge said.

Everly patted Colt on the shoulder. "Cheer up. Remi is probably just afraid to tell you how she feels."

"Does she like me? Did she tell you that?" Colt asked quickly.

"Well, no, but I'm sure she does. You're a great guy."

"And I'm handsome, right?"

Everly nodded. "Totally handsome."

Colt wrapped an arm around Everly's shoulders. "Blake, your girlfriend is hitting on me."

Blake didn't look up from the taco he was building. "Fiancée. She'll be my wife in a few days. And trust me, I'm not threatened by you at all."

Everly smiled and stepped up to Blake's side. "He's right. I've found my one and only."

"I have too, but she doesn't know yet," Colt said as he flopped some shredded lettuce onto his plate.

"Are you making a taco or just throwing all the ingredients onto your plate?" Ridge asked.

"It's all going to end up in my stomach anyway. I'll just scoop it up with tortilla chips."

Blake shook his head. "You're a monster. No wonder Remi isn't beating down your door."

"Speaking of my door. I have a new one now." He pointed to the ornate front door of the house. "Call before you come over and knock before entering."

Ridge chuckled. "I don't think Blake is going to be spending much time over here after this weekend."

"True, but I've been living with Linc for years, and he never announces his presence. In fact, he hardly acknowledged I was his roommate."

"Are you upset about that?" Ridge asked, barely containing his grin.

"No, but it would have been nice to talk to someone every once in a while," Colt said.

Ridge sat down at the bar with his plate of tacos. "I'm not going to have girls' night with you, so don't get your hopes up."

Colt threw open the fridge and grabbed a can of Dr Pepper. "Whatever. You know what I mean."

Blake held up a finger. "No, you picked another bad roommate if you want a gossip girl. I only know so much about Ridge because I used to read his emails when I was his agent."

"Will you read my emails?" Colt asked.

Blake chuckled. "Do you even get emails?"

"No. Well, I get a lot of spam."

Everly sat between Blake and Colt at the bar. "I can set you up with someone."

Colt sighed. "I don't want to be set up with anyone."

"Except Remi? Why don't you just ask her out?" Everly asked.

Colt looked down. "I did once. Kinda."

"Wait, wait," Blake said, holding up a hand. "You did?"

"It was a long time ago. She shot me down. Big time. It's fine. I'm fine."

Blake stared at Colt with his mouth gaping. "Dude, that sucks."

"Are you sure she said no?" Everly asked. "Maybe she misinterpreted you, or you misinterpreted her."

"Nope. She definitely said no. Not even 'No, thank you.'"

Ridge rapped his knuckles on the counter. "Somebody say the blessing so I can eat while you all chitchat."

Blake bowed his head. "Father, thank You for this food, thank You for these friends, and thank You for the hands that prepared this food. Amen."

Everly's head snapped up at the end of the prayer. "Ridge. What about Cheyenne?"

Ridge's shoulders tensed at the mention of Cheyenne. He'd been discreet when it came to anything to do with his new co-worker, but had Everly seen through his mask?

"What about her?"

"Are you going to ask her to be your date to the wedding?"

The wedding. He hadn't thought about taking a date at all. "Um, I wasn't going to."

Everly sighed. "You're clueless."

"I am?"

Blake finished chewing a bite. "Yep. She likes you."

Ridge's breath halted halfway between his lungs and his mouth. He liked Cheyenne, and he couldn't deny it. That didn't change the fact that it wasn't smart to get involved with her. His focus was the program, and he wasn't willing to sacrifice their working relationship if things went south.

Colt propped his elbows on the table and rested his chin in his hands. "Go on. I want to hear this."

Ridge pointed at Colt. "We're not girl talking."

"Pretty sure we are," Colt said.

"Are you still planning to stay here?" Blake asked.

"I guess so. I just bought a house," Ridge said as he waved a hand in the air, indicating the house he'd sneakily bought from David. For Ridge, getting back at David wasn't about money. It was about taking something David had foolishly taken for granted.

"Then you should start dating," Blake said.

"Says who? I don't have to date to be happy."

Blake and Colt laughed. Everly tried to hide her grin.

"Wait. Wait. Wait." Blake waved a hand in the air. "I know relationships aren't for everyone, but I *know* you're lonely."

Ridge huffed, pretty confident Blake was all talk. "Oh, you think so?"

"Please tell me you read his diary," Colt said.

Blake shrugged. "I just know you. You'd make a good family man."

Ridge huffed. "Right. Who is going to date a convicted felon?"

"You said that about getting a job too," Blake said. "Mr. Chambers hired you."

"Riddle me this," Ridge said. "I meet someone, we fall in love, and then, one day, I want to ask her to marry me. How is the conversation going to go with her parents? Hi, I hit a man who fell onto the bumper of a car that crushed his face, and I served time for it, but don't worry about that. I love your daughter, and I want to marry her."

"She'll know the truth by then," Everly said.

Ridge looked at his plate. His appetite was fading. "It's not fair to ask someone to overlook my crime because I had a good excuse."

"It's not fair to punish yourself forever because you did everything in your power to protect me," Everly said.

Blake jerked a thumb at Everly. "What she said."

Everly held up her hands. "I didn't say you should come clean to her about your past yet. I asked if you were going to invite her to the wedding."

"And I'm not planning to." The more Ridge thought about the crazy things a woman would have to believe, overlook, or forgive to have a healthy, trusting relationship with him, the more he knew it was wrong to even ask at all.

Everly put her hands together. "Please. I want her to feel included. I want her to come to the wedding, and you have a plus-one that you're not using."

Ridge looked at the taco he held. "Can't I just eat my lunch in peace?"

Everly lifted her chin. "Fine. Colt, will you ask Cheyenne to come to the wedding with you?"

The bite Ridge was chewing turned to lead in his mouth. He didn't want Cheyenne going on a date, even one that was basically a social obligation, with anyone except him, but having his mouth full left him unable to object.

"I would. Trust me, I would. But I already asked Remi, and she said yes."

Ridge took a deep breath and swallowed the food. He shouldn't be so relieved, but he was. Why did Cheyenne have to be his new kryptonite, and why did his sister have to be right all the time?

"Oh, you did?" Everly drawled. "So, she is interested in you."

"No, she made it clear–again–that she doesn't date. Not even me," Colt said.

Blake chuckled. "So, it's not you, it's her."

"Maybe Remi is just happy being single. The two of you can still be friends," Everly said.

Colt looked down at his food, but even Ridge could see the disappointed look on his face. "Right. I guess I'll take what I can get."

Everly rubbed a hand over Colt's back. "It's okay. Ridge is going to be single for the rest of his life too."

"He'll be a grumpy old man!" Colt said. "I get why no one would settle down with him. Me? I'm a romantic. I want to spoil my wife one day."

"You are so sweet, Colt. You'll definitely find a good wife one day," Everly said.

Colt threw his head back and sighed. "Remi thinks marriage is just a way to make two people hate each other."

Everly sucked in a breath through her teeth. "Yikes. I think she told me once that her parents were hostile toward each other. Surely, she'll see that marriage doesn't always end that way."

Blake stood and tossed his empty plate in the trash. "Yep. Maybe her mom and dad were just wrong for each other."

Ridge scooped the stray meat and cheese from his tacos onto a tortilla chip. What kind of family life did Cheyenne have growing up? She hadn't talked about her parents much, but neither had he. The subject hadn't come up yet, like so many others. He didn't know much about her, aside from her day-to-day work ethic and how she was always there when someone needed a hand or a comforting hug. The first group of kids had grown so close to her, they'd lingered on the evening of the last day to stay with her just a little longer, and she hadn't rushed them off despite her exhaustion.

"Give her time," Everly said. "Maybe she's just scared to open up to someone."

She was talking about Remi, but Ridge could relate. The thought of telling anyone about who he really was or what he'd done had him breaking out in a cold sweat.

Everly turned back to Ridge. "So, are you going to ask her?"

Ridge took a deep breath. He could handle one evening with Cheyenne. They worked together every day, and the wedding didn't have to be any different.

"Fine. I'll ask her."

Chapter Fifteen

Cheyenne

Cheyenne rapped her knuckles on Ava's open office door.

Ava looked up from her laptop and smiled. "Hey! Did my text wake you up this morning?"

"Nah. I'm turning into an early riser."

Ava opened a drawer in her desk and pulled out a single key on a ring. "Are you as excited as I am?"

Cheyenne laughed and reached for the key. "There's no way you could be as excited as I am." She'd been here two weeks, and the cabin was finally ready for her to move into. The Kellerman Hotel wasn't terrible, but she'd been dreaming about that cabin since Ridge took her to see it.

"I'm glad you'll be here full time, but don't think that means you're always on call. You still get time off, even if you live on site."

The metal was cool on her fingertips, and the small key was heavier than she'd expected. "Thank you so much for this. I've completely fallen in love with this place."

Ava leaned against the filing cabinet and smiled. "It didn't take me long either. Wolf Creek Ranch is different from any home I've ever had before."

Cheyenne looked at the silver key in her hand. "I know what you mean." This was a step closer to the ranch–a step closer to Ridge–but her reasons for digging her heels into this place weren't the same as when she arrived two weeks ago.

"You can move your things in whenever you're ready. It's the first cabin," Ava said.

Cheyenne chuckled. "I actually packed my car and checked out of the hotel as soon as I got your text."

Ava opened her arms and wrapped Cheyenne in a hug. "I'm so glad you're here!"

Cheyenne closed her eyes and squeezed Ava's small frame. "I'm glad I'm here too."

Cheyenne and Ridge had wrapped up their first week with the kids last night, and she'd left the ranch feeling hollow and afraid. After a night of praying, she knew she needed to come clean to Ridge. The problem? She had to figure out how to get out of the deal she'd made with David without getting her mom kicked out of the new facility and losing Hadley's home.

Ava leaned out of the hug. "Do you need some help with your stuff? I can ride over there with you and help you unload."

"I've got it, but thanks. I didn't bring much with me."

"You sure? Just call me if you need me. Ridge is probably available to help too."

Of course her handsome, good-hearted boss would be around to help. Life was cruel that way. She still hadn't figured out how to tell him about David. She hadn't mustered up the courage either, and she was hoping that would come whenever she figured everything else out.

"Thanks. I'll see you later." Cheyenne waved over her shoulder as she walked out of Ava's office.

Cheyenne had lucked out on the way in and missed Bethany. Now, the receptionist was at her post. Cheyenne had apologized to Bethany for her rudeness when they first met, but the young girl's narrowed eyes said she hadn't forgiven or forgotten the exchange.

"Hey. You having a good day?" Cheyenne asked.

Bethany looked up from the article she'd been reading on the computer. "Yep. You?"

"I guess so. It's my day off, but I'm headed over to the cabins on the western ridge. I remember you asked Ridge to show you around the place where we're holding the youth program. Did he ever take you out there?"

Bethany's eyes crinkled at the corners. "No. He's been busy."

"You want to come out there with me now? I can show you around?" Cheyenne jerked a thumb over her shoulder toward the door.

The tension in Bethany's posture eased, and she cut a glance to the gift shop where Stella was bagging a customer's trinkets. "Thanks, but I probably need to stick around here. The shop gets busier in the afternoons when guests get back from their rides."

"Okay. Maybe some other time. Or you could come out to the barn for lunch sometime. The kids would like to see a new face."

Bethany glanced back at the article she'd been reading. "Thanks. I might do that."

"I'll see you later." Cheyenne waved at Stella as she headed out the door.

The offer hadn't completely fixed things between them, but Bethany hadn't been as snippy during their conversation as she'd been the past few weeks.

Cheyenne slipped back into her car and closed the door, muffling the chatter and laughter of the guests heading to the dining hall. Why was she trying to make friends with Bethany? Why did it even matter?

It mattered because Cheyenne wanted to stay, and she'd been avoiding thinking that dangerous thought for days.

She backed out and headed toward the trail leading to the new cabins. The bright sunshine covered every sweeping hill, and she drove slower than usual. With the window down, the crisp scent of fresh-cut grass tingled in her nose.

Until further notice, this was her home.

Ridge's truck crested the hill ahead of her. Of course he was at the ranch on his day off. Did the man ever go home? When she turned toward the cabins, he followed, and anticipation bubbled in her middle.

She parked in front of the first cabin, and Ridge parked beside her. She got out and waved. The key to her new cabin was burning a hole in her pocket, and she shifted her weight from side to side to keep from running to the door.

"Hey. Fancy seeing you here on your day off," she said.

Ridge rolled his eyes. "I came out to feed the horses and fill up their troughs."

"Work never ends for you, does it?"

Ridge looked at the cabin. "Not really. You moving in?"

"Yep. Ava just gave me the key." She pulled it out of her pocket and held it up. The shiny metal glinted in the sunlight.

"You need help moving in? We can use my truck to haul your stuff over." He jerked his head toward the vehicle behind him.

"Actually, it's all in my car." She shrugged. "I don't have much."

Ridge walked toward the trunk. "I'll carry the stuff in."

"You don't have to do that." She rushed to get ahead of him.

"Can you get the door?" he jerked his head toward the cabin.

Cheyenne hesitated. She didn't want him to move her stuff by himself, but she was itching to see the cabin. She opened the trunk and jogged up the two small porch steps to the door.

The key fit perfectly, and cool air hit her face as she opened the door. A window unit on the back side of the cabin had cut right through the dry summer air. The small kitchen was empty with cream countertops and brown cabinets. An open living area to the right of the front door had only a small fireplace and hearth.

The thud of Ridge's boots on the porch snapped Cheyenne out of her daydream, if she could even call it that. This wasn't a dream.

Ridge hefted two large suitcases over the threshold. "Where do you want these?"

"You can just leave them there by the door. I'll unpack them in a little bit."

Ridge nodded and walked back out to her car. She hadn't paid for a moving service, but it seemed that perk had fallen into her hands anyway. She rolled one of the suitcases across the main room and opened one of the doors. The bedroom was finished now, and much more homey and quaint than the last time she'd seen it covered in sawdust. By the time she got the second suitcase to the bedroom, Ridge was back with the last one.

"Thank you for bringing that in. You made it look easy. I bet someone in town got a good laugh this morning watching me shove those bags into my car."

"You could have called me," Ridge said.

"I know, but it's your day off, even if you don't actually take a day off."

"You can call me anytime."

A chill raced down Cheyenne's back. It would be so easy to read more into those words, and she wanted to give in and savor them for just a second. Even with his eyes covered in the shadow of his hat, his intense gaze made her want to do crazy things like lean in.

But Ridge wasn't about to kiss her, and this wasn't some fairytale. He was her boss, and she hadn't come clean to him about the mess she'd gotten into with David.

Ridge cleared his throat and removed his hat. His dark hair was tousled, and he ran his fingers through it. "I actually wanted to ask you if you wanted to go to Blake and Everly's wedding with me next Saturday."

Cheyenne gasped, and the whoosh of air got caught in her throat. She doubled over in a coughing fit. After she'd coughed for a few seconds with no end, Ridge's heavy hand rested on her back.

"Are you okay? Do you have asthma or an inhaler or something?"

Cheyenne shook her head. "No." Another cough. "I'm fine. Just a little startled." With her hand on her chest, she croaked out a few more coughs.

"I didn't mean to just blurt it out like that, but–"

"Yes, you did. You're not a man who beats around the bush about anything," Cheyenne said, wiping the moisture from her eyes.

Ridge grinned. "I guess you're right." He shifted his weight from side to side and rubbed the back of his neck. "Listen, don't feel obligated to say yes. I'm the best man, and I have a plus-one. Everly would love it if you came."

Cheyenne cleared her throat one last time. "Are you saying it's not a date?"

Ridge looked at the floor and then back up at her with a surer expression. "It's not a date unless you want it to be."

Cheyenne's breath halted in her chest. Ridge was asking her to be his date to a wedding, and she wanted to say yes more than she wanted air.

But she should say no. A warning string pulled in the back of her mind. She enjoyed being around him way too much, and she could admit that to herself. The dark secret between them was growing, and attending a wedding–a romantic affair–with Ridge was just asking for a broken heart.

She would either betray him and leave them both scarred, or she would confess her mistakes and lose his trust in the process. Neither situation ended well for either of them.

Why did Ridge have to be so different from the way David described him? She came here with hate in her heart, and Ridge had turned that anger into respect. He was selfless, hard-working, not asking for a handout, and earning his keep and keeping his word.

Her mission from David was to get close to Ridge, and she had, but now she was left wanting more. Not for David, but for herself.

"I'd love to go with you," Cheyenne finally answered.

His grin sealed her fate. She was falling for Ridge Cooper, and not even the impending heartbreak could stop her now.

Chapter Sixteen

Ridge

Ridge pulled up in front of Cheyenne's cabin and stared at the door. He hadn't been this nervous since his first college game. No turning back now. The wedding would start in forty-five minutes, and his date was waiting.

Cheyenne was waiting. She was the cause of all this sweating. It had been years since he'd picked up a woman for a date. He hadn't been out with a woman since moving to Blackwater, and before that, most women opted to meet him at the restaurant. Call him old-fashioned, but there was something about picking up a woman at her place that started the date off on a different, more personal note.

After wiping his sweaty palms on his gray slacks, he got out of the truck. *Now or never.*

On the small porch, he adjusted the collar of his shirt and stretched his neck from side to side. *Here goes nothing.*

Ridge rapped his knuckles on the wooden door and shoved his hands into his pockets. *Breathe. It's just a date.*

Seconds later, Cheyenne opened the door, greeting him with a full smile that showed off the dimples in her cheeks. "Hey!"

Ridge stood there, gaping like a fish out of water. Half of her blonde hair was pulled back in loose curls that fell over her shoulders like water cascading down a mountainside. The emerald-green dress she wore fit tight at the top and flowed out at the bottom, hanging in folds at her knees.

Cheyenne's gaze traveled down to his feet and back up again. "You look handsome."

He was still staring, and it took him a few seconds to comprehend what she'd said. "You're beautiful," were the only words he could muster.

She grinned and pointed toward the small kitchen. "Let me grab my clutch."

Ridge watched her walk away and threw his head back. He'd need some major resolve to keep his sanity if he was going to be seeing her in that dress for the rest of the day.

She returned moments later and held up the silver purse. "Ready."

Ridge stepped to the side and offered his arm. "You're beautiful."

Cheyenne laughed, free and joyful with her head tilted back just a little. "You said that already. Thank you." She reached for his arm and rested her hand in the crook of his elbow.

When he walked her to the passenger side of his truck, she didn't try to beat him to it. Instead, she let him open the door and hold her hand as she slid into the seat. He rounded the truck and got in on the other side.

"Have you been posing for photos all day?" she asked.

"Surprisingly, no. Everly is going for a simple wedding, and I'm glad. We took a few earlier, and she said there would be more before the reception, but the photographer promised she wouldn't keep us from dinner for too long."

"That sounds like Everly. She's always so thoughtful."

"She didn't invite a lot of people, and she hasn't been demanding at all. Blake said he felt like he was forgetting something because she hadn't asked him to do anything except show up."

Cheyenne laughed. "So she's the opposite of a bridezilla?"

"Pretty much."

When the chapel and reception hall came into view, Cheyenne gasped. "I haven't seen this part of the ranch yet. It's gorgeous."

"Everly and Linda have put a lot of work into this place in the last year. Everly used to work at the front desk where Bethany is now."

"Who's Linda? I don't think I've met her."

"Linda is Ava's mom. She came to the ranch a while back, and she's kind of starting over."

Cheyenne hung her head and picked at the skin around her fingernail. "I know what that's like."

Ridge wanted to ask. He wanted to tell her he knew about starting over too. He wanted to reach for her hand and assure her that everything would work out for her here the way it had for him, but he couldn't say any of that right now. They were pulling up at the chapel, and he needed more than a few stolen seconds to tell her the story.

When he shifted into park, he turned to Cheyenne. "You ready?"

Cheyenne inhaled a deep breath that swelled her shoulders. "Ready as I'll ever be."

Ridge got out and jogged around the truck to get Cheyenne's door. She was already halfway out of the truck and rolling her eyes when he got to her side.

"I thought we talked about this." Her words were soft, and her smile said she wasn't irritated.

"We did, but it's a wedding. Will you let me open doors for you just for today?"

He couldn't put his finger on the real reason why it mattered to him, but he wanted to pull out all of the stops for their first date.

Cheyenne stepped out of the truck and threaded her arm through his. "I guess I'll let you spoil me this once."

Ridge placed his hand over hers as they walked toward the chapel. He opened the door for her, and she walked in first.

"Ridge!"

He'd know that voice anywhere. His mom hastened toward them with a bundle of her long dress in one hand, looking down every few steps to be sure of her footing in the silver heels she wore.

His mom panted softly as she reached him and placed a hand on his shoulder. "I've been looking for you."

"Everything okay?"

"Of course. I'm actually looking for Blake. Have you seen him?" She scanned the vestibule of the small chapel as if she might have overlooked him.

"No, but I don't think he's a runaway groom. He'll turn up."

His mother's gaze circled back around and stopped on Cheyenne. "Oh, hello there. I'm sorry. Where are my manners? I'm Emmaline Cooper."

Ridge wrapped his arm around Cheyenne's back. "Mom, this is Cheyenne Keeton."

His mother's eyes widened as she gasped. "You're the one I've heard so much about."

Cheyenne jerked slightly, and a flicker of panic tensed Ridge's muscles. His mom didn't know how to beat around the bush. He'd gotten his own directness from her. And while he hadn't told his mom much about Cheyenne, she'd obviously been talking to Everly too.

Cheyenne gently grasped his mother's outstretched hand. "I hope it's all good."

His mom wrapped her other hand around Cheyenne's, gently cradling it. "Of course. Getting Ridge to talk is like wringing water from a stone, but Everly filled in the gaps for me."

Cheyenne glanced up at him, and her easy smile from a moment ago now seemed forced.

Was she disappointed that Ridge hadn't been the one talking to his mom about her?

Still holding Cheyenne's hand, his mother looked at him with a knowing grin. "Ridge told me about how great you are with the kids."

Well, apparently, his mom knew how to summarize two weeks' worth of things he'd told her about Cheyenne into one sentence all while making him look good. He'd have to buy her an exceptionally amazing gift for her birthday.

"Oh, thank you, Mrs. Cooper. Ridge is doing a great job," Cheyenne said.

"He's been working so hard on this program. I know it means so much to him, and I'm so glad he has a good woman by his side. It's been tough for him after what happened, and I think this program is just what he needs."

A sharp chill raced down his spine. Why was his mom bringing up the past? He'd been so careful not to slip up and tell Cheyenne anything about what happened before he came here, and his mom had opened the can of worms in the first three minutes of meeting her.

The hand on Cheyenne's back tensed against her smooth dress. "Mom, weren't you looking for Blake?"

"Oh, yes. I have to run. I'll catch up with you more after the ceremony." His mother released Cheyenne's hand and wrapped her arms around Ridge's neck, reaching up onto her tiptoes to plant a kiss on his cheek. "Love you." She turned to Cheyenne. "It was so nice to meet you."

"You too," Cheyenne said as she waved.

Ridge didn't breathe until his mom was out of hearing distance, but his palms continued to sweat even after she was gone.

He gestured toward the seats in the chapel. "You want to sit in the front or the back?"

Cheyenne shrugged. "Either is fine. Are you the usher?"

"No. Everly wanted the guests to sit wherever they wanted, and she said she wanted everyone to enjoy the wedding instead of having a job to do."

"Then I'll leave the front pews for close friends and family."

She wrapped her hand around his elbow again, but her grip was tense now. His mom's slipup played on repeat in his mind.

After what happened.

He'd been grappling with himself and praying for the words to tell Cheyenne for days now, but if he waited for the perfect time to tell her, that day might never come.

Chapter Seventeen

Cheyenne

Ridge hadn't been kidding when he said Everly wanted a simple wedding. The ceremony was understated and beautiful, focusing on blessing the new union before their friends, family, and God.

The whole thing had Cheyenne sniffling back that tickling in her nose that said tears were near. She'd shed more silent tears over the last two weeks than in the last two years of her life.

It was the emotional struggle. That had to be it. She was stuck between a rock and a hard place with no one she could turn to. She couldn't ask her sister, Sadie, Ava, or Everly for guidance when no one knew about the mess she'd gotten herself into. The Lord was her only confidant, and if He knew the answer to her problem, He hadn't let her know about it yet.

After the ceremony, Ridge had stayed close to Cheyenne's side, only leaving when he was called to be in some of the wedding photos. Within the first half hour, she'd officially been introduced to all of Ridge's relatives and friends, and aside from the influx of introductions, she was having a great time.

Now, Cheyenne had somehow ended up in a never-ending conversation with Ridge's grandma.

"I told him, 'Don't get muddy.' I said those exact words. But did he listen?"

Cheyenne smiled. "I'm guessing he didn't."

"Of course not. In fact, he got my golf cart stuck in the stream! He knew I used that golf cart to get to my garden at the bottom of the hill every day, and he took it on a little joy ride and planted it in the muddy bank. Everly ran in covered in mud and crying. She told me what Ridge had done and that they couldn't get the stupid golf cart out of the stream."

Cheyenne glanced over to where Ridge was talking with his uncle Henry. In the few seconds she watched him, his gaze darted to hers no less than three times. "I bet he was a handful."

"You have no idea. I still love that booger. He was always so sweet. I had some of the most beautiful flowers in my yard, and he'd pick one and bring it to me every once in a while. At first, I wanted to throttle him for picking my good blooms instead of the dead heads, but then I realized the kitchen was a little brighter whenever he brought one inside. You know, he did some of the sweetest things when he was little, but he never said a word about them. He'd hand me those flowers and run off without a backward glance."

Cheyenne glanced at Ridge again, who was now making his way back toward her. "I know what you mean. He's a quiet one."

Ridge's grandma patted Cheyenne's shoulder. "His actions speak louder than words, and that's okay."

Ridge stepped up beside Cheyenne and wrapped an arm around her waist. "Granny, are you telling embarrassing stories again?"

"I don't know what you mean," Granny said with a stern expression. "I was just telling this young girl about the flowers you used to bring me."

Ridge stepped away from Cheyenne to wrap his granny in a full-on hug. "Sorry I haven't brought you any lately."

"It's fine." Granny lifted her chin, and Ridge bent so she could kiss his cheek. "Georgia isn't right up the road from here."

"Was your flight okay?" Ridge asked.

Cheyenne rested a hand on her chest. If Ridge didn't stop being so sweet to his grandma, she was going to be head over heels before the end of the night.

"I don't like planes, but it was fine," Granny said. She had a way of making everything sound snippy, but her actual words were mild. It was like she'd been scolding children for fifty years and couldn't get out of the habit.

"You need something to drink?" he asked.

Granny waved him off. "I'll get it myself." She turned to Cheyenne. "It was nice talking to you."

"It was nice talking to you too," Cheyenne said as Granny opened her arms for a big hug.

"I'm glad Ridge finally found him a good woman. Keep him in line, won't you?"

Cheyenne released the hug and nodded. Was she Ridge's "good woman?"

No. If she was Ridge's woman at all, things had started off all wrong between them. The secret she harbored rolled around in her stomach like rocks in a tumbler.

Granny set off for the drinks table, and Ridge stepped up beside Cheyenne, blocking out the room full of happy guests.

"You okay? I know Granny can be a little forward."

"I'm fine. She was so sweet."

Ridge shook his head, but his grin said he knew Cheyenne was right. "Once Granny starts talking, she doesn't know when to stop."

"It's fine. I wanted to hear more stories about you as a kid."

Ridge huffed. "Granny has them in spades. She never forgets anything."

Cheyenne looked down and bit her lips between her teeth. When the truth came out about David, Granny wouldn't forgive and forget. Cheyenne shouldn't care, but she did. Ridge had a huge, amazing family, and none of them deserved David's wrath–especially Ridge.

Ridge tilted his head toward the food table. "Are you ready to eat? The line is short right now."

"Sure." Cheyenne threaded her arm through his. Was she hungry, or was it the gnawing secret that had her stomach in knots?

When they reached the buffet table, Cheyenne chuckled. "Of course Blake and Everly would serve tacos at their wedding."

Ridge handed Cheyenne a plate. "Ava tried to talk them out of it. She said guests would mess up their nice clothes. Blake and Ev wouldn't budge."

"Good for them. I could eat about ten tacos right now. This all looks so good."

With their plates full, they found seats next to Colt and Remi at a table near the dance floor.

Remi greeted them with a big wave. "Congrats, Ridge!"

Ridge took his seat and raised one eyebrow at Remi's comment. "Um, thanks. Why am I getting congratulated?"

"Blake is officially your brother now," Remi said with a flippant eye roll. "You were friends, and now you're family."

Ridge rubbed his chin. "I guess I hadn't thought about that. Are you saying I can't return him if I decide I don't like him anymore? I kept the receipt."

Remi jerked her head toward the front of the room where Blake and Everly stood close to each other as they chatted with Ava and Linda. "I think you're stuck with him. Those two are a perfect couple if I ever saw one."

The pumping beat of a pop song blasted through the sound system, and Remi gasped. "It's my song!"

Colt rolled his eyes. "You think every song is your song."

Remi grabbed his arm, unfazed by his comment. "Dance with me!" she shouted.

Colt's eyes widened. "What? I was told there'd be cake, not dancing."

She tugged at his arm. "On your feet, soldier!"

With a heavy sigh, Colt stood and let Remi drag him to the dance floor.

Cheyenne covered her mouth to hide her chuckle. "Those two are so cute."

Ridge leaned toward her to be heard above the music. "It's kind of a sad story."

Cheyenne raised her eyebrows. "You're kidding. Those two?"

"Yep. I don't know if it'll ever happen."

An older couple sat down beside Ridge and Cheyenne, and the conversation about their friends was replaced by a friendly chat with Blake's great aunt and uncle.

Remi ran up behind Cheyenne just as she swallowed the last bite of her taco. Remi's excited smile either said she'd enjoyed dancing with Colt or she had a trick up her sleeve.

"Hey, kids. Look alive." She pointed to the ceiling. "It's a slow song."

Cheyenne hadn't noticed the change in tune, but Remi was right. Ridge looked around for a second, seeming unsure.

"We don't have to dance," Cheyenne said.

"Do you want to?" Ridge asked.

"I want to if you're comfortable with dancing. It's really fine if you don't want to." The man hid out in every corner of the ranch. Dancing at a wedding didn't seem to fit the image she'd been painting of Ridge in her mind.

He stood, scraping the legs of his chair over the floor. "May I have this dance?"

Unable to deny him, Cheyenne took his outstretched hand and let him lead her to the back of the dance floor. She gulped down a wad of nervousness as he pulled her close, resting a warm hand on her lower back. She took a few deep, calming breaths, but nothing could stifle the fire that stemmed from his hands on her.

When she looked up at him, the pain in his expression caught her off guard. "Are you okay?"

His hand tensed on her back. "Yeah." His gaze trailed to her right where his parents were dancing.

In a brave moment, Cheyenne asked, "Is it about what your mom said earlier?"

Ridge's attention snapped back to Cheyenne. He hesitated a moment before answering. "Yeah."

After what happened. His mom had to have meant the arrest. And the wounded look in Ridge's eyes confirmed that whatever happened was haunting the strong man standing before her.

"Do you want to talk about it?" she asked, almost too quiet to be heard above the soft music.

Ridge shook his head slowly. "Not here."

That was more than she deserved. Those two words held a gentle yes. Did he really mean to tell her about his arrest? The cowardly side of her that hadn't mustered the courage to tell him her own secret sank deeper into a hole. She wanted to hear his side of the story. Why had he hurt that man? What had he been forced to overcome in the months after his sentencing?

She knew him well enough now to understand that she was missing some crucial part of the story. If Ridge had done something in his life he wasn't proud of, he could join her club.

Her secret, however, was as black and white as a newspaper: she'd accepted money from a stranger in exchange for finding out anything she could about Ridge Cooper. She'd learned enough to know he was a good man, and he probably didn't deserve David's wrath.

She'd stopped cashing the checks, and she'd started putting every cent she could back into a savings account she'd created just for gathering up the money to pay back what she'd already accepted from him. If she didn't figure something out soon, her mom was going to have to move to a different, less expensive and less inclusive facility.

Ridge halted the swaying of their dance and focused on something behind her. When she turned, Everly and Blake were talking with someone Cheyenne didn't know, but their facial expressions were grave.

"I'm sorry, but I need to find out what's going on. I'll be right back."

Cheyenne nodded, but Ridge was already headed for his sister and friend. If David had two brain cells, he'd know the one surefire way to get on Ridge's bad side was to mess with his sister.

Maybe that was the real cause of the rift between the two men. David did seem like a determined businessman, but if he cheated on Everly, Ridge wouldn't let the insult to his sister slide.

Remi stepped up beside Cheyenne to watch the confrontation the bride and groom were involved in. "Wonder what's going on."

Cheyenne shrugged. "I'm not sure."

"Probably Everly's stupid ex. I wouldn't put it past him to try to crash the wedding."

Cheyenne pulled her attention from the couple and Ridge. Remi's red hair fell in a curly ponytail over one shoulder and down the seafoam-green dress she wore. "Who?"

Remi waved a hand in the air. "David. He was a loser, and he didn't know how to take no for an answer. He crashed a wedding here earlier this year to get to Everly. Thankfully, Blake gave him the ol' one-two. I thought Ridge was going to lose it on the guy too, but a police officer escorted David out with a bloody nose." Remi shrugged. "He deserved it."

Cheyenne stared at Remi with wide eyes. "What did he do?"

Remi made a motion like she was slapping someone with the back of her hand. "Pow."

"You're kidding. David hit her?" Cheyenne could barely say the words. The guy had accused Ridge of being violent, and he'd hit Everly. Cheyenne turned her attention back to where Everly and Blake were talking to Ridge. The other person had left the conversation while she'd been listening to Remi.

"He was the worst. I'm so glad Everly dumped him when he cheated on her."

Cheyenne gaped. David cheated on Everly, came all the way out to Wolf Creek Ranch, hit her, and was escorted out by the police.

Everything clicked into place. Ridge wasn't the bad guy. It was David.

Chapter Eighteen

Ridge

Ridge stopped beside Blake. "What happened?"

Everly's eyes were red-rimmed, and she averted her gaze. Whatever happened was still bothering Everly. Ridge crossed his arms over his chest, waiting to hear who needed a throat punch for making his sister cry.

Blake looked around to see if anyone else was listening. "Asa stopped David at the entrance."

Ridge's tense jaw was starting to ache. The loser actually tried getting in–again. "David needs to get a clue before trouble comes looking for him, and Officer Scott needs a raise."

"Asa wants us to come to the station after the reception to talk about the threat David might pose to us... and the ranch."

"You're kidding." Ridge looked from Everly to Blake.

Blake hung his head. "Afraid not. He wants you to come by too."

Ridge rubbed the back of his neck. Everly couldn't catch a break from David. Not even on her wedding day. Ridge wouldn't be surprised if David followed them on their honeymoon.

"Does Asa need help?" Ridge asked.

Blake shook his head. "He has backup, and I think you're the last person we need to call to diffuse a situation where David is involved."

Ridge lifted his chin. "What's that supposed to mean?"

Everly rested a hand on Ridge's arm. "It means we need to keep the peace as much as possible."

"I won't maim the guy, but he could use a broken finger," Ridge said.

"Like I said, we don't need anyone getting hurt."

Heat rose from Ridge's neck to his face. "I'm not hardwired for violence, Ev."

Moisture glistened in her eyes, and her chin quivered when she looked up at him. "I know that, but I also know you won't sit back and let anyone hurt the people you care about."

"And?" The bite in his tone meant he needed to take a step back. "What's your point?"

Everly wrapped her arms around his neck and buried her face in his chest. "My point is that I love you, and I don't want you anywhere near David."

Ridge wrapped an arm around Everly. "Right back at you. Can I stick his feet in wet cement and chuck him in the Pacific?"

Everly chuckled and released him. "If he follows us on our honeymoon, I'll do it myself."

Blake held up a finger. "I've thought about tying him to Thunder's saddle and letting the stallion loose on the ridge."

"Blake!" Everly shouted.

Blake shrugged. "It would be fun to watch."

"Agreed." Ridge turned to Everly. "Can Asa bring David to the stables?"

Everly rolled her eyes. "No. Asa is taking care of the situation, and no animals or construction materials will be involved."

"Fine. I'll give Asa my statement later." Ridge looked at his watch. "Do you two need to cut out early? Don't you have a long drive to the airport?"

Blake wrapped his arm around Everly's shoulders. "We'll leave after we make the rounds and tell everyone good-bye."

Ridge wiped a tear off Everly's cheek. "Be safe, and keep an eye out for Blake."

Blake held out his open hands. "I can take care of myself. You're the one who can't even read your emails."

"Correction. I got you to read the emails for me without even asking. I'd say that was pretty smart."

Blake's brows furrowed, and his mouth gaped. "Are you serious right now?"

Everly wrapped her arms around Ridge's neck again. Despite David's intrusion, she was smiling again. "Love you," she whispered.

"Love you too," Ridge whispered back before releasing her and giving Blake a slap on the back hug.

Blake pointed over Ridge's shoulder. "You need to get back to your date. Remi is sharing all of your dirty secrets."

Ridge looked over his shoulder to see Remi waving her hand in the air while Cheyenne watched intently. "That's why I never tell Remi my secrets, but Cheyenne probably does need saving. See you two in a few weeks."

Just as Ridge started making his way toward Cheyenne, she held up a finger and pointed to her phone. Remi waved Cheyenne off to a corner and set her sights on Ridge.

Remi was a force to be reckoned with, and she didn't pull punches. If she was headed his way, the smart thing to do would be to change course.

"Ridge! Is David being a weirdo again?"

Ridge stopped and turned to face the music, or the flaming-haired loudmouth of the ranch. "Can you keep your voice down?"

"This is my indoor voice." Remi blinked at him as if daring him to try to stifle her again.

"Right. There's no problem. Blake and Everly are about to head out."

"Good! I'll go say my farewells!" Remi shoved an empty cup at him as she walked past.

Ridge set the cup on the table and looked for Cheyenne. She was still on the phone. With her shoulders raised and her elbows tucked in close, she stared at the floor. Ridge's hands fisted at his sides. The urge to go to her grappled with the warning to keep his distance. He still didn't know much about her, and from the look of worry on her face, she was dealing with something she hadn't told him about yet.

Yet. As if uncovering the mysteries of Cheyenne Keeton were inevitable. Sure, he wanted to know, but was it fair to ask her to open up to him if he wasn't ready to do the same?

A few seconds later, Cheyenne ended the call and cradled her phone in her hands. She looked up and met his gaze, but there was a flicker of unease in her eyes before she smiled at him.

The smile was her tell. It was that stifled, put-on expression she'd given him on her first day, not the easy, genuine smile he'd come to love in the weeks since.

Love. What did he know about love? Love was patient. Love was kind. He could be patient if it meant he could earn the love of a good woman. Cheyenne was that woman–the only one. The truth settled something inside him as he took the first step toward her.

He slipped his arm around her waist when they met. "Are you okay?"

She hesitated. "I'm okay." She looked at her phone and shoved it into her clutch. When she looked back up at him, the determination he'd come to know in the last few weeks working beside her flared in her eyes. "That was someone from my old life. Someone I need to cut out."

The resolve in her tone calmed any uncertainty he'd been holding onto. Still, she hadn't told him the whole truth. He could only hope she would in time. "If you tell me you have a husband back in Tennessee, I might lose my mind."

The joke earned him a smile–the real one. "No. Nothing like that." She shook her head and reached for his arm. "Don't worry about it. Let's just enjoy the night."

Enjoy the night. That's exactly what he wanted to do. "I hate to spoil the fun, but I have to cut the night short."

Cheyenne glanced to where he'd been talking to Blake and Everly. "Did something happen?"

This was a chance to let her in on something, but he hesitated. Was he ready to lay out the skeleton in the closet?

Remi had probably already told her about David. She'd guessed what was going on before being told. If he kept it under wraps now, he wouldn't earn any of Cheyenne's loyalty. "Everly has an ex who causes trouble from time to time. The police are handling things, but they want me to give a statement at the police station tonight."

The color drained from Cheyenne's face. She opened her mouth a few times, but she didn't speak.

Ridge reached for her hand and threaded his fingers in hers. "Everything is fine. I promise."

"Who is it?" Cheyenne quietly asked. Her hand was still tense in his.

"His name is David. He cheated on her, so she broke up with him. I've known him for years, and he doesn't like it when his plans don't turn out exactly the way he thought." Ridge scoffed. "He's kind of like a toddler throwing a fit."

Cheyenne squeezed his hand and nodded slowly. "Okay. We can leave whenever you're ready."

"I think Blake and Everly are getting ready to head out. We can leave after them." Ridge tilted his head toward the table where Blake and Everly were standing beside a simple two-tiered cake. "Want some cake before we go?"

Cheyenne took a few deep breaths before answering. "Maybe a small piece."

Her color was still pale, and her chest rose and fell in deep waves. "Are you sure you're okay?"

"Yeah. I'm fine."

Google translation: Cheyenne was not fine. Why wouldn't she just tell him? Seeing her upset was simultaneously shutting down the logical side of his brain and firing up his need to protect her from whatever was causing her to worry.

"Let me say good-bye to a few people, and we can head out," Ridge said.

Cheyenne stayed by his side as he let his parents and grandparents know he was leaving, and when Blake and Everly made their exit, Ridge watched Cheyenne for any signs of what might be bothering her.

Half an hour later, they walked out of the reception hall toward his truck. Cheyenne's anxiety seemed to have settled a little, and she let him open her door for her. Neither of them spoke until they'd almost reached Cheyenne's cabin.

"The sunset is beautiful," she said quietly.

Ridge studied the orange-and-pink sunset. It looked like the sky was on fire. "I'm usually out here at sunset, but I hardly ever stop to look at it."

"I've been sitting on the front porch in the evenings. I can't get enough of it."

Ridge's tense shoulders relaxed. At least she was talking now. "Did you have a good time?" he asked as he parked the truck in front of her cabin.

"I did." She looked down at her hands, and her words didn't match the sullen expression on her face.

Unsure what to say to bring back her happiness from earlier, Ridge got out of the truck and walked around to Cheyenne's side. This time, she waited for him to open the door for her.

When they reached the front door, Cheyenne turned instead of opening it. Was she ready to tell him about whatever was bothering her?

"What's wrong? Did I do something to upset you?" he asked.

Cheyenne shook her head and looked up at him. "Your family is great. I really liked your mom."

"She's the best."

Was Cheyenne still thinking about his mom's slipup earlier? The heavy question rose in his throat and threatened to choke him. Should he tell her about the arrest? Would she even let him explain?

Cheyenne picked at her fingernails as she spoke. "I don't have much family. Just my mom and sister. Seeing your family tonight made me miss them."

"I'm sorry. I didn't even think about that when I introduced you." He reached for her hand, and she didn't resist. When their hands were linked, she squeezed lightly.

"It's okay. I don't think I ever told you about my mom. She had a stroke a few months ago, and she needs constant supervision and health care."

Ridge's throat tightened. "I can't imagine going through that with my mom. I'm sorry."

"I lost my job right around the time she had the stroke. My younger sister, Hadley, was the only one working, and I couldn't find a job in Bear Cliff."

"Is that why you took the job here, even though it was far away from home?"

She looked up at him and hesitated before nodding. "You're lucky to have them."

Ridge gently tugged on her hand, and she took a step toward him, erasing the distance between them and resting her head against his chest. His arms wrapped around her, hoping to shield her from the sadness that had crept into their evening.

His hand lazily rubbed up and down her back. "Is your dad around to help?" he asked.

Cheyenne lifted her head from his chest. "My dad hasn't ever been around." She hesitated a second before continuing. "My dad is some famous football player, and he never claimed me or even acknowledged I exist."

The words hit Ridge like a kick in the gut. "Football player?"

"Jerry Keeton."

Ridge's eyes widened. "He's your dad?"

She shrugged. "That's what Mom tells me. I've seen pictures of him."

Ridge stared at Cheyenne. The mention of the sport he used to play had knocked the breath out of him for a second, but now, he could see the truth in what she'd told him. The dimples in her cheeks when she laughed, her dark-brown eyes, and the point of her chin all came from her dad.

"You look a lot like him. I know you don't want to hear that, but I think your mom is right."

Cheyenne looked down. "I've heard that before."

Ridge couldn't believe what he was hearing. He'd met Jerry Keeton a dozen times, and the man didn't seem like the kind of guy to abandon his kid. In fact, he had two sons with his wife, and Ridge had met them too. They were always around to support Jerry.

Would knowing any of that help Cheyenne? The information would probably hurt her. Still, he couldn't piece together what Cheyenne was telling him and what he knew of the man.

He could tell her. He could tell her everything. She'd mentioned football, and now he had a chance to come clean without having to drop the news on her out of nowhere.

Say it. I played in the NFL. I met your dad.

He couldn't do it. The words wouldn't come out.

Cheyenne rested her hand on the doorknob. "Thanks for taking me tonight. I had a good time."

A rock settled in Ridge's middle. Those words felt hollow. Was she pulling away from him? What had happened tonight to bring on the change?

"I did too." He meant it, and he held his breath waiting for her to say something to validate the way he felt.

"Good night," she whispered.

Cheyenne looked up at him, and the urge to kiss her had him leaning in.

No. Not yet. He couldn't. It was their first date, and the feeling that something was bothering her didn't sit well with him. Not only that, but he hadn't been honest with her. She should know what she was getting into before he kissed her.

"Good night," he said, tipping the imaginary hat he wished he wore to hide the concern that was probably written on his face. He walked slowly back to the truck, reluctant to leave Cheyenne. Was she upset because she was missing her family, or was something else bothering her?

He got in the truck and waited until Cheyenne was inside and the light came on in her cabin. If he didn't have to give a statement at the police department, there was no way he would leave. She was just starting to open up to him. She told him a little bit, but there had to be more.

Was the ball in his court? Was it his turn to fess up? Maybe he should ease her into things. He could tell her about the NFL first, and then tell her about the assault charge later. But would she think he'd kept the truth from her for too long?

For the first time in six years, he wanted to open up to someone. He only talked about the things that happened before coming to the ranch if he absolutely had to. Was this one of those times when he needed to get the ugly truth out in the open?

Would Cheyenne judge him? Would she leave? It was crazy to ask her to believe the truth, and he wouldn't blame her if she walked away.

No, Cheyenne would understand. She'd do anything for her family just like he'd done for his sister.

At least, that's what he wanted to believe.

Chapter Nineteen

Cheyenne

Cheyenne reached her hand into the shallow water at the edge of the creek. Her jaw twitched as she pulled out the tadpole. "Eww," she whispered, trying not to look like a coward in front of the kids.

"She did it!" Eric yelled "Told you!"

Cheyenne turned toward the three teenagers and opened her hand. The tiny tadpole rested in her palm.

Remi leaned over the tadpole to get a better look, and her red hair fell in a curtain over her shoulder. "That's the cutest thing I've ever seen!"

Tiffany, a friendly girl who'd developed a little crush on Ridge, leaned close to Remi. "Cuter than Mr. Cooper?"

"Who in the world is Mr. Cooper?" Remi asked.

Tiffany pointed to Ridge where he was showing some of the teens how to tie a fly on a line.

"Eww! He's a boy. He has cooties." Remi scrunched up her nose.

"Not cuter than Colt," Lucy said. She sighed and fanned her face.

Remi held up her hands. "Stop it. You're going to make me lose my lunch."

They'd brought a picnic to the creek and ended up staying for hours. It was the first day of camp for the fourteen and fifteen year olds. Everyone was enjoying the beautiful weather and getting to know each other.

Cheyenne laughed at Remi as she walked off to join the fly-tying lesson.

"What about you?" Tiffany asked. "You don't think the icky tadpole is cuter than Ridge or Colt, do you?"

Cheyenne looked at the blob in her hand. It was kind of adorable, but telling the truth right now would only bring trouble. "I need to get this guy back in the water."

"She totally has the hots for Ridge," Tiffany whispered to Lucy.

Cheyenne squatted beside Wolf Creek and gently tipped the tadpole back into the water. She definitely had the hots for Ridge, but things between them had been awkward since her freak-out at the wedding.

Hearing Ridge talk about David had completely immobilized her. Panic and fear had choked her, and she hadn't been able to tell Ridge the truth.

When she finally did tell him, it would ruin everything. She'd kept the secret for too long, and he was going to hate her. That crippling fear only served to scare her into keeping the secret for longer.

A girl down river let out a blood-curdling scream, and Cheyenne jumped to her feet. A group of the teens were huddled back from the creek, and Ridge was crouched by the bank.

Cheyenne jogged to the group. "What's wrong?"

"There's a snake in the water!" Tiffany said, pointing to where Ridge leaned over the water.

"What's he doing?" Cheyenne asked.

Just as the words came out of her mouth, Ridge's hand darted out in a blur. He held the snake right behind the pointed head.

"What is he doing?" Cheyenne screamed again. She wasn't terribly afraid of snakes, but never in a million years would she touch one.

"That was so cool," Hudson said behind her.

Ridge stood and grabbed the snake's tail with his other hand. He took a few steps back from the creek and lifted it up toward her.

Don't flinch. Don't let the kids see fear.

"I'm taking this guy a little farther downstream so he won't bother us. It's just a garter snake," Ridge said.

"Um. Okay," Cheyenne squeaked. That explained what he was doing; she just couldn't fathom touching a snake on purpose.

"My sister is going to flip out when she hears about this," Nathan said.

Cheyenne turned to the kids and took a deep breath. "Well, it looks like Mr. Cooper has saved the day. Nothing to see here."

"Next one to spot another snake gets an extra ride on Sprinkles this evening!" Remi shouted.

The boys jogged off in different directions, while the girls huddled next to Cheyenne.

Tiffany watched the boys and shook her head. "I've had enough wildlife for one day."

Cheyenne wrapped an arm around the girl's shoulders. "It's almost time to head back to the barn, and I'm sure Mr. Cooper will handle any other critters we might find."

Remi belted out the chorus of "Fight Song" by Rachel Platten as she tied a fly on the line of a fishing pole. A few of the girls chimed in too. Working with Remi never felt like work, and it was no secret why the kids at the ranch loved her.

Colt walked out of the trail in the woods and shouted, "What in the world are you singing?"

Remi halted her song and looked over her shoulder at him. "It's my anthem."

"Your anthem?" Colt asked as he stepped up beside Remi.

"You know, my jam. Cause I'm single as a Pringle."

Cheyenne leaned toward Lucy and whispered, "You were right about those two." She tilted her head toward Colt and Remi.

"I know. They're so cute," Lucy said.

Colt looked at the ground and shook his head. "You're ridiculous."

"Remi. My name is Remi," she corrected.

"Whatever. Ava sent me out here to tell you to please come to her office. She's been trying to call you, and you haven't answered."

"Okay," Remi said as she swung the fishing rod behind her.

"I think she meant now, Remi," Colt said.

Remi looked at him with one brow lifted. "Oh, well why didn't you say that?"

The girls giggled, and Colt walked off shaking his head.

Remi handed her rod to Cheyenne. "I'll meet you back at the barn."

"See you there," Cheyenne said.

Remi bent down as she passed the picnic area and plucked a triangle of cornbread out of the food basket. "I'm takin' my cornbread with me," she said before shoving a big bite into her mouth.

Ridge walked up beside Cheyenne. Thankfully, the snake was nowhere in sight.

"Where's she going?" he asked.

"Colt said Ava wanted to talk to her. She'll meet up with us later." Cheyenne looked around. "You take care of the snake?"

"I took care of it." Ridge gave her one of those heart-stopping winks.

A pang of pure regret shot through her. Ridge was efficient at taking care of unwanted snakes. What would he do when he found out there was a figurative snake in his own life?

Ridge pointed at the rod Remi had handed her. "You fishing?"

Cheyenne looked at the rod. "No. Not me."

"You want to?" he asked.

"I don't know. I've never used one of these before."

Ridge rested a hand on her back and urged her toward the creek. "I'll show you." He turned and shouted over his shoulder. "Fishing lesson, guys!"

A crowd of teenagers pushed and shoved each other as they huddled near the bank.

Ridge stood behind her, wrapping his arms around her. "You want to hold it like this."

Cheyenne's breath hitched as Ridge's hands rested on top of hers. His warm chest pressed against her back, and his big arms shielded her on both sides.

Ridge moved the fishing rod, showing her how to cast. The lure flew over the water, and he wrapped his hand gently around hers and turned the reel. He could have let go now, but he didn't. Inside, her lungs were screaming for air, but her head and heart were in agreement. She didn't need air. She needed Ridge to stay firmly pressed against her like this.

He rattled off instructions through a few more casts. The kids were probably hanging on his every word, but Cheyenne was tingling from her head to her toes.

When he released her, cold slid down her back in all the places he'd been, and she couldn't focus on the line at all. That was a good description of her life with and without Ridge in it. Warm or cold. Safe or lonely.

"Okay, folks. Start loading up," Ridge said. "Half of you get the picnic and half of you get the fishing gear."

She turned around to start gathering things up when Ridge stopped her. With one hand on her arm, he leaned in close and whispered, "I could get used to fishing with you."

And Cheyenne melted into a puddle. What was this man doing to her?

"Want to try it again sometime? Without the audience?"

The best response she could muster was an excited nod. Shaking her head up and down meant yes, right?

Ridge slipped past her, and her face and fingers began tingling. Nope, she couldn't be trusted to go fishing alone with Ridge. Not yet. She'd turn into a pile of goo and babble out her whole life story, effectively sending him running for the hills.

She had to be at her best when she finally worked up the nerve to tell him. Today wasn't that day.

Cheyenne brought the rod to the flatbed trailer they'd used to bring the kids and stuff out to the creek. She turned around to gather up more of their things when her phone rang in her pocket. Ice froze in her veins when she saw Jaden's name on the screen.

"Hey. Is everything okay?" Cheyenne asked quickly. Jaden never called her in the middle of the day.

"Hey, um. I was just wondering how things were going today," Jaden said. Her usual peppy assurance was laced with worry.

"Fine. I'm at work. Are you sure everything is okay?"

Jaden hesitated. "I think so, but I'm not sure."

Cheyenne glanced at Ridge, who was busy gathering up the fishing supplies. "Is it David? Did he do something?"

Whatever David was into, it would be terrible for everyone around him. He was a liar, and she didn't trust anything about him now.

"I don't know. Really. He didn't show up for work this morning. I know Everly's wedding was on Saturday, and I've been worried he would try to do something. I just don't know what he's up to, and the possibilities are endless."

"Thanks for the warning. Are you okay? Is he a threat to you?" Cheyenne had come to know

Jaden in the last month, and the woman seemed just as trapped as Cheyenne.

"I don't think so. I'm not sure. Just keep your eyes open, okay?"

"Okay."

"I'm sorry, I have to go. He just walked in," Jaden said.

The fear in Jaden's tone had Cheyenne gripping the phone. "Call me if you need me."

"Thank you." Jaden ended the call without a good-bye.

Cheyenne looked around at the kids and caught Ridge watching her. She smoothed the lines of her forehead and prayed he hadn't caught onto her concern.

Whatever David was up to was going to be bad, and she needed to warn Ridge. They had another few hours before the parents came to pick up the kids, but she would tell him today.

Chapter Twenty

Ridge

Ridge waved at Liam as he got into his dad's truck. There were only two kids left to be picked up. Once Ridge could get Cheyenne alone, he'd ask her to go out on a date with him. Maybe if they talked over dinner, he would be comfortable enough to tell her everything she needed to know.

He cut a glance at her while she let the remaining girls teach her a handshake. It was past time he told her the truth, and he couldn't let another night pass without coming clean. He'd been praying for the words to say to her for weeks now, and he'd recently been feeling the push to just go for it. If God had a plan for them to be together, they'd be able to talk through everything and trust each other from here on out.

Two more cars parked at the barn, and Lucy ran off waving. "That's my mom."

Cheyenne followed Lucy toward the car. She'd gotten into the habit of talking to the parents in the evening. Lucy had been extra attentive with the horses this afternoon, and Cheyenne would probably be gushing about how great Lucy did today.

A woman got out of the other car and walked toward Ridge. He went to meet her, despite the inkling that Cheyenne should do all the talking. She connected with people in ways he didn't.

Tiffany stepped up beside him. "That's my mom."

The woman's black hair was pulled up into a messy bun, and she wore a tank top and jean shorts that were a few inches short of appropriate.

"Hi. I'm Kaylee. Tiffany's mom." She reached her hand out to Ridge.

"Ridge Cooper. I'm the manager of the youth program." He turned to Tiffany and held out his fist for her to bump. "Your girl did a great job with the horses today."

Tiffany touched her knuckles to his and glanced at her mom. "I'm ready to go."

"Go on to the car, and I'll be there in a second," her mom said.

Tiffany looked from Ridge and back to her mother before walking off toward the car.

Kaylee tilted her head and propped her hands on her hips. "Ridge, have you been doing this for a long time?"

Ridge tensed. Was she asking to make friendly small talk or was she vetting him as an appropriate guardian for her daughter this week? "I've been working at the ranch for a few years, but this is the first year we've put on this program."

She grinned and tilted her head to the other side. He'd seen Tiffany make the same movement whenever C.J. had come around today. "I can't believe I haven't seen you around town." She looked around and then back at Ridge. "I guess you've been hiding out on this ranch."

"Yeah, I don't get out much." Ridge looked for Cheyenne, but she was still talking to Lucy's mom. "So, Tiffany said she's really interested in the garden project we're starting tomorrow. Does she have a place at home where she could plant her own garden?"

Kaylee's loud laugh caught Ridge off guard. When he looked the other way, Cheyenne,

Lucy, and Lucy's mom were watching them now too.

Kaylee finished her exaggerated laugh and slapped her hand on Ridge's chest, leaving it there as she composed herself. "No, we live with my parents, and there definitely isn't any room for a *garden*."

Ridge took a step back, and Kaylee's hand slid down his chest. His skin tickled where her fingernails grazed him, and he fought the urge to rub the remnants of her touch away.

Kaylee propped a hand back on her hip and pulled her shoulders back. "What are you doing tonight? Want to get a beer?"

Ridge coughed and beat his chest. He was a straight to the point kind of guy, but he hadn't had a proposition like that since he set foot in Wyoming. Bethany didn't hold a candle to this woman when it came to advances.

He looked for Cheyenne, and she was looking back to him. It was like she knew he was thinking about her. Now he just needed her to read his mind and come save him.

Instead of running to his rescue from the she-wolf, Cheyenne smiled. That little lift of her lips always made his heart beat a little faster, and he'd come to think of it as a reward for persisting through the long, tough days.

"Ridge?"

He snapped his attention back to the woman. What was her name again? "Yes?"

"You want to get a beer?"

"Thanks for the offer, but I'm still on the clock."

"What about after you get off work?" she asked.

"I don't drink."

That earned him a scowl. She looked him up and down as if checking to see if he had extra arms like an alien. "Like, not ever?"

"Not ever." He wasn't a fan of anything that impaired his judgment, and he'd seen too many of his teammates lose everything over alcohol and drugs.

She touched the bun her hair was knotted in and looked at the ground. "Oh, well, we could grab something to eat."

Soft hands wrapped around his upper arm, and his impatience with the woman eased.

"Hey, I'm Cheyenne, Ridge's assistant here at the ranch. You must be Tiffany's mom."

Cheyenne held out a hand, but Tiffany's mom hesitated before reaching out. "Yeah. Kaylee."

Kaylee. He needed to remember that name and run fast if he ever heard it.

Ridge wrapped his arm around Cheyenne's waist and pulled her flush against his side. She let out a soft gasp, and the little slip of surprise did crazy things to his chest. Her warmth had his brain firing on all cylinders.

"Cheyenne's the real brains of the operation." He looked down at her, and the fire in her eyes had his grip tightening on her hip.

"Oh, well, that's cool," Kaylee said.

A clap of thunder drew their attention to the sky. The western sky was dark, and the air was thick and charged.

Tiffany stuck her head out of the car window. "Mom! Let's go!"

Kaylee pointed to the ominous sky. "I should run. Bye." She barely waved as she ran toward her car.

Cheyenne chuckled beside him. "She can't get out of here fast enough."

"Thanks for marking your territory," Ridge whispered.

Her dimples were on full display, and she batted her lashes. "I don't know what you mean." She slapped her hand on Ridge's chest and let her fingers trail over his abs the way Kaylee had done.

The sparks that spread through his body from the place she'd touched could burn down the entire town. There was no denying Cheyenne's hold on him.

Another clap of thunder snapped him out of the trance she'd put him in. "We'd better get things cleaned up before we get rained out."

Cheyenne looked up. "I'll get the gardening tools. You get the trailers into the barn."

"You got it, boss."

She narrowed her eyes at him. "You're the boss."

"Sometimes, I'm not so sure. You definitely have authority over me."

Cheyenne bit her bottom lip and looked away from him. "Stop flattering me and get to work."

They jogged off in different directions, and the thunder was like a timer. Ridge pulled the trailers inside and ran to get Vanilla from the pasture. The young horse was afraid of thunderstorms, and Jess had been adamant about bringing her in when the weather was bad. By the time he got to the horse, rain poured over the brim of his hat.

He led the horse to the barn, catching resistance every time thunder clapped in the sky. Cheyenne bolted out of the barn, heading back out for another load of tools from the garden.

"Just leave it!" Ridge shouted, but the torrential rain drowned out his words.

He ushered Vanilla into the stall and went to find Cheyenne. The sky lit up in bright white, and a deafening clap of thunder rolled through the air, shaking the ground beneath his feet. Vanilla squealed in the barn behind him. Ridge crouched low and scanned the area for Cheyenne, but the heavy rain was impossible to see through.

"Cheyenne!"

"Coming!" Her yell was barely audible over the rain.

She burst into view a second later, and he reached for her, taking the gardening tools from her hands. "Are you okay?"

She panted and pushed her wet hair from her face. "Yeah. That was scary."

Ridge tried to calm his breathing. Scary didn't begin to cover the fear that had gripped him when Cheyenne had been out in that storm.

Cheyenne squeezed water from her hair. "I'll dry off the tools, and you'll want to unhook the trailer." She jerked her head toward his truck attached to the trailer.

Ridge stared at her, unable to move away from her yet. He needed the assurance of her safety a little longer.

She righted her shoulders and looked at him. "You okay?"

"Yeah. Just trying to calm down," Ridge said.

Her hand rested on his upper arm and trailed down, leaving a warm trail to his hand. "Everything is fine. We're safe."

Ridge nodded and removed his drenched hat. "Right. I'll get the trailer."

Cheyenne had the tools dried and put away before he finished the trailers. She snuck off into the office and came out with a small bag. Holding it up with one hand, she pointed to the office with the other. "I'm going to change into some dry clothes."

He'd backed the trailer in far enough to pull his truck into the cover of the barn, and he rummaged in the back seat for his extra clothes. He'd kept the emergency bag since the time he'd been dragged into a creek by a horse on a trail ride, and Cheyenne had taken her hint from Preston's fall into the manure the first week of the program.

Cheyenne walked out of the office wearing dry clothes and squeezing the ends of her hair. "Your turn."

Ridge hefted the bag over his shoulder and took his turn. The soaked clothes clung to his body and left a freezing chill when the air hit his bare skin. After changing, he dug into the bag of dry clothes and pulled out a thick coat.

Out in the barn, Cheyenne was comforting Vanilla, running her hands over the horse's mane. Ridge walked up slowly and wrapped an arm around her shoulders.

She sank into his embrace. "Thank you. Are you warm enough?" she asked.

"I'm fine. There's a heater in the office. Let's wait out the storm in there."

With one last look at Vanilla, Cheyenne followed him to the office. He closed the door behind them to trap in the heat. He picked up the coat and held it up for Cheyenne. She stared at the coat and hesitated for a second, then she slipped her arms into the sleeves and tugged it tight around her. She looked down at the coat then up at Ridge.

He reached out a hand, and she took it. With her icy hand in his, he led her closer to the small heater. "Is that better?"

She nodded but kept her gaze pointed to the floor.

Ridge leaned down to get in her line of sight. "What's wrong?"

Cheyenne shook her head. "Nothing is wrong. I just don't know many people who would give me the shirt off their back."

Ridge slid his hand behind her head and pulled her close to kiss her forehead. "Now you know at least one."

She looked up at him, and the pull toward her came straight from his chest. "I can't decide if I should keep my distance or pull you in and never let go." He leaned in closer to whisper, "You're making me crazy."

He leaned in closer but stopped an inch before touching his mouth to hers. His breaths mingled with hers as she kept her gaze locked with his.

If she didn't want this, now was the time to speak. Her trembling hand slid up his chest and wrapped around his neck, gently pulling him down to her.

That was the signal he needed, and Ridge didn't resist. He leaned down and pressed his lips to hers, breathing in the crisp air from the rain. Her warmth and softness pulled him in, and he wrapped his arms around her. He kissed her hard, then soft, pushing and pulling until his world turned end over end.

He broke the kiss and studied her, waiting for any sign of doubt. When none came, he kissed her again, savoring the brush of her mouth against his. His hands tightened against her waist, pulling her in when he got lost in the kiss.

She tilted her chin up, breaking the kiss before he was ready. When his heart rate slowed, he registered the slight narrowing of her eyes and the shallow marks between her brows.

"Are you okay?" He relaxed his hold on her waist. "Should I not have done that?"

Cheyenne shook her head. "No, it's just… Can we go somewhere to talk?"

Talking. Right. That was probably a good idea since he had some major things to tell her. He nodded and took a step back. "Right. Let's check on Vanilla, and we can go."

The light flickered, and the room went dark. Cheyenne pulled out her cell phone and turned on the flashlight, shining it to light their path out of the office. The air was growing thicker with the storm, and Vanilla was still bucking in the stall.

"There's a battery powered lantern in the tack room." He pointed to the door across the barn. Inside, they both searched for the light until they found it in a corner. Cheyenne held up the beacon while they both headed to check on the horse.

Ridge's hands shook as he reached for the latch on the stall door. Between the kiss and the storm, his adrenaline would be running high until morning.

Cheyenne lifted the light high, and Ridge reached for Vanilla. If he could calm himself enough to convince the horse, she might settle. Vanilla huffed and threw her head from side to side.

"Easy, girl," Ridge said loud enough to be heard over the torrential rain.

Instead of calming, Vanilla reared up, pawing her front hooves in the air. Ridge stepped to the side, but Cheyenne was behind him, and they fell hard against the side of the stall.

"Oww!" Cheyenne screamed.

Ridge turned, lifting her to her feet. "Are you okay? What hurts?"

Cheyenne held the lantern with one hand and lifted her ankle. She grabbed at it, then quickly jerked her hand away. "My ankle. I twisted it."

Vanilla had backed into the far corner and was still on edge. Ridge wrapped his arms behind Cheyenne's back and lifted her into his arms. Careful not to jostle her, he kept his back to the horse and sidestepped out of the stall.

"Ridge, you can't carry me."

Instead of diving into an explanation of how he definitely could carry her, he jerked his chin toward the lantern. "Just guide me."

Back in the dark office, he gently lowered her into a chair and pulled the other chair over to prop her foot in. He crouched in front of her and asked, "Where does it hurt?"

"Don't worry about me," Cheyenne said. "Go check on Vanilla."

"I'm not leaving you. You're hurt."

Cheyenne shook her head. "I'm okay. It's probably just a sprain." She put the foot down and tried to press her weight on it, but she quickly pulled it back up when the joint started to bend. "I'm fine. I'll just stay here."

Ridge looked up at her. The lantern scattered shadows over her face, but the restrained pain in her expression wasn't masked. "I don't want to leave you."

Cheyenne rested her hand on his cheek. "I'm really okay." Thunder rumbled again, and Vanilla knocked against the walls. "Please check on her. I'm fine here."

Ridge pulled out his phone. "I'll call Brett to help with the horse."

Cheyenne sighed. "Ridge, please."

Brett answered on the second ring with a twangy, "Yel-low."

"Can you come up to the south barn? Vanilla is losing her mind in the storm, and Cheyenne is injured."

"Is she okay?" Brett asked.

"She hurt her ankle. Can you come?"

"Already on my way," Brett said.

Ridge pocketed his phone and turned his attention back to Cheyenne. "You need ice." He looked at the small fridge in the office that definitely didn't have a freezer. "It might need to be wrapped too."

"Ridge," Cheyenne said as she placed her hands on both sides of his face and turned his attention to her. "I'm fine. Go. Take the light."

He wanted to argue, but the note of finality in her voice said he should obey. "I'll be right back. As soon as Brett gets here, we'll get some ice and bandages."

"Go, Ridge!" She pointed to the door.

He rushed out of the office, determined to calm the wild horse so he could tend to Cheyenne. Seeing her in pain had his stomach in knots, and he still had a lot to tell her before the night was over.

Chapter Twenty-One

Cheyenne

Sitting in the dark wasn't Cheyenne's cup of tea, but she would rather pick up a slithering snake before calling for Ridge like a scaredy cat.

Snake. She'd forgotten about the snake Ridge had handled earlier. The memory reminded her of Jaden's call and everything Cheyenne needed to tell Ridge. She couldn't keep putting it off. With David showing up at the ranch and Jaden's concern for his stability, the man could cause all kinds of damage, and she had to get a handle on her part in the mess.

The storm was calming, but her heart raced on. She had to tell Ridge, and the impending fallout had her stomach rolling.

Ridge burst back into the office without the light. "Cheyenne?"

"I'm here."

He moved toward her slowly, careful not to trip over anything in the dark. "Brett is here. He's going to stay with the horse for a while. I'll take you home."

"But my car is here," Cheyenne said. It was a futile argument. She couldn't drive when her right foot was injured.

"Brett said he'd bring Jess over here later and she could drive it over to your place. Just leave the key on the desk."

Cheyenne pulled her purse out of the desk drawer and left the key beside the computer. She steadied her hand on the arm of the chair and pushed up.

"I'll carry you. Just wrap your arm around my neck," Ridge said as he leaned down to slide his arms beneath her.

He lifted her and pulled her close to his hard chest. His warmth wrapped around her, and she settled into the safety of his arms. Ridge's truck was parked inside the covering of the barn, and he walked around to the passenger side. He gently lifted her into the truck and supported her leg until she was comfortable.

He closed the door and jogged around to the driver's side. There was no way this man could have hurt someone the way she'd been told. He was so gentle with her. He cared about her safety. He always worried over the kids when they were at the ranch. His friends and family here loved him.

Ridge was a kind man. Kind men didn't hurt other people. At least not in the way David had painted Ridge.

Ridge reached for her hand and threaded his fingers in hers. "Are you okay?"

"I'm fine. Really. You're overreacting," Cheyenne said with a chuckle. Her ankle pulled and ached, but she was pretty sure there wasn't any major damage.

Ridge's expression remained stoic. "I can't help it. I don't like seeing you hurt."

Warmth flooded Cheyenne's chest. No man had ever been as good to her as Ridge, and the awful truth that shadowed their relationship would turn his care into hate.

He parked the truck in front of her cabin and released her hand. "I'll come around to get you."

He didn't wait for her to respond before dashing out into the sprinkling rain. The storm on the ranch might be passing, but the one in her heart was raging. This was her moment, and she couldn't chicken out.

Ridge opened the door and carefully lifted her into his cradling arms again. She clung to him as the cool rain fell on her face and hair. This might be her last chance to be held by him, and the loss was already seeping into her soul, leaving a hole as big as the Wyoming sky.

Inside, he rested her in the old recliner she'd bought from the thrift store and positioned her ankle on the coffee table. "I'll be right back."

He rummaged in the kitchen for a few minutes while she stared at the ceiling. Each breath was labored as if the air were mud instead of oxygen.

Minutes later, Ridge returned with a grocery bag of ice cubes. "I refilled the ice tray, so you should have ice to put on it in the morning."

She held out her hand for the bag, but he crouched to lay it on her ankle himself. After adjusting the cubes to hang evenly on both sides of her ankle, he sat on the couch and rested his elbows on his knees.

"How do you feel?"

Cheyenne swallowed. "I'm…" This was her chance. She could lie and say she was fine, but that would give her the out she needed to put off the talk they needed to have tonight.

Ridge pushed a hand through his damp hair. "I need to tell you something. I'm sorry I've waited so long to say anything, but I didn't want to bring it up if it wouldn't matter. Now, it does matter, and you need to know."

Cheyenne held her breath. What was going on? She was supposed to do the talking.

Ridge looked at the floor, then lifted his attention to her. "Before I came to the ranch, I was a professional athlete. I had trained for it my entire life, and my family supported me. I was drafted out of college and played for the Colts for four years. Blake was my agent."

Cheyenne relaxed a little. If he was going to tell her about his time in the NFL, maybe she would have a lead in to confess about David.

"I don't want you to think I'm living a double life, but… I actually am, so I guess it doesn't matter what I want. I don't live on the ranch because I have a house right outside of town–a pretty sizable place. That's why Colt moved in with me. I lived off the ranch with Blake until a couple of months ago. My place isn't a cozy little cabin. It's ridiculously big, even for the two of us. And there's a big long story behind why I bought the house, but I'll get to that later."

"Ridge," Cheyenne whispered. "I–"

"Wait. Let me tell you everything." Ridge held up a hand, then balled it into a fist. "I didn't leave the NFL quietly." He stood and linked his hands behind his head as he paced the small room. "There was this guy. He kept showing up. Every place I went. Every press conference, every gala, every charity auction, he was there. I thought he was a fan. Some people are really into pro sports teams. Some get angry when their bets don't pay out, so I knew the things I needed to watch for when fans popped up more than once. But this guy, he was quiet, and he didn't cause trouble."

His words were coming quickly now, but Cheyenne wanted him to talk even faster. She needed to know if Ridge could really be innocent.

He turned and faced her. "It was Everly. She was part of my PR team at the time, and she went everywhere with me. Blake was always there too. He's the one who figured out the guy was watching Everly, not me."

Cheyenne gasped. Of course. Ridge would do anything for his sister, just like Cheyenne had done the unthinkable with the intention of helping her mom and sister. Family. That was the piece of the puzzle she'd been missing.

"I kept my eye on him a while longer, just to be sure we were right about his attention to Everly. We were at a dinner one night when Everly left before the rest of us. The guy was there, watching, and when she left, he followed her. I followed him and sent Blake to make sure Everly made it home safe."

Cheyenne felt the remnants of Ridge's fear for his sister. It would tear him apart if anything happened to her. He would do anything for her. What had he done?

"I confronted him in the parking garage, and he pulled a gun on me. I was planning to tell him to stay away from Everly, but things spiraled before I could get a word in. I was wrestling the gun away from him, and he fought back hard. I panicked because a guy carrying a gun had been following Everly, and he moved from a nuisance to a lethal threat in seconds."

Ridge started pacing again and threw his hands in the air. "The whole thing happened so fast. I know I elbowed him in the face once, and once I wrestled the gun away from him, he came at me. I landed a few punches, but I only know that because I saw the parking garage security tapes. I remember the rage and fear of what he could do to Everly. He wasn't some harmless guy watching her. He came unhinged in a split second." Ridge snapped his fingers.

Cheyenne pushed up on the arms of the recliner. "Ridge–"

Ridge interrupted, "I hit him once, and he fell. He hit his head on the bumper of a car, and he was out. I didn't find out until later that he'd broken his neck and he was paralyzed."

Cheyenne hadn't eaten since the picnic at lunch, and the ham sandwich threatened to climb up her throat. "Ridge, stop."

"I called the police. I told them everything," Ridge continued. "There was a trial, but the man couldn't testify. I was charged with second-degree assault, but there were gray areas. The man didn't have a license to carry a concealed weapon, and the security videos proved that he pulled a gun on me first. I stuck to the story that I thought he was following me, and I left Everly out of it. She's always been a private person, and she came to all of those events with me, even though she hated being around groups of people. She would have been terrified if she knew a man had been following her. I spent three months in prison."

His last sentence shot straight through her chest, and she covered her mouth to stifle her gasp. The truth was so much worse than she'd feared. He'd been trying to protect his sister, and he hadn't set out to hurt anyone.

"After I was released, I came here to leave everything behind. Blake and Everly came too. I would do it again if I had to. I would do anything to keep Everly safe, and the thought of what that man could have done to her will haunt me forever."

"Ridge?" she said softly this time. She'd been trying to stop him from continuing before, but now she was glad he'd pushed through and finished the story, despite what it meant for her.

God, please help. I need the words, and I'm terrified.

His hands were propped on his hips, and he kept his chin down. "Yeah?"

"I already knew," she whispered.

His head jerked up. "What?"

"I already knew most of that. I have something to tell you too."

Chapter Twenty-Two

Ridge

What did she say? Why was she so calm? He'd just told her he spent time in prison for a criminal offense. A felony.

Before he confessed the first word, he'd known their time together was over. He'd lose her now.

But she already knew? Ridge hadn't considered that she might already know. She never mentioned it, and after her first few rocky days at the ranch, she hadn't looked at him with anything but trust. She couldn't have known about Everly and what really happened back then, and the media had painted him a criminal, another athlete who couldn't control his temper.

"I knew you were a professional athlete," she said quietly.

Something else clicked into place. "I know you told me about your dad, and I should have told you then."

Cheyenne shook her head. "You're nothing like him. Before I came here, I thought you were an entitled jock just like him, but you're not."

Ridge frowned. "You knew before you came to the ranch?"

Cheyenne's phone rang in her pocket, and she pulled it out. She looked at the screen and set it on the coffee table next to her swollen ankle. She covered her face with her hands.

Ridge sat down on the side of the couch closest to her. "Why didn't you tell me you knew?"

The phone on the table rang again, and Cheyenne moved her hands away from her face. She stared at the phone, and her chin quivered.

Ridge looked at the lit up screen. "Jaden?"

He knew someone named Jaden, but it couldn't be the same person. With no last name to go on, it could be anyone.

Cheyenne's breaths came quicker as she stared at the phone. "David Lang sent me here."

"David Lang!" Ridge shouted. Of all the people who could ruin his relationship with Cheyenne, he'd never expected David.

Cheyenne flinched at his booming words.

Ridge stared at the floor and tried to make sense of what she was saying. "David," he growled.

"I didn't know you. He told me you were a terrible person. He told me about the assault, the sentencing, and other things about you that were awful. He sent me here to spy on you." She squirmed in her seat, unable to get up because of her injury.

Ridge breathed slowly through his heavy chest. Nothing could hurt worse than this. Not getting kicked out of the NFL. Not having to give up the game he loved. Not anything.

Cheyenne adjusted in her seat again and reached for his arm. "This wasn't the plan."

Ridge sat back, pulling his arm from her reach. "What was the plan?"

The hurt in Cheyenne's eyes shot through him like a cannon. Why did he still care that she was upset? She'd sold his secrets to his enemy.

Yes, David was an enemy. Ridge hadn't associated the word with David until now, but the shoe fit.

She cradled her hands in her lap, twisting her fingers. "I didn't know you."

"You said that," Ridge retorted.

"My mom couldn't get approved for the treatment she needed. I had no job, no money, and I was about to lose the house where I lived with my sister."

"So that part was true? Your mom did have a stroke?"

"Yes! I promise I didn't lie to you about who I am."

"Just who you work for?" Ridge asked with a bite in his tone.

Yeah, he'd kept a secret from her, but his secret wasn't meant to hurt her. She'd come here with the sole purpose of tearing his words apart and handing them to David for cash.

The first tear slid down Cheyenne's cheek. "Please listen to me. I didn't know what I'd done until I got here."

"So if you hadn't been interested in making out in the barn, you'd have just handed over my secrets to David? For how long?"

"I couldn't! I couldn't do it. He offered me so much money, and he was going to pay for my mom's medical bills."

"How much?" Ridge asked.

"He told me you were buying hotels he wanted and–"

"How much?" he asked again.

Cheyenne huffed out a breath. "Fifty thousand dollars a month, plus the medical bills."

Ridge scoffed. "At least it was a lot of money."

She reached for him again. "I'm so sorry. I didn't want to do it. You don't deserve to be hurt like that–like David said. I didn't know him. I didn't know he was so awful."

"You finally figured it out?" Ridge stood and walked to the other side of the room. He couldn't sit while Cheyenne tore apart every moment of the time they'd spent together.

It was all a lie. His neck tightened. How could she go all in with David?

She scrambled to get up and limp on her injured ankle. "I'm sorry. I was wrong. I wanted to get out of it, but now I don't know how. He made me sign contracts."

Ridge rounded on her. "What kind of contracts?"

There were tears on her face, but she ignored them. "A non-disclosure agreement. And one that said I'd pay back the money if I couldn't complete the job."

"What were you supposed to do exactly?"

Cheyenne shook her head as if disagreeing with herself about everything she was saying. "I was supposed to report to Jaden about everything you were doing. I was supposed to tell her everything you said. David wants to know what you love most so he can ruin it."

"Mission accomplished," Ridge muttered as he paced toward the small kitchen.

Cheyenne limped after him. "Listen. You're not a man who deserves to be ruined. I know that now. David lied to me." She reached Ridge's side and reached for his arm. She looked up at him. "I stopped telling them anything I thought could really be used against you. You have a dangerous secret–one worth protecting from him."

Ridge stared back at her. She had no idea how right she was. "I was so careful around everyone, so tight-lipped about everything in my past. I finally opened up to you."

"And I want to know you!" Cheyenne interrupted. "I wanted you to tell me everything, but I wanted to keep it to myself and save you from him. I didn't tell him about how protective you are of Everly, but he already knows that. I didn't tell him about how much you love this ranch and the program you've worked so hard to build. I couldn't tell him any of that! David painted you as a monster, but you're far from it. He's the–"

"You spied on me. You deceived me. You betrayed me," Ridge said.

"No–"

"Everything between us was a lie." Ridge swallowed hard and looked down at her hand resting on his arm. "You made me trust you. You made me…"

She made him fall in love, and his chest twisted into an ugly knot. He'd finally trusted someone, and it had all been a mistake.

Cheyenne's tears continued, and she gasped through sobs with every few words. "I promise I'm telling you now because I can't do what he asked me to do. I can't betray you the way I was supposed to."

Ridge wanted those words. He wanted them to be true, but he couldn't trust them. Not now. He stared at her, restraining his features and shoving down the ache her tears built inside him.

"I came here to be left alone. I didn't let anyone in… until you."

Cheyenne's hand on his arm gripped tighter. "Please."

"I shut everyone else out. Until you. You were the only exception."

"I'm so sorry," Cheyenne cried. "I didn't know you. I trusted the wrong person. I didn't want to do it. I thought I didn't have a choice!"

"Do you know what David did to Everly? He hit her. Knocked her to the ground! If you know I'll do anything to protect my sister, then you know all there is to know about me. Blake got to David first, but it took every bit of my restraint not to beat him into the ground that day."

Cheyenne nodded furiously. "I know, and I don't blame you. I didn't know about any of that."

"And I bought my house from him. He'd planned to live in it with Everly when they married, but he ended up kicking her out with three days' notice after she found out he cheated on her. She loved that house! I lowballed the offer, and he took it. I knew he would be furious when he found out it was me, and he was!"

Ridge rubbed the back of his neck where his hair stood on end. "I bought a handful of hotels I knew he wanted. I did it all to get back at him because the only thing he cares about is the next item on his to-do list, and he can't stand to have his plans go wrong. My assistant has been remodeling those hotels and turning them into affordable family hotels. It's the opposite of what David would have done."

Cheyenne bit her lips between her teeth and sniffed. "I know. You're nothing like him, and I made a huge mistake."

Ridge couldn't look at her. The pain in her voice rivaled the breaking in his chest. "I need to go."

"Wait." Cheyenne reached for him as he stepped back.

"Rest your ankle. I'll send Ava over to help you." He couldn't look at her right now, but he also couldn't leave her alone.

"Ridge, please."

He stopped with his hand on the door but didn't turn around. "I need some time to think. I'll see you in the morning."

He walked out of the cabin and closed the door behind him with a bang. David had gotten the better of him again.

Chapter Twenty-Three

Ridge

The rain had stopped, but a storm still raged inside as Ridge stalked to his truck.

Cheyenne and David. It didn't make sense, and yet, it was somehow true.

Ridge got into the truck and jerked the door closed, releasing some of his anger on the sturdy metal. Truth. He didn't even know the meaning of the word anymore. It might as well be some imaginary fairy tale because he couldn't believe much anymore.

He slammed his fist against the steering wheel and yelled into the quiet cab, "You've got to be kidding me!"

Sitting still would only make him want to tear up his truck. He shifted into gear and headed toward the check-in office. Blake and Everly would lose their minds over this when they found out, but he'd let it ride until they got back from their honeymoon. David just didn't know when to give up.

Ridge parked in front of the office and barged in. Bethany stood from her desk, but he didn't slow down. His boots thudded against the wooden floor as he marched toward Jameson's office.

The door was open, but there wasn't any sign of the foreman. He turned and knocked on Ava's office across the hallway. Jameson opened the door a second later.

"Hey, man." Jameson's expression fell almost immediately. "What's wrong?"

Ava stood from where she'd been sitting behind the desk. "Is everything okay?"

"Did you know Cheyenne is a spy?" he asked.

"A spy? Like an espionage agent?" Jameson asked.

Ridge scoffed. "David sent her here to get close to me so he could find out the best way to hurt me."

Ava gasped. "No, he didn't. You can't be serious."

"I am. She just told me everything."

"So she came clean?" Jameson asked. "Does that mean she's blown her cover on purpose?"

"I don't know why she told me. I told her about the NFL, and she went into this story about how she already knew who I was before she came here."

"She changed her mind about working for David?" Ava asked.

Ridge shrugged. "I guess so! He tried to ruin Blake and Everly's wedding, and now this. He's been planning this for months, if she made the deal with him before she came here. She could have told me sooner!"

Ava glanced at her husband, then back at Ridge. "What did David offer her?"

"He said he would pay for her mom's medical bills and pay her fifty thousand a month to tell him everything I was doing and saying."

"And did she?" Ava asked.

Ridge tried to remember everything Cheyenne had told him, but his memories were blurred. Rage had the blood pumping loudly in his ears. "I think she said she hasn't been telling him everything."

Ava and Jameson were quiet. They glanced at each other as if they could read what the other was thinking.

"What? Say something. She tricked all of us," Ridge said, pointing to Ava, Jameson, and himself.

Ava walked around her desk and leaned against it. "David has been causing trouble here for a while. Everly was in a relationship with him for years, and I believe he hid his true self from her that entire time."

"Yeah. He's a whack job," Ridge said. "We all know that."

"But she doesn't," Jameson said. "We've had time to see what he's capable of doing. Cheyenne didn't know."

"Are you defending her?" Ridge asked.

"Yes," Jameson and Ava said in unison.

Ava held out a hand. "Don't mistake what we're saying. You're our friend, and we would never think it's okay to do what she did. But I've seen you with Cheyenne, and I don't think she truly wanted to hurt you. I know about her mom, and that's an awful situation to be in. No job, and the bills are piling up. She was desperate."

Ridge tugged on his short hair. His whole body was as hot as a wildfire, but he wanted to give in to the cooling logic Jameson and Ava were offering.

"I came here to tell you she hurt her ankle today and might need some help," Ridge said.

Ava shook her head. "You should help her. And while you're there, maybe listen to her a little more. Pray first, then listen to her."

Pray. He hadn't cooled down enough to do that yet, but he could definitely use some guidance.

Jameson rested a hand on Ridge's shoulder. "What if the Lord sent her here, not David?"

"I know you want to believe that. I do too. But how can I trust her now?" Ridge asked.

"I can't answer that," Ava said. "But it sounds to me like she was coming clean and asking you for help at the same time."

"Help? What kind of help?"

"Her mom," Jameson said. "If she didn't have a way to get her mother the help she needed before her arrangement with David, I doubt she'll have any help now that she's told you. She gave that up by telling you."

"And David will be angry when he finds out," Ava added. "We all know how unpredictable he can be when his plans don't pan out."

Ridge looked at the floor. "What are you saying?"

"That Cheyenne did what she thought she had to do to help her mom. I know you would do anything for your family too," Ava said.

Ridge looked up at her. He'd done the unthinkable to protect his family–committed a criminal offense and served time as punishment.

"Cheyenne got caught up in the wrong side, but she did tell you the truth," Jameson said.

"It's been a month. She could have told me sooner," Ridge said.

Ava tsked behind her teeth. "I can think of a million reasons why it would be hard for her to tell you." She started ticking off the list on her fingers. "You're not easy to talk to. She's afraid of David. She didn't want to lose you. She likes it here–"

"I get it," Ridge interrupted. "You know you sound a lot like Everly?"

Ava grinned. "That's a good thing. And if Everly was here, she would probably tell you to calm down and then go talk to her."

Ridge looked at Jameson. The foreman nodded, agreeing with his wife.

Jameson looked at his watch. "It's suppertime. Maybe take her a plate and an ice pack."

Remembering Cheyenne's grimace every time she'd put weight on her ankle made him want to run back to her cabin. How did she have that kind of power over him? She'd betrayed him, sold him out. Why was he considering running back to her?

Because he wanted to believe her. Because he wanted to work things out with her. Because he loved her.

The bold and scary truth hadn't hit him until now when she was so far from him. He loved her, and he trusted her. If she needed his help with her ankle, with her mom, and with David, he should be there for her.

"I'll go talk to her," Ridge said. "Can you get her car to her cabin in the morning? She couldn't drive it this afternoon."

"Does she need to see a doctor? Do you need help with the kids tomorrow?" Ava asked.

The anger in his heart had diminished, leaving exhaustion and regret. "I'll ask her if she wants a ride to the doctor, and I'll be fine tomorrow. She might need someone to help her around if the ankle isn't feeling better."

Ava reached for him, halting him at the door. "Wait. Remember that she was probably desperate, and rock bottom is a terrible place to be. Remind her that she has our help if she needs it."

Ridge nodded and headed for the dining hall. He'd planned to talk to Cheyenne over dinner tonight, but this was far from what he'd imagined.

Chapter Twenty-Four

Cheyenne

Cheyenne rested her chin in her hand and stared at the wall of her cabin. The new wood was crisp and straight with a small picture window in the center. She'd foolishly fallen in love with the charming little home when she should have been guarding her heart.

But she hadn't just loved the cabin. She'd let herself become completely consumed with the ranch, the kids, the people, and Ridge.

Ridge. A sharp pain pierced her abdomen. She'd fallen for him head over heels, and then she'd dug her own grave. He had every right to hate her.

She'd have to go back home. There was no way she could keep her job and work with

Ridge now. Then she'd have to pay David back. She'd been desperate before, but now she had a life of servitude ahead of her. She'd probably still owe David five figures when they laid her in the ground.

Cheyenne wrapped her arms around her abdomen. The pain of losing Ridge was worse than any sprained ankle. Something inside of her was breaking–irreparably damaged now that the best part of her life was gone.

She heard the rumble of a diesel engine and sat up quickly. One of the ranch workers would be bringing her car over, and she didn't want to answer the door looking like she'd just dunked her head in the sink. She pushed up on the arms of the chair and limped across the room. The knock on the door sounded before she'd made her way around the couch.

"Coming!" She rubbed her face on the sleeve of Ridge's coat, and his woodsy smell sent a fresh wave of ache down her throat to the bottom of her stomach.

She opened the door and gasped. Ridge stood on the porch with a bag in each hand. The sun was setting, and the faint light from inside her cabin illuminated his face.

"Ridge, I–"

"Can we talk?" he interrupted.

"Yes." The word was a sad squeak. Getting the chance to talk to him at all was more than she'd expected. Maybe he would let her down easy.

She hopped to the side, and Ridge walked in. He headed straight for the kitchen and put the bags on the table before coming back to where she stood. He moved to her side and held out his arm to her.

Cheyenne bit her lips between her teeth and wrapped her hands around his offered arm. Even in his anger, he was helping her. She limped to the small kitchen table where he waited for her to take a seat before pulling another chair over. He lifted her leg and propped it up. She didn't say a word–couldn't even thank him through the tightening of her throat.

He washed his hands in the sink and said, "I brought you something to eat." Without looking at her, he unpacked the to-go boxes and pulled an ice pack from the other bag. He laid the cold pack over her ankle and went back to setting the table for the meal.

Cheyenne inhaled a shaky breath as he positioned the plate heaped with food in front of her. He opened the fridge and pulled out two Sprites, the only beverage she kept in her cabin.

When he took his seat beside her, he laid his hand on the table with his palm up. Cheyenne looked at his big open hand. That hand had caused destruction and pain, but it had also built, helped, and comforted.

How could she have been so wrong about him?

Cheyenne laid her hand in his, and he bowed his head.

"Father, I pray You would bless this food. I pray You would give Cheyenne healing and give me the words to say and the ears to listen. Guide my heart. In Jesus's name I pray. Amen."

Cheyenne's hand slipped out of his as he moved to pick up his fork.

"Let's eat. Then we'll talk."

Cheyenne scraped small bites onto her fork and chewed slowly. She wanted the food, but her stomach was in a state of complete upheaval. She used the time to say her own silent prayer for guidance. Ridge was here, and this chance to explain was more than she deserved. Was it too much to ask if she prayed for forgiveness? She didn't deserve it, so how could she genuinely pray that Ridge or God could overlook what she'd done?

After a few minutes, Cheyenne stopped trying to eat. Emotion clogged her throat, making it hard to swallow the meatloaf, even if it was one of her favorites.

Ridge cleared the table and sat back down, finally looking at her. "You talk first."

Cheyenne straightened in her chair and cleared her throat. "I lost my job at the grocery store right around the time Mom had her stroke. The whole time I was going to her appointments and staying with her, the bills were piling up. I was able to get out of the lease for my apartment, and I moved into Mom's house with Hadley. She has a job at a bistro, and she makes good money in tips, but it still wasn't enough." Cheyenne lowered her chin. "I'm sorry."

"Keep going," Ridge said.

"I applied for any job I came across. All over the country. If it was a good enough job, I'd leave Bear Cliff. I finally got a call back about a PR position at Lang Corp. I interviewed with his assistant, Jaden, then David told me the position had been filled, but he wanted to offer me a different job. That's when he told me about you."

When she didn't continue right away, Ridge asked, "What did he tell you?"

"That you were an entitled athlete." She picked at her fingernails and kept her head down. "He also told me about the assault, and he sent photos and articles. It looked terrible, and he claimed you hadn't been punished enough for what you'd done."

Ridge rapped his knuckles on the table. "He was probably right about that."

Cheyenne shook her head. "No. He wasn't. When I met you, I knew there had to be a reason for what happened. I believe you." She scoffed. "But I made the mistake of believing David first. When he offered to pay for Mom's medical bills and pay me fifty thousand a month on top of that, I said I'd do it."

She jerked her head up and reached for Ridge's hand, but she quickly changed her mind, pulling her hand back and resting it in her lap. "Once I started to put the pieces together, I was afraid to tell you the truth. I stopped spending the money because I'm going to have to pay it back now. Jaden told me David has been angry and unpredictable lately, and now that I know what he's already done to you and your family, I'm terrified of what he'll do when he finds out I told you everything. I don't have a clue how I'll pay him back the money I've already spent."

"Don't worry about–"

"And I knew that once I told you, I would lose you." She sniffled and continued quickly. "And now I'll have to leave, and I loved it here."

Her sniffles had turned into sobs, and she furiously wiped at the tears on her face. Ridge looked around before grabbing a paper towel from the counter and handing it to her. She took it and wiped her face.

"I've never been out of Bear Cliff before I came here, but this place felt like home. You felt like home," she whispered.

Ridge scooted his chair closer to hers. "Calm down. We're going to figure this out."

"We?" she asked. The ache in her heart eased a little bit.

Ridge nodded slowly, almost imperceptibly. "We."

Cheyenne shook her head. He couldn't help her. She'd committed so many wrongs.

Ridge reached for her hand and cradled it in both of his. "It sounds like you made a decision to protect your family, and I know what that's like. Whatever happens, we'll figure it out together."

Cheyenne bit the inside of her cheek and inhaled a deep breath. "I'm so sorry."

"There's one thing we have to do if we're going to have a chance of getting you away from David."

"Anything," she said quickly.

"You have to tell me everything. Be honest with me. I should have told you about the NFL and what happened with the guy and the assault charges earlier. I know it's hard to come clean. It was hard for both of us, but if we start with honesty from here on out, we can get through everything together."

Cheyenne leaned toward him, but her injured foot that was propped in the chair prevented her from getting closer. "I'm so sorry. I'll never tell him or anyone else anything again."

Ridge stood and wrapped his arms under her, hoisting her into the cradle of his arms. Cheyenne gasped, and Ridge stilled.

"Are you okay? Did I hurt you?"

"No! I just wasn't expecting that." She wrapped her arms tightly around him, holding on to the grace she'd been given.

"I'm sorry I left," Ridge whispered.

"I'm just glad you came back."

He carried her to the living room where he sat on the couch, cradling her in his arms. "We need to talk about your mom."

Cheyenne leaned back to look into his dark eyes. "I'll tell you anything."

"Let me take over her bills," Ridge said.

"What!" Cheyenne tried to scramble out of his arms, but all she managed to do was send her hurting ankle flying in the air.

Ridge steadied her in his lap and braced her ankle. "Careful."

"Sorry. What did you say?" Cheyenne asked in a pitch higher than normal.

"I have the money. I hate seeing you worry about getting her the help she needs, and I want David's name out of everything." He looked at her with a pained expression. "I don't want him in our relationship."

Cheyenne's eyes widened. "Our relationship?"

"I mean, if you'll have me."

Cheyenne's eyes filled again. She'd hurt him so deeply, and he was still here, telling her he wanted to be with her. "I want you more than anything."

Ridge's gaze lowered to her mouth, and his lips quirked up in a smile. "Good." He slowly pulled her closer, bringing his mouth within an inch of hers. "Because you're the only one for me."

Cheyenne cradled his face in her hands. "Ridge, I–"

"I love you," he interrupted.

"I was–"

"I know." He smiled and looked up at her. "I wanted to say it first."

Cheyenne closed her eyes tight, pushing out the tears that blurred her vision. When she opened them, Ridge's forgiving eyes were looking back at her. "I love you too."

He pressed his mouth to hers, and she breathed in the happiness around her. His hand slid up her shoulder and behind her neck, pulling her closer as he kissed her hard and sure.

When they pulled away, Ridge rested his forehead against hers. They each took a few deep breaths before speaking.

"Don't worry about anything. I'll make sure your mom and sister have everything they need, and I won't let anything happen to you." He brushed his thumb over her cheek and slid his hands into her hair. "You're mine to protect, and I'll guard you with my life."

Chapter Twenty-Five

Cheyenne

Cheyenne pulled up at the barn and grabbed the bag from her passenger seat. She rushed inside and scanned the first few stalls. Jethro whinnied at her as she walked past.

"Ridge?"

"Tack room!" he yelled from the other side of the barn.

She walked in and handed him the bag. "Sorry it took so long. Grady wanted to talk. He said to tell you to be good."

Ridge scoffed as he took the bag from her. "I'm always good."

He leaned in and kissed her sweetly on the forehead. The heat of that touch was hotter than any Wyoming summer. "I'll be back soon."

"Take your time. I have registrations to enter."

Ridge stopped in the doorway and turned. "Dinner at my house tonight?" he asked tentatively.

Cheyenne's eyes widened. "That's a big step." She'd yet to see his place, and she'd been careful not to pry about where he lived. Did she want to know? With the money he had, it could be a shocker.

Ridge shrugged. "Not really. I've seen your place."

"You designed my cabin. Of course you've seen it." Yes, it was her cabin, and she wanted to claim it in every way she could. When Ridge told her he paid for the building of the extra cabins, she had one more reason to love her little home.

And Ridge. She had a million reasons to love him, with more showing up daily. Every evening, he told her stories about growing up, playing football, and learning to work at the ranch. In exchange, she told him the deepest secrets of her heart. She wanted to give him everything.

"We can eat by the fire pit," Ridge offered.

"No." She wanted him all to herself. "Let's go to your place."

"You sure?" Ridge asked with a raised brow.

"I'm sure."

"Good. I'll tell Colt to get lost for a few hours tonight." Ridge winked at her and stepped out of the tack room.

Cheyenne sighed and leaned against a saddle rack.

Ridge stalked back into the room and wrapped one arm around her, pulling her in for a soft, slow kiss. She hadn't even had a chance to breathe, but she didn't need air. She needed Ridge.

"What are you doing?" she whispered as they parted.

"Kissing you. I wanted to remind you that I love you."

Oh, her heart. "I love you too."

He pressed one more quick kiss to her mouth. "I'll be right back."

She placed her hands on his chest and gently pushed. "You keep saying that, but the horses are going to be halfway to Texas if you don't fix that gate."

"Right. Gate. Then dinner." He smiled and looked down at her with narrowed eyes. "Then dessert."

"Go!" she shouted, but there wasn't a hint of bite in her order. It was silly, but she wanted him to stay just as much as he didn't want to go. Being with him–all day, every day–never got old.

"I'm going. I'm going," he said as he walked out.

Cheyenne propped her hands on her hips and took a breather. Kissing Ridge always left her dazed. The man had some weird ability to leave her knees weak.

Work. Focus. She did have some work to do before she could have dinner with Ridge.

The office always seemed too quiet after the noise of the day. She'd learned one thing this summer, and that was that kids never stop talking. It was a good thing because she got to know them all so quickly. This week's group was especially chatty, since the fifteen and sixteen year olds all went to school together and hadn't seen each other much over the summer. The biggest task had been keeping their focus on the work instead of their friends.

Cheyenne's phone rang, and she checked the clock. Jaden. Right on time.

"Hello," Cheyenne answered.

"Hey. How are things?" Jaden asked.

"Pretty good. Sorry, but I don't have anything new for you today. The kids kept us busy."

Stalling. That was the plan Cheyenne and Ridge had decided on. They were ready to come clean to David and sever all ties, but Ridge wanted Blake and Everly safely home from their honeymoon before they rocked David's world with the news.

"That's fine," Jaden said. She let out a heavy yawn. "Sorry. I didn't sleep much last night."

Cheyenne had been debating about how much to tell Jaden. Would she side with David? She seemed troubled by the things David was doing but unwilling to sacrifice her job.

"Is everything okay?" Cheyenne asked.

"Yeah. Just a lot of work to do. I'll talk to you tomorrow. Stay safe."

Jaden's recent farewells had included the ominous "Stay safe" or "Be careful," and the warnings weren't lost on Cheyenne.

"Talk to you tomorrow."

She disconnected the call and started logging registrations. The remaining summer sessions were almost full, and there were a dozen fall field trips scheduled. With this kind of reception, the program could grow exponentially over the next few years.

Cheyenne's phone rang, and she answered the call on speakerphone when she saw her sister's photo on the screen.

"Hey. I'm just finishing up today. Can I call you back in half an hour?"

"No, but I'll make this quick. Something is wrong with Mom. I went to visit her after my shift, and she was fine for the first hour or so. Then she... Long story short, Dr. Krenshaw thinks Mom has an infection that is causing her stroke symptoms to return."

"What?" Cheyenne pushed away from her desk and stared at the phone.

"She called it recrudescence of deficits or something. She said it started with a kidney infection."

"What does this mean? How is she?" Cheyenne asked quickly.

"They transported her to the hospital, and Dr. Krenshaw ordered some tests."

Cheyenne couldn't move. "Are you there with her?"

"Yeah." Hadley's usually upbeat tone was somber. "I just stepped out of the room to call you."

"Tell me more. How is she? What are they planning to do?"

Hadley let out an empty half-breath. "I don't know. She's not communicating at all. She won't look at me. It's like she can't hear me. And the paralysis is back in her left side."

"So it's like the stroke all over again?" Cheyenne asked. Blood pulsed loud and hard in her ears.

"And they haven't told me what they plan to do," Hadley said. "She's in ICU right now, so I can only stay in her room during visiting hours."

Cheyenne looked at the clock on her screen. "When's your next shift?"

"Seven in the morning. I already called in."

"No. You can't do that. We can't afford to lose your job too."

Hadley let out a small whimper. "I can't leave her like this."

Ridge stepped into the office and halted. The look on her face must have told him everything. "What happened?"

"It's Mom," she said.

Hadley spoke again. "Is that Ridge?"

Cheyenne looked from the phone on her desk to Ridge. "Yes."

"I'll let you go. I'll call you when I hear more," Hadley said.

Cheyenne stared at the phone until her sister ended the call.

"What happened?" Ridge asked again.

"She said something is wrong with Mom. Her stroke symptoms are back, and they think it's because of an infection. She's in the ICU."

Ridge rounded the desk and pulled Cheyenne to her feet before wrapping her in his arms. "Is she okay?"

"I don't know," Cheyenne whispered against his chest. "They're still doing tests. Hadley doesn't want to leave Mom, but she could lose her job."

Ridge took a step back and looked down at Cheyenne. Tears welled in her eyes, and she begged them to retreat. She needed to stay strong.

Ridge jerked his head toward the laptop. "Let's get you home."

"What? No. I can't leave. We have the kids tomorrow."

"And I can manage without you. We'll find someone to fill in until your mom is better."

"I'm supposed to be here," she said.

"You're supposed to be with your mom and sister," Ridge said. His jaw was tight, and his brow furrowed. "You need to go."

"What about... what about reporting to Jaden? Blake and Everly aren't back yet, and if I leave, we'll have to put off telling him for even longer."

Ridge wrapped her in his arms again. "I know you're ready for this to be over. Trust me, I am too. As long as David still thinks you're determined to keep reporting to him about me, I don't think he would bother you. He still thinks you're his ticket to getting back at me." He wiped at the tear on her cheek. "You should go be with your mom."

Cheyenne wiped at her face and noticed the dirt on her hands. "Let me clean up, and we'll talk more about it."

Ridge kissed her forehead and released her. She walked out of the barn toward the outhouse. For once, she was glad the primitive bathroom offered such privacy. As strong and determined as Ridge had sounded about her mom, she didn't have any of that assurance. She splashed water on her face and washed her hands before trudging back to the barn.

When she made it back to the office, the swirling emotions hadn't subsided. Ridge stood to meet her at the door. "Can you get packed and ready in an hour?"

Cheyenne narrowed her eyes at him. "Are you serious? I can't leave the camp, and I can't get a flight out that soon. If I'm not using David's money, I definitely don't have the money for a last-minute flight."

"You can. I promise we'll make it a few days without you. I just talked to Jordan. He manages my properties, and he's getting a plane ready for you now."

"What? No. You can't do that."

"I can get you back to your mom tonight. It's already in motion."

"No–"

"Yes, I can," Ridge said. "Let me help you. I'm smart with my finances."

Cheyenne scrunched her nose at him, still reeling from the news he'd dropped on her. A private plane.

Ridge shrugged. "Maybe not all the time. Buying hotels just to spite David started as a game, but the first one I bought is already remodeled and open. So far, the reception has been great."

"I have no idea how you manage hotels and work all day here."

"Jordan is the manager, and he's good at what he does."

Cheyenne looked around the small office. She wanted to be with her mom, but what Ridge was offering was beyond her comprehension. And she needed to be here to help with the kids. "I don't know."

Ridge cupped the side of her face, gently pulling her attention back to him. The hard lines of his jaw, the scruff on his face, and the sincerity in his eyes held her captive. "I hate seeing you upset. You need your mom just as much as she needs you."

Cheyenne bit her bottom lip and reached up to wrap her arms around his neck. "I'll never be able to pay you back," she whispered.

Ridge stroked his hand over her hair. "I don't need a payback. I need to know you're okay."

The fear that had been growing inside her since Hadley called slowly evaporated in the warmth of Ridge's arms. "I will be."

Thanks to Ridge. Whatever life threw at her, she would have him by her side.

Ridge whispered against her ear, "Father, please keep Your hand on Cheyenne. Please give her mom the healing she needs. Please protect both of them."

Cheyenne tightened her hold around him. No one had ever prayed for her by name or cared enough to beg the Lord on her behalf. Never in her life had someone stood beside her when everything else crumbled.

Until Ridge. The Lord had been too good to her and had led her to a man who walked in faith. He was a steadfast reminder to speak truths, pray for thanks and forgiveness, and trust that God had a plan she couldn't always see.

Chapter Twenty-Six

Ridge

Ridge nudged Liam's shoulder. "You have a good day today?"

Liam shrugged and watched his dad's pickup crest the hill. "Yes, sir."

Ridge would never get used to being called sir, but the kids always did it. Liam was a rare one though. He didn't seem to be looking for trouble all the time.

"When is Cheyenne coming back?" Lucy asked from behind them.

There was that familiar tugging in Ridge's chest again, the one that happened whenever thoughts of Cheyenne entered his mind. "I don't know. Her mom is sick, and she had to go take care of her."

Lucy dragged the toe of her shoe through the dirt. "I miss her."

The fourteen and fifteen year olds had spent one day with Cheyenne, and they were just as attached as Ridge. She had some kind of super attractive power that he couldn't understand.

Ridge looked up at the cloudy sky, begging the hollow ache in his chest to ease. "I miss her too."

Cheyenne would come back. He had to believe she would or he'd lose his mind. The unwelcome thought entered his head at the most inconvenient times, and his fortitude was slipping.

She loved him. She'd said the words. He had to believe she meant it. She'd told him the truth about David, and they'd agreed she should keep feeding him useless information until she was safely back at the ranch.

Ridge should have gone with her. He'd offered, but they both knew the kids program would have to be canceled for the week if they both left. Colt and Remi had been able to fill in for half a day each, but only Ridge and Cheyenne knew the ins and outs of the program.

Tiffany sighed as her mom's car came into view. "There's my ride. See you tomorrow."

Ridge headed toward Liam's dad's truck, careful not to even acknowledge Tiffany's mom's approach.

Remi skipped up to Tiffany and threaded their arms together. "Let's go. I want to tell your mom about that massive worm you found."

Tiffany groaned. "Please, don't remind me. I'll be having nightmares for weeks."

Ridge walked up to Liam's dad's truck and propped his arms on the window. "Your boy is smart."

The man's proud grin told Ridge all he needed to know. This kid had a dad who supported him, and Ridge knew that comfort well. His own dad had sacrificed his own wants to give him the best future.

"Yeah, he's a good one." Liam's dad ruffled the kid's hair.

"Dad," Liam drawled.

"See you tomorrow," Ridge said. "Don't forget to wear long sleeves. We're clearing a hill near the blackberry bushes, so expect thorns."

"Yes, sir," Liam said with a nod.

Ridge stepped away from the truck as Colt parked beside the barn. He'd helped all morning and tagged out with Remi at lunchtime, but Ridge needed an extra hand bringing a new horse over from the main barn.

Ridge hopped in Colt's truck and threw his hat on the dash. "Thanks for the hand. The trailer is at the main barn."

Colt backed out and turned toward the trail. "No problem." He spotted Remi walking back to the barn and his eyes narrowed. "I bet the kids had a blast with Remi today."

Ridge bit his tongue. Colt only had one thing on his mind–Remi. He'd been hung up on the woman as long as Ridge had known him.

When Remi was only a few feet from the front of the truck, Colt pressed his hand against the horn on the steering wheel. The deep bellow sounded through the whole valley, but Remi didn't flinch. She gave Colt a playful smirk as she walked past the truck.

"Man, I love her." Colt jerked back, and his eyes widened. "Did I say that out loud?"

Ridge shook his head. "You didn't have to."

Colt fixed his attention back on the trail ahead. "You heard from Cheyenne?"

Ridge checked his phone.

Cheyenne: Just saw the doctor. They said her vitals are stable. She'll have a few more tests in the morning, but they're pretty sure the antibiotic they're giving her will clear up the infection and she'll be able to discharge to the rehab facility as early as Thursday.

Ridge typed up a quick reply.

Ridge: Good. Are you okay? Did you get some sleep?

"Looks like her mom is on the mend," Ridge said.

Colt sighed. "What's it like being in a relationship?"

"I said we're not doing the girl talk thing."

"But you talked to Jameson and Ava about her! Don't think I didn't hear about that through the grapevine."

Ridge sighed. "People always talk."

"So, what's it like?" Colt asked again.

When Ridge didn't answer right away, Colt cleared his throat. "I haven't been on a date since I met Remi. I'm wondering if I should try to move on."

"Sorry. If you want me to tell you it's a piece of cake, I can't. It's ridiculously terrifying."

Colt smirked. "You're a softie after all."

"I'm not scared of much, but–"

"What if she doesn't come back?" Colt interrupted.

"Thanks for your consideration."

"What?" Colt shouted. "You want me to pretend like we aren't all thinking she's a long gone runaway?"

Ridge threaded his fingers through his hair and pulled. "This is why I don't want to talk about women with you."

"Oh, maybe you've got a point there."

Ridge jerked his head up. "Are you kidding me? I'm glad you came to this realization at my expense." When the truck pulled up at the barn, Ridge grabbed his hat and jumped out.

"Dude, I'm sorry!" Colt shouted.

Ridge kept walking. He didn't need Colt's extra assurance that Cheyenne might not come back. He'd been pushing past that doubt all day, ignoring it every chance he could. Now, it was front and center in his head. Would anyone miss Colt if he ended up in the river?

"Come on, man," Colt said as he caught up with Ridge.

Ridge slapped his hand down on Colt's shoulder and leveled his gaze with his friend's. "If you say another word, I'll lock you in the stall with Thunder."

"You–"

Ridge slapped a hand over Colt's mouth. "I said not another word."

Colt nodded, and Ridge let his hand fall. "Now, get the trailer attached to the truck while I get the horse."

Colt gave an exaggerated salute and marched off. Ridge breathed a sigh of relief. Colt was one of the best guys, but he wasn't good for Ridge's confidence right now. Was there a way to kick him out of the house until Cheyenne came back?

They loaded the horse without another word from Colt. The old mare was a calm one, and she was used to moving in the trailer. The trip across the ranch was a breeze, and Ridge and Colt had the horse in the new pasture before suppertime.

They'd almost made it back to the barn when Colt asked, "Can I talk now?"

Ridge sighed. "Sure."

"Can we watch *The Replacements* tonight?"

"No way. That movie was awful when it came out over twenty years ago."

"Don't think of it as a football movie–"

"But it *is* a football movie," Ridge interrupted.

"No, it's a ragtag band of misfits who work together to win it all," Colt said wistfully.

Ridge frowned at his friend. "What are you talking about? The plays aren't real, they skip around the field in the same play, and the acting is terrible. Don't even get me started on wimpy

Keanu Reeves trying to pass as a professional quarterback."

Ridge's phone rang in his shirt pocket, and he pulled it out. "It's Cheyenne."

"Good. Ask her if she's flaking on you," Colt said.

Ridge gave Colt's shoulder a nice shove, sending him stumbling into the door of the tack room. "Get lost."

"Does this mean we're not having dinner together tonight?" Colt shouted as Ridge shut himself in the barn office.

With the door firmly shut between him and his chatty roommate, Ridge answered the call. "How's my woman?"

Cheyenne's bubbly laugh was music to his ears. "Hello to you too."

He hung his hat on the hook by the door and let his head rest against the old wood. "I miss you like crazy."

Her answering sigh calmed every doubt in his mind. "I miss you too."

"You sound sad," Ridge whispered.

"I'm okay. Mom is doing a little better, and Hadley is here now. I'm just… scared."

Her confession had Ridge's fingers and toes itching to move. He should be with her. "Why?"

"I was afraid Mom had taken a turn for the worse. Then I hated leaving you and the ranch. I'm scared David will know we're planning something. It's like there are storms all around us."

Us. They were hundreds of miles apart, and Cheyenne still thought they were the only people in the world.

But she was right. The wolves were closing in, and he couldn't protect her when they were apart. "I'm coming. I'll be on a flight tonight."

"No! Ridge, I'm sorry. I'm really fine. You don't have to come. We'll have to cancel the rest of the week."

"I don't care. I wanted this program to work, but I *have* to keep you safe. Do you see the difference?"

Cheyenne was quiet for a moment before she said, "I do. The difference is that I love you and you love me. I know you want to be here–"

"Need. I need to be with you," Ridge corrected.

"No. I'm fine here. I promise. I want to be with you more than anything right now, but we have to be smart about this."

Ridge grunted. "I don't want to be smart. I want you. Here. With me. Now."

Cheyenne chuckled. "Is that a caveman I hear? What have you done with my Ridge?"

My Ridge. The truth of those words hit him square in the chest. He was hers through and through.

"What can I do to make things better for you?" he asked.

"Pray. That's all you can do. And trust me. You can do that too."

Ridge ran his fingers through his hair. "Why do you say that?"

"Because that's what I'm always worrying about–that you won't ever really trust me after what I did."

"I do trust you. You've done enough to prove that I can."

She sighed. "I'm afraid it won't ever be enough."

"Stop, please. I can't stand it when you're upset."

There was a quiver in her voice when she spoke again. "Why are you so good to me?"

Ridge cleared his throat. Why was it so hard to be away from her? "Listen. I care about you. I love you. I'm sad and empty when you're gone, and I hope you're not feeling the same things I am."

"Sorry, but I am," she said with a sniffle.

Ridge swallowed the burning in his throat. "I'll do anything to make you smile again."

The sound Cheyenne made was half chuckle and half sob. "I wasn't supposed to love you like this."

Ridge walked over to her desk and picked up a thin, colorful band. She'd called it a friendship bracelet when he asked what she was doing with Lucy. He picked it up and rubbed the delicate thread in his calloused hand. "Looks like I didn't have much of a choice in the matter either."

"I'm not complaining," she said, sniffling again.

Ridge laid the bracelet down and sat in Cheyenne's office chair. "Go be with your mom. Call me before you go to sleep. I want to tell you good night."

"Okay. Ridge?"

"Yeah."

"I miss you," she whispered.

"I miss you too." He clenched and relaxed his hand against the desk. Every cell in his body was being pulled toward her, but she'd told him not to run after her. It would blow their cover if David found out they'd both left the ranch.

"I love you, Cheyenne."

"I love you too."

Ridge hung up the phone and let it fall onto the desk. He'd told Colt that being in a relationship after spending so many years alone was terrifying, but that was an understatement compared to the storm raging inside him when Cheyenne was gone.

Chapter Twenty-Seven

Cheyenne

Cheyenne zipped her luggage and tugged it off the bed. "I don't think I could fit another thing in here."

Hadley rushed into the bedroom shoving a sweater at her. "Wait! You have to take this one."

Cheyenne held up a hand and laughed. "I don't need another sweater."

"Wyoming is freezing in the winter, and you might not come back before the whole state is under twelve feet of snow!"

"Twelve feet? I don't think that's accurate."

Hadley propped a hand on her hip. "You never know. You might get snowed in with *Ridge*."

Cheyenne grabbed her purse and positioned the strap on her shoulder. "I should have never told you about him."

"No! You should have! I'm a sucker for a good love story, and yours is…" Hadley sank to the floor and laid a hand over her forehead. "So dreamy!"

"Pick yourself up. You're like a lovesick teenager," Cheyenne said as she stepped over her sister.

"I love that you're in love! When can I meet him?" Hadley asked as she crawled across the carpet toward the door.

Cheyenne stopped and looked back at her sister. "I don't know."

"Oh, come on! If I get a weekend off, he could send his super fancy plane to get me."

"No, no, no." Cheyenne held a finger in the air. "I'm not asking him to do that for me again."

"But it's me! Your sister! Your blood!"

"Would you stop shouting at me? We're two feet apart."

Hadley sighed, and her shoulders slumped. "I'm sorry. I just get so excited about your super cool new life in the wilds of Wyoming."

Cheyenne's phone pinged, and she checked the message. "Sadie is here." She pocketed the phone and wrapped her sister in a hug. "You should be the one running off to some exciting new place."

"Nah. This is your time, sis. I've got my whole life to have adventures and find love."

Cheyenne sniffled in her sister's hair. "Are you saying I'm old and this is my last chance to be happy?"

"Kind of," Hadley said.

Cheyenne pushed her sister away and laughed. "I see how it is."

"Wait!" Hadley grabbed Cheyenne's arm and turned her around just before the front door. "Remember what Mom says?"

"Take care of her flowers?" Cheyenne asked.

"Well, yeah. Us flowers have to take care of each other. But that's not what I meant. Remember who you are and whose you are."

"And return with honor," Cheyenne finished.

Hadley tilted her head and tightened her jaw. "I think your home is there now."

Cheyenne hugged her sister again and whispered, "You'll always be my home too."

"I know, but you have a chance to get out of here, and I hope it works out for you."

Cheyenne pulled back and looked Hadley in the eyes. "I don't hate it here. I'm going to miss you and Mom."

"We'll miss you too. Now get out of here." Hadley pushed Cheyenne's shoulder toward the door.

"I'll call you when I get there."

"Video call. I want to see Ridge this time," Hadley said.

Maybe it was time Cheyenne let Ridge into this part of her life. He'd helped her get back to her mom when her health was bad, he wanted to pay her mom's medical bills, and he'd sent money for Hadley. He was saving all of them, even after she hurt him.

Cheyenne tugged her suitcase behind her and met Sadie at her sedan in the driveway. Her friend was poised and perfect in a flowy blouse and neat pencil skirt.

"Ready to go?" Sadie asked.

"That's the question of the day."

Sadie grabbed the bottom of the suitcase and helped Cheyenne lift it into the trunk of the car. "You don't want to go."

"I do, but I don't."

"Ah. Your heart is in two places?" Sadie asked.

Cheyenne closed the trunk. "Yeah. I want to go back because I miss Ridge and the ranch and the kids, but I miss Mom and Hadley too."

"And me. You forgot me."

Cheyenne chuckled as she got into the car. "I could never forget you."

Sadie started the car and reached for Cheyenne's hand. "Let's start this journey off with prayer."

"Please. I need a lot of it."

Sadie squeezed Cheyenne's hand. "I haven't stopped."

"And it's been working. I'm back in church, right where you always hoped."

"It's not just me," Sadie said.

"I know that. Thank you for never giving up on me."

"I'm always a phone call away," Sadie said with a wink before she bowed her head and prayed.

***

Cheyenne clung to the armrests as the plane touched down. She'd gone her whole life without flying, and she wasn't ready to do it again. The sounds were loud, and the landings were bumpy. She kept her eyes closed tight until

THE ONLY EXCEPTION | 345

the plane was coasting on the ground. She'd kiss the ground as soon as she got off this thing.

The flight attendant, a sweet young woman with bright-red lips appeared by her seat. "You can take your phone off airplane mode now, but please keep your seatbelt fastened."

"Thank you." Maybe this flight didn't even count as a first. Ridge had chartered a private plane, and she'd bypassed all the usual airport measures. The only other people on the plane were the two pilots and one attendant.

Cheyenne pulled her phone from her bag and turned it on. She had two messages: one from Ridge and one from David.

Her heart jumped into her throat. Why was David texting her? He'd only called her himself three times since their initial interview.

David: When will you be back in Wyoming? Call my cell when you land.

That was a simple enough question. She'd given Jaden her flight information though. She checked the message from Ridge.

Ridge: I can't wait to see you. I love you.

Her heart settled back into her chest. Whatever she encountered with David, she wouldn't have to face alone.

She texted Ridge first, hoping to put off responding to David until she was back with Ridge.

Cheyenne: Just landed. I love you too.

Ridge: I know. I just watched your plane come in.

Cheyenne looked out the small window and saw Ridge standing by another man close to the hanger. The man was talking, but Ridge was facing toward the plane.

A few seconds later, the plane coasted to a stop, and the flight attendant appeared again. "You can unbuckle your safety belt now. We'll be opening the door soon."

"Thanks." Cheyenne stuffed her phone in her pocket and grabbed her purse from the seat beside her. The whole ride in a private plane had been surreal. What had it cost Ridge to send her to Tennessee and back this way? She didn't want to know.

Thunder rumbled as she stood to make her way toward the door. Seconds later, the rain came in earnest, thudding loudly on the plane.

"Oh goodness. I'm sorry, Miss Keeton. Let me get you an umbrella." The flight attendant zipped into a back room and rummaged around until she reappeared with the umbrella.

"Thank you. You've been so kind."

The woman smiled. "As have you."

Cheyenne had no idea how the wealthier class lived. She knew Ridge had made millions each year during his time in the NFL, but he hadn't really showed it until he helped pay for her mom's expenses and chartered the private flight.

The flight attendant stood at the open door and spoke loudly to be heard above the rain. "I hope you had a nice flight."

"I did. Thank you."

Cheyenne turned to the pouring rain out the door just as Ridge was bounding up the steps of the moveable stairs beside the plane. He took the steps in twos, rushing to the top until his arms were around her. The cold rain that drenched him seeped into her skin, but his warmth quickly dissolved the chill. The scent of crisp summer rain filled her, and she was reminded of home.

Not Tennessee. Here.

Ridge released his hold on her only long enough to place his huge hands on her face and pull her mouth to his. With a deep inhale, she drank him in, moving with an urgency that matched his need.

He broke the kiss before she was ready, and the flight attendant behind her sighed.

Ridge leaned down to whisper in her ear, and her stomach flipped with every breath against her ear.

"Let's go home."

Cheyenne relaxed at the sound of those words on his lips. She'd missed him so much more than she would have thought possible.

She turned to grab her suitcase, but the whole world tipped, stealing her breath as Ridge swept her into his arms.

"Ridge!"

"Jim is going to get your bags," he said as he descended the stairs into the pouring rain.

"My purse too!" It had fallen off of her shoulder when Ridge had taken it upon himself to serve as her carrier.

Ridge jogged for the hangar, keeping her wrapped tightly in his arms. Once inside the massive room, he rested her on her feet while she gaped.

"Wow. This place is huge!" The ceilings must have been more than one hundred feet tall, and two planes were parked inside. She'd been in such a rush when she left, she hadn't taken the time to check the place out.

"It has to be to get the planes in to service them." He took her hand and led her toward the back of the building. "Let's get you home."

"What about my bags?" she asked.

"I told you, Jim is getting them."

Cheyenne tugged on his hand. "I know, but who is Jim, and why am I trusting him with my bags?"

Ridge turned to her, giving her his full attention. "Sorry. Jim is a driver. He's worked for me on and off for years. Jordan sent him when he scheduled your flight."

"Why do you need a driver?" she asked with a smirk.

Ridge rubbed his calloused thumb over the soft skin of her hand. "I don't, but we have a long drive, and I wanted to spend it with you."

Heat raced up Cheyenne's cheeks. "You're crazy."

He leaned down until his lips were an inch from hers. "I definitely am."

"People are going to see us," she whispered.

"There are maybe half a dozen people here, and I don't care who sees us." He leaned back, putting a foot of distance between them. "But I can wait until the drive home."

Driving back into the ranch after four days away was like watching an old favorite movie. The gently rolling hills were familiar and welcoming, and the ranch had a rugged beauty that was almost dangerous. She could wander the vast reaches of this place for years and never see it all. It was endless and beckoning–never satisfying.

Ridge rested his hand on her knee in the back seat of the car as Jim drove. "I have a surprise for you."

Cheyenne perked up. "A surprise? What kind of surprise?"

"It's not really from me. It's from the kids last week."

"Really? That's so sweet!"

Ridge's truck was parked beside her car in front of her cabin, and that was all she saw before he said, "Don't look yet."

Cheyenne squeezed her eyes closed. "Oh. What is it?"

"Wait just a second." Ridge moved in the seat beside her, and the car came to a stop. "Thanks, Jim."

"Always a pleasure, Mr. Cooper," Jim said.

"Wait just a second," Ridge repeated.

The car door opened, then closed. A few moments later, the door beside her opened. The rain had stopped, but the thick humidity hung in the air.

"Don't open your eyes yet."

"I won't," Cheyenne said, keeping her eyes closed tight.

She gasped as Ridge swept her off her feet again.

"Ridge!"

"No peeking," he said.

Cheyenne chuckled and wrapped her arms around his neck. When he set her feet back on the ground, he kept his arms around her until she regained her balance.

"Okay. You can look now."

Cheyenne opened her eyes to see a rectangular planter positioned on both sides of her door. Beautiful flowers popped up from the planters, spreading color where there had once been only muted brown.

"Are you serious?" she shouted.

"The kids thought you would like the color."

Cheyenne looked up at him and nodded. "I do. It's beautiful." She looked back to the little cabin. How long had it been since she'd had this kind of love, support, and acceptance? "It's home."

Ridge wrapped his arm around her and kissed the top of her head. "Wait till you see my place."

Cheyenne wrinkled her nose. They'd both been tiptoeing around the topic of his money for days, but she would have to see his house eventually.

Ridge laughed at her expression–a scrunched-up nose and a twisted mouth. "You don't have to like it. I'd prefer something like your cabin anyway."

"You're lying," she said.

"No. I really love your place. I designed it, remember?"

"But you're used to fancy things," she said.

Ridge held out his arms. "Do I look like I'm used to fancy things?" he asked.

Cheyenne pointed to the cloud of dust that followed Jim's car over the hill. "You chartered a plane to get me to and from Tennessee, and you're on a first-name basis with a personal driver."

"Fair enough. I haven't used any of those perks in a while, and what better way to use them than to spoil you?"

Cheyenne stepped up onto the porch, admiring the flowers. "I definitely appreciated it."

Ridge grabbed her bags and followed her inside. She breathed a loud sigh and let her shoulders fall.

"I'm glad you're home," Ridge said as he put her bags down by the door.

"Me too."

She turned, and Ridge wrapped his arms around her waist. "I love you. I know I've said it before, but…"

"But what?" she asked.

"But love is an all or nothing thing for me. My family? Love. Football? Love. This place? Love. It's always been very black or white to me." He tilted her chin up, focusing all of his attention on her. "And then there's you. Love. You've been the biggest love of all, and I don't know how you did it, but you turned my world upside down. When you were gone, nothing felt right."

Cheyenne slid her arms up and around his neck, pulling him closer. "You're not alone. This has been scary for me too, but I know what I want. You."

Ridge leaned down and pressed his lips to hers. He sweetly adored her with his slow movements, and she memorized the silent promise in his kiss. When he broke the connection and looked down at her, heat flooded her face. His intense stare said they shared more than just a kiss.

Cheyenne took a deep breath. "What a welcome home."

"I'm glad you're back, and that things are better with your mom and sister."

Cheyenne gasped. "Speaking of my sister, she wanted me to call her when I got here safely." She pulled her phone out of her pocket and saw more messages waiting from David.

David: I need answers, Cheyenne.

David: He's a criminal. Never forget that.

She stared at the screen for a moment before turning it to Ridge. He read the words, then took her hand in his, leading her toward the couch. When they sat, he pulled her close and kept his hold on her hand. "Don't answer it."

"He'll know something is up. It sounds like he already does."

"Blake and Everly are back, and I talked to Linda and Mr. Chambers last night. They're ready to reach out to him." He jerked his chin toward the phone. "Tell him you'll call him tomorrow evening at six. You have something big to tell him, but you need to get a few others onboard."

Cheyenne stared at the phone cradled in her hands. "This is risky," she whispered.

Ridge pulled her close and kissed the top of her head. "It's risky now, but we have to cut all ties with him. This is the best way to get him out of our lives."

There was truth in his words. She'd been chained to David Lang for weeks now, and she'd do anything to break free.

Chapter Twenty-Eight

Ridge

Ridge parked the truck in front of the reception hall and glanced at Cheyenne beside him. "Are you ready?"

Cheyenne looked around. "As ready as I'll ever be. What about you?"

Ridge grabbed her hand and squeezed. "I'm so ready I wish it was already over."

She chuckled and gave his hand a little squeeze back. "It'll all be okay. We're cutting all ties."

"Right." Ridge wanted to believe everything they were saying, but it was a stretch to think the people he loved would ever really be out of whack job David's grasp. "Can I have just one punch?"

Cheyenne laughed and grabbed for the door handle. "He's not even here."

"That doesn't stop me from wanting to introduce my fist to his face," Ridge said.

They got out of the truck, and he reached for her hand as they neared the door. "Looks like Linda, Blake, and Everly are here, but I don't see Mr. Chambers's truck."

Cheyenne tugged on his hand and pointed to the decorated arbor next to the reception hall. "That's so pretty. This place is gorgeous. I bet tons of people want to get married here."

"They do. Linda and Everly have put a lot into this place since it opened. Blake and I built the arbor about a month before you got here."

"You built that?" she asked.

"Why do you sound so surprised?" He opened the door to the reception hall and stepped aside to let her enter first. "I have skills."

Cheyenne laughed. "I know you have skills, but I saw you renovating a barn, not building pretty scenery pieces."

Linda, Blake, and Everly sat at a round table in the wide-open reception hall. White fabric was draped over the exposed wooden beams in the ceiling, and other tables were scattered throughout the room. Other than that, the place was empty.

Everly gasped and jumped up from her seat. "You're back!" She barreled into Cheyenne, wrapping her in a bear hug.

"You're back too! How was Grand Cayman?"

"Beautiful!" Everly exclaimed.

"Well, the bungalow was nice. I didn't get to see much else," Blake said.

Ridge shoved his friend's shoulder. "That's enough honeymoon talk."

"She asked," Blake said with a shrug.

"Yeah. I didn't," Ridge grumbled. "I have innocent ears."

Blake bent over laughing, and Everly bumped him with her hip in a silent command to straighten up.

"Tell me about this mess with David," Everly said.

Cheyenne glanced at Ridge, and he gave her an encouraging nod. "I made a mistake. I had no idea who he was."

Everly held up a hand. "Trust me. You're not the first one he fooled."

"So I've heard." Cheyenne ducked her chin. "Whether I knew that in the beginning or not, I shouldn't have agreed to spy on anyone. I knew that was wrong."

"But you needed money. I get it. None of us are innocent here. He's always been obsessive about his business, but I think things turned personal for him when we broke up. He wouldn't let it go if things didn't go his way. When Ridge started messing with the hotels, I think he took it as a double blow."

Cheyenne looked up at the ceiling and blinked rapidly. "I'm sorry for what I've done to your family."

Ridge reached for her, but Everly pulled her in first, wrapping her arms around Cheyenne's shoulders.

"I know what it feels like to be deceived by him. He has a way of manipulating that makes you think you don't have any choice but to go along with what he's saying. I'm just glad you were brave enough to come clean." Everly stepped back and looked Cheyenne in the eyes. "We can take care of you. There's no one in the world I trust more than these people."

Cheyenne looked around just as the door to the reception hall opened.

"I'm here. What'd I miss?" Mr. Chambers asked.

Blake slapped the older man on the shoulder. "We're having a meeting of the minds. Nobody showed up yet."

Mr. Chambers greeted each person with a handshake, including Cheyenne. "What's this I hear about that David guy again?" He looked at Everly with narrowed eyes. "I thought you got rid of him."

Everly held up her hands. "I didn't do anything. The man doesn't know when to give up."

"This is my fault," Cheyenne said. "David wanted to get back at Ridge for buying up hotel properties he had his eye on, and he sent me to spy on Ridge."

"What is this? A 007 film?" Mr. Chambers asked.

"Might as well be," Linda said.

Ridge studied the woman. He'd been skeptical of her intentions here for months, but Everly worked with her every day and swore Linda had changed her ways. Asking her to pretend to be that person she used to be was asking a lot of her if she was genuinely trying to do the right thing now. Ridge knew the stigma of bad decisions was hard to shake, and it was even harder to get out of that shadow when everyone expected the worst from you.

"You don't have to do this," Everly told Linda.

"It's okay. I think David needs a taste of his own medicine." Linda gave Cheyenne a friendly wink.

Ridge slipped an arm around Cheyenne's waist. "We've tried being direct with him, and that hasn't worked so far. Are you sure this is the best plan?"

Blake huffed. "No, but it'll either work or it won't."

"Thanks for your wise words," Ridge said.

Blake rubbed his hands together. "You ready to give him a call?"

Cheyenne scrunched her nose. "No, but I guess it's now or never." She pulled out her phone and made the call, leaving it to ring on speakerphone.

"David Lang."

Ridge stared at the phone, ignoring the pounding of blood in his ears. The man was on the other end of that call, and he wanted nothing more than to make David pay for what he'd done. To Cheyenne. To Everly.

"Hey, I have some big news for you." Cheyenne swallowed hard and continued. "Do you know a woman named Linda Collins? She works here at the ranch."

"I've heard the name," David said.

"She told me yesterday that her dad is putting the ranch on the market," Cheyenne said.

"She told you that?" There was a hint of skepticism in David's tone.

"That's what she said. And I thought you would want to know. It doesn't have anything to do with Ridge, but–"

"I understand. Have Linda call me."

Ridge fisted his hands and glanced at Blake who was white-knuckling the back of a chair. He'd seen that tense jaw on Blake a few times. Ridge was fired up too, ready to throttle David for talking to Cheyenne like she was his to command.

"Should I tell her anything else?" Cheyenne asked.

"No. Not yet," David said.

David disconnected the call, and everyone breathed a sigh of relief.

"How long do we wait before Linda calls?" Everly asked.

"A few minutes," Ridge said. "We want him to think Linda is eager to talk to him."

Linda huffed, and Everly rubbed a hand over her friend's back. They'd come so far since Linda tried to take the ranch from her dad, but Ridge still kept an eye on her. Wanting to believe she'd changed was one thing. Actually believing it was another.

Everly started talking about her honeymoon in the Caribbean, but Ridge cut the story short after a few minutes. Cheyenne gave Linda the number, and the call was made.

"Hi, this is Linda Collins. I'm calling for David Lang."

Ridge wrapped an arm around Cheyenne as they listened to Linda's half of the conversation.

"I've heard about you too. I know things were rocky between you and Everly, but she told me a little about how you're a successful businessman. Now Cheyenne tells me you might be interested in the ranch. My father only mentioned it to me last week. But he's only willing to sell a piece of the ranch, not the whole property. He wants the dude ranch to continue, but the western side is mostly unused right now."

Linda looked up at Ridge and nodded as she listened to David.

"Yes, the basin was surveyed for gold decades ago. The mineral rights alone would be worth it. Now, I'm sure my father won't let it go without a hefty price." Linda gave a thumbs up. "Yes. I believe the area he is considering is about two hundred acres. There are a few structures on the property, but they're all dilapidated except one. We recently started up a youth program here, and they use one of the barns as an office."

"That was a nice touch," Ridge whispered to Cheyenne.

She hugged closer to him. "Yeah, but a little scary. How awful would it be if Mr. Chambers did sell our part of the ranch to David?"

Ridge grinned down at her. "Our part?"

"Well, not ours really, but it feels like ours." She shrugged. "At least it's nice to pretend."

Linda looked up at Ridge. "No, I don't think Ridge knows about this yet. My father told me and Ava and asked us not to tell anyone else yet." She grabbed a pen from the table and scrawled a number in a notebook. "Thank you. I'll get back to you about a time and date to meet with him if he's willing to talk. Thank you, Mr. Lang."

Linda disconnected the call and exhaled deeply. "I'm glad that's over."

Blake rested a hand on Linda's shoulder. "You did great. Thanks for doing this. I know it's not easy for you."

Linda's grin was forced. "Thanks. Now that I'm back here, it's hard to think about the ranch being in anyone else's hands. Dad, Ava, and Jameson do a great job of running things."

"You've got that right," Blake said.

Ridge's jaw tensed. He was lucky Mr. Chambers had agreed to hire him with a felony charge on his record. The man was more forgiving than most.

Mr. Chambers stood from the chair where he'd been sitting. "Well, tell him he can meet us at the main house any evening after six. Ridge and Cheyenne need to be there."

"Are you sure you want him here?" Everly asked.

"I'm sure. We need to talk man to man, and I don't want to do any of that computer video stuff. If he's as serious about buying a piece of this place as I am about getting rid of him, he'll get his fancy pants behind to Wyoming."

Linda called the number David had given her and said, "Jaden? Hi, this is Linda Collins. David said I need to talk to you about setting up a time for him to meet with Mr. Chambers."

Cheyenne tucked closer to Ridge's side. "I can't believe he's coming here," she whispered.

Ridge kissed the top of her head. "Don't worry. I won't let him hurt you."

It was the truth, but a stirring of fear mixed with the anger churning inside him. Ridge had something to lose, and he'd have to be careful to stay one step ahead of David.

Chapter Twenty-Nine

Cheyenne

Cheyenne swiped her damp palms on her jeans and looked at the old clock on the wall. David should be walking in any minute now. She tried focusing on the family photos on the wall, but each smiling face reminded her of happiness that David could steal.

She cared about these people. Mr. Chambers, Linda, Blake, and Everly had all stepped up to help her when she came clean about her connection to David. She'd brought this problem to their doorstep, and they were still willing to help her.

Ridge wrapped his arms around her and kissed her forehead. "You don't have to be here."

She shook her head. "I do. I have to face him. I have to tell him that I'm backing out. No one else can do that for me."

"I can–" Ridge began.

Cheyenne interrupted. "You can't. I have to do it."

"I can at least be here beside you," he said.

"I would love that, but wait until we get him in the office. If he sees you, he'll know something is up."

"He's here!" Everly shouted from the front of the house.

Ridge tightened his hold on Cheyenne. "I don't want to leave you."

"It's just for a second. Let him walk in, and you can be right behind him."

Ridge stared at her, barely controlling his protest.

"I can do this," Cheyenne said. Her words didn't waver this time. It was now or never, and she had to appear strong when David walked in.

They both looked up when they heard the knock on the front door.

"That's your cue," Cheyenne said. Thankfully, her words didn't tremble like her knees.

"I won't let anything happen to you," Ridge promised.

"I know. Now go before he gets in here." She shooed him out of the office and looked around. The desk was worn and nicked, and the window looking out to the ranch was open, letting in a warm breeze.

"Mr. Lang. I've heard about you," Linda said from the front of the house.

"Ah, I hope only good things," David said.

Linda's sing-song laugh echoed through the house, but her words were quieter. "Well, I can't say it was all good. You've stirred up some dust here."

The voices were getting closer, and Cheyenne gripped the back of a chair to steady herself. *Don't let him see you sweat.*

"I assure you, I'm not the man you've heard about. I'm here for business, and business only," David said as he stepped into the office. If he was surprised to see Cheyenne, he didn't show it. She had no business being here if the meeting was about selling a portion of the ranch.

He extended a hand to her. "David Lang."

She took the hand and shook it, grateful she'd just wiped her hands again. "Cheyenne Keeton." Was that all she was supposed to say if David thought they should act like strangers?

David smiled, but the grin only served to turn her stomach.

Linda followed him into the office. "Have a seat Mr. Lang." Linda jerked her head toward the other chair in front of Mr. Chambers's desk.

Slowly, Cheyenne sank into the chair. Was she supposed to speak first?

Linda made her way to the other side of Mr. Chambers's desk and sat. "My father will be here soon, but I wanted to prepare you for what might be coming. Cheyenne told me you would be interested in the land at the ranch, but I don't know why."

David leaned back in his chair and crossed an ankle over his other knee. "I have many reasons, but I'll wait to hear the details from Mr. Chambers. I'm not sold yet."

Cheyenne looked down at her hands in her lap. David was in businessman mode, and the whole act sounded ridiculous. She knew exactly how much he wanted this land, and his casual brush off was comical.

"Did you get a chance to look over the mineral survey I sent you?" Linda asked.

"Yes, and while there are thought to be quite a few deposits here, I'd like to speak to Mr. Chambers regarding the accuracy and any clearances that have been conducted since the original survey."

"Are you aware of the youth program the ranch hosts on the western ridge? You would need to decide what to do with it if that portion of the land is included in the sale."

David held up a hand. "I'm still not sold on the property, but I would carefully weigh all options after closing."

"The program is run by a man named Ridge Cooper, and Cheyenne here is his assistant," Linda said.

David's grin widened. He thought he had Ridge in the palm of his hand. "I'll be sure to speak to Mr. Cooper when the time comes."

Mr. Chambers walked into the office, and Linda stood from the seat behind the desk. Her acting skills were spot-on as her eyes widened like she was a kid who'd been caught in her dad's office.

"Mr. Lang," Mr. Chambers said as he extended a hand. "I hear you came a long way today."

David stood and shook the older man's hand. "Just a few hundred miles, but I agree with you. Business should be conducted man to man."

Cheyenne's palms were sticky as she watched the men greeting each other. Linda made a show of slipping out from behind the desk and trying to blend into the wall.

Mr. Chambers took his place at his desk with a few grunts, then he clasped his hands together. "Mr. Lang, let's get to the point. We're not here to talk land and dollars. I'll never sell this ranch. Not a single acre. You say you're a businessman, but you've meddled in my business."

David straightened. "I don't know what you've been told, but–"

"I've heard enough. Cheyenne told me about how she met you. You see, I would call this meddling in my business because you're trying to harm my employees."

David stood and placed his hands flat on the desk. "Listen here, old man. What I do with my money is none of your business."

Cheyenne stood and pulled the check from her pocket with a shaky hand. She shoved it toward David. "I told Ridge about you. Here's the money I owe you."

Her plan to draw David's ire away from her real boss succeeded, and David snatched the check from her hand. "What is this?" His chest rose and fell in deep waves as he studied the check.

Almost one hundred thousand dollars. She'd lost her lunch in Mr. Chambers's bathroom when Ridge handed the check to her. Her neck was hot thinking about that money being in David's hands now.

Cheyenne took another shaky breath. "I signed a contract saying I would repay the money you'd given me if I didn't fulfill my part of the bargain."

David stepped toward her. "You signed a non-disclosure agreement too."

Mr. Chambers stood. "I see you're still harassing my employees, Mr. Lang."

David's gaze was locked on hers. His face was turning red, and his jaw was set so stiff that she could see the muscles in his face tighten. Every instinct told her to run, but she held her ground. She'd brought everyone into this mess, and she couldn't leave when things got tough.

"I'll make you pay for this," David growled. He leaned away from her, and his right arm lifted at his side.

Cheyenne ducked and shielded her face with her hands. Her stomach sank, and her skin heated.

But the impending blow never came. When she lowered her hands, Ridge was in front of her, holding David's fist in his hand. The room was silent as the two men came nose-to-nose.

Slowly, Ridge started to move, pushing David back toward the wall where Linda slipped out of the way. Cheyenne couldn't see Ridge's face, but David's squinted eyes slowly widened.

When David's back hit the wall, he started to squirm, trying to pull his hand from Ridge's grasp.

Cheyenne held her breath, but one word slipped out as Ridge took a last step toward David.

"Ridge…"

David thrashed his shoulders and pushed at Ridge's chest. "Get your hands off me!"

"It's over," Ridge said calmly. "Take the money and get out. If you ever think about hurting someone I love again, I'll let you meet your maker."

David turned and pushed against Ridge, who now had an extra hold on David's shoulder. "Is that a threat?"

Cheyenne gasped for breath. *Please let David leave. Please let this be over.*

"You bet it is," Ridge said. "I'm not playing your game anymore. Buy hotels, sign contracts for players, you can buy an island for all I care. I'm not asking you. I'm telling you. Leave us out of it."

David stopped bucking against Ridge's hold, and his gaze locked on Cheyenne. Slowly, his smile grew until he laughed.

Laughing was not the reaction she expected right now, and dread settled heavy in her stomach.

"The joke's on you, Ridge. I always knew how to cut you to the core." David jerked his head toward Cheyenne. "She was always the plan."

She was the plan? That wasn't true. Was it?

David laughed again. "When I heard her telling her sob story to Jaden, I knew you wouldn't be able to resist her. I knew Ava would hire her, and you'd fall for her. It was a given. When you found out about what she'd done, it would cut you to the core."

"Too bad. Your plan didn't work," Ridge said.

"Or did it? Are you ever going to be able to trust her? She sold out to the highest bidder. Then she switched sides. She'll leave you if she gets a better offer."

"Stop it," Cheyenne said. Her entire body burned under David's words. Would Ridge believe him? She'd really done those things, but she was loyal to Ridge now.

How could he ever trust her?

"What, you don't like the truth?" David asked. He looked back at Ridge with a triumphant smile. "I think my work here is done."

"If you're finished playing games, then you're right. I know where my loyalties lie, and so does Cheyenne. Now take the money and go," Ridge said.

David relaxed his fisted hand in Ridge's and stopped fighting back. After a few seconds, the two men stepped away from each other. Ridge pointed toward the door. "You're not welcome here anymore."

David huffed. "You think you own the place?"

Mr. Chambers crossed his arms over his barrel chest. "You're not welcome here anymore."

"Fine." David smoothed a hand over his tousled hair and raked his gaze from Ridge to Cheyenne. "There's nothing here I want."

Cheyenne took a step closer to Ridge as David left the room. They all stayed still and quiet, until they heard the front door close behind David.

Linda sighed and fell into a chair. "I think it's over."

Ridge wrapped an arm around Cheyenne's shoulders. "I hope so."

Cheyenne tightened her hold on him. "I'm sorry. This is all my fault."

Ridge tipped her chin up. "No, it's not. I was doing things to make him angry, but he took things too far. I brought this mess to the ranch."

She shook her head. "I hope that's the last we see of him."

Everly came running into the office with Blake only a step behind her. "Did it work? Did Jaden get what she needed?"

Cheyenne gasped. "Oh, I need to call her." She pressed to call and left it on speakerphone.

Jaden answered on the second ring. "Hey!"

"Did you get it?" Cheyenne asked.

"Oh, I got it. And a lot more."

"A lot more?" Cheyenne looked at everyone in the office.

"This is huge." Jaden's joyful tone turned somber. "Which means he'll definitely be out for my head after this."

"Don't worry about that," Ridge said. "I've arranged for protection for you."

"I really appreciate that, but I won't have a job in a few hours. I can't afford to pay for that protection."

"It's on me," Ridge said. "He's on his way to meet you at Lang Corp. right now. Mr. Nathan Fox is coming from Boston."

"I can't thank you enough," Jaden said.

"We really appreciate what you've done," Cheyenne said.

"I'm happy to do anything to help you," Ridge added.

"Good because David was into a lot of shady business. I was pretty sure he was committing tax fraud because he didn't claim any income from the storage facilities he leases. But get this: he was money laundering with the hotels!"

Blake whistled. "That's steep. How many hotels was that?"

"Half a dozen. I'm still digging for more contacts, but there was easily a few million dollars in dirty money passing through those properties in the last three years."

"I'll tell Nathan to send reinforcements so you can have time to get everything you need," Ridge said.

"Thanks. This is huge. He could get years in prison."

"Don't get your hopes up. I'm sure he has a well-paid defense team," Ridge said.

"I don't think anyone could save him from this," Jaden said.

Cheyenne reached for Everly's hand and squeezed. This was their chance to get David out of their lives for good.

Chapter Thirty

Ridge

Ridge pulled the burger patties off the grill as Cheyenne walked out onto the patio. The sun was starting to set, and the view from his backyard over the hills beat a cityscape any day.

She inhaled a deep breath and sighed. "That smells delicious."

"You're just hungry because we barely ate lunch," Ridge said as he put the patties on the table next to the condiments.

Cheyenne walked straight into his arms, and he leaned back against the railing, holding her close.

"Kendrick and Penny asked questions all day long!" she said. "I couldn't chew because they kept talking."

"I can't decide which age is the toughest," Ridge said.

Cheyenne laughed, and the rumble vibrated against his chest. "I don't know either. The ten and eleven year olds really wore me out today, but the older teens are challenging in their own ways." She tilted her chin up to him with a smile.

Ridge pressed his lips to hers, moving slowly until her wide smile pulled them apart.

"The food is going to get cold," she whispered.

Ridge let his arms fall from around her, and she walked straight to the patio table, sinking into a chair. She leaned back and sighed as if the stress of the day melted from her shoulders.

There was something about that content look on her face that filled him with hope. She'd been reluctant to see where he lived, but she'd made herself at home in tiny ways.

She looked around and reached for Ridge's hand. That little movement was always a confirmation for him. She expected him to bless their food. She expected him to be consistent and strong, and he would always be that for her. Knowing she was as dedicated to prayer as he was drove out all of those doubts David had tried to plant in his mind.

Ridge took her hand and prayed, then they started building their burgers. Cheyenne's was simple with only ketchup and mustard, while his was fully loaded.

She swallowed a big gulp of water and sighed.

"Everything okay?" Ridge asked. She'd been quieter than normal over dinner.

"Everything is great. I'm still getting used to this massive place you have."

It took every ounce of restraint not to tense at her words. Cheyenne had walked around gaping for half an hour when they first arrived. Would she ever get used to it? Did he even want her to get used to it? He'd be much happier in a smaller place, and now that they were trying to cut all ties with David, the place was excessive and useless.

"It's not practical. We could find a place that's best for us. Or we could build a cabin," Ridge said with a shrug.

Cheyenne tilted her head. "Best for us? A place?"

Ridge's ears heated. "Not right now. Just in the future. Maybe."

Cheyenne smiled and leaned in to kiss him on the cheek. "I like that idea, but I'd be happy anywhere with you."

Cheyenne's phone rang on the table beside her. "It's Jaden."

"Answer it," Ridge said.

"Hello," Cheyenne said as she put the call on speakerphone.

"Hey. How is everything there?" Jaden asked.

"Great. No word from David. I have you on speakerphone with Ridge."

"Hey, Ridge," Jaden said. "Just wanted to give you two an update. The investigator called me yesterday and said he would be starting his audit tomorrow."

"That's good," Cheyenne said.

"I expect he'll find a lot more than I did," Jaden said.

"How are you? Has David caused any trouble?" Ridge asked.

"A little, but Mr. Fox has been wonderful. I don't expect David to give me a problem, as long as my beefy bodyguard is around."

"Mr. Fox," Cheyenne repeated as she wiggled her brows at Ridge. "Is he nice?"

"Very, but he's a little rigid," Jaden said.

"I expect that's just part of the job," Ridge added.

"Right. Anyway, I think my work at Lang Corp. is finished. Mr. Fox went with me to clean out my things yesterday."

"I'm so glad you're out of there," Cheyenne said.

"You and me both," Jaden added.

Cheyenne gasped. "You should come to the ranch. The high season is almost over, and we'll only have about one or two field trips a week once school starts back."

"I'd love that. Looks like I'm a free agent until I can find a new job."

Another call interrupted the conversation, and Ava's name flashed on the screen. "Hey, Jaden, can I let you go? My boss is calling."

"Sure. We'll talk later about that trip. I'd love to meet you in person."

"Bye," Ridge and Cheyenne said in unison before the call ended.

"Hello," Cheyenne answered the new call.

"Cheyenne? What's going on? I just got three phone calls from irate parents."

Cheyenne straightened in her chair. "What? Why?"

"They all know about Ridge's arrest, and they're upset that we didn't disclose Ridge's felony charge before the kids signed up for the program."

Ridge rested his forehead in his hands. There had always been a kindling of fear in the back of his mind that his charge might come up again like this. The program had gone almost too well this year, and he'd forgotten about the dangerous possibility.

"That's another call. Have you checked the email?" Ava asked.

Cheyenne stood, and her chair scooted across the patio. "No, but I'll check it now. Thanks for calling. I'll let you know more once I check the emails."

"Thanks. And Ridge?"

Ridge lifted his head. "Yeah?"

"We'll get through this. It might not be easy, but this doesn't change your position here at the ranch."

Ridge scoffed, clearing the lump in his throat. "Don't speak too soon. The mob might demand my head on a platter."

Cheyenne ended the call. She grabbed his hand and pulled him from his seat. "Come on. Let's find out what's going on."

Ridge let her lead him inside, then directed her toward his home office. They started the laptop in silence and checked the email. There were fifteen messages.

Cheyenne scooted the chair closer to the desk. "Let me handle this."

"I'm not leaving," Ridge said, pulling up a seat beside her.

Cheyenne read the first message. "I can't believe I left my child in the care of this man. Anyone who could do that to someone should be locked up." Her words faded toward the end.

Ridge stood. "Okay. Let me take you home."

Cheyenne whirled on him. "What? I'm not leaving."

"This is my mess, and you don't have to be a part of this. I should have seen this coming and let someone else take over the program."

"No. It's *your* idea. It's *your* mission. You're the one who wanted to teach the kids how to work and have fun building and doing things that matter."

Ridge stared at the screen where an inbox full of hateful messages waited. His breath seized in his chest. "David wanted to take something from me."

Cheyenne stood and placed her hands on both sides of Ridge's face. "Don't let him win. I know he's the one who spread these articles and photos. I know he's going down swinging, but we can't let him win. This program is worth fighting for."

Ridge shook out of her hold. "I know, but I don't think we'll have much choice." He pointed at the laptop. "The damage is done."

"We haven't even read all of the messages."

Ridge leaned down and read the subject lines. "Registration cancellation. Important message regarding enrollment. Terminate enrollment. Yeah, those don't sound like good news."

"We'll set the record straight," Cheyenne said.

Ridge opened the next email and read, "Is this photo real? I want to remove my daughter from the Wolf Creek Ranch Youth Learning Program immediately." He opened the attachment to see the photo of the man he'd assaulted. His eye was purple and swollen shut, and he had an open gash down the side of his face. He pointed to the screen. "The parents think I'm a dangerous criminal."

"But you're not," Cheyenne said.

"But do you blame them? The evidence is right there!"

"I know what happened. They just don't know the whole truth." She wrapped her arms around his waist and rested her head on his chest. "You're not the dangerous one. David is."

Ridge's arms rested around her, but he felt the pulling away inside. His past wasn't her problem, and he should protect her by distancing her from his mistakes.

"I love you. We'll get through this together," Cheyenne said. She took a step back. "I'll get our burgers, and we can eat while we work through this mess."

Ridge watched as another email popped up in the inbox. The program slipped further and further away from him with every minute.

"I'm sorry," Cheyenne whispered.

Ridge lifted his attention to her. "For what?"

She pointed to the screen. "For the part I played in this. He wanted to take something you loved, and I was supposed to help him. I can't–"

"That's over. You didn't do this."

She pressed her lips into a thin line and walked out of the room.

Settling into the chair, Ridge rested his head in his hands. The things he loved were pulling away from him, and what right did he have to drag them back into his life?

Chapter Thirty-One

Cheyenne

Cheyenne picked at the hem of her blouse as she waited in the parking lot at the local airport. She checked the clock again. Jaden's plane should be landing right now.

Everly typed away on her laptop in the passenger seat. Her phone dinged with another text, and she checked it. "Mrs. Scott is confirmed. We'll stop by the antique store before we go to Grady's." Her phone dinged again. "That's Jenny. She's meeting us at the law office."

Cheyenne checked her phone for a message from Jaden. Nothing yet. "You think this is going to work?"

"Of course. Camille is a good attorney, and Jenny's spotlight at the news station is a local favorite."

"I can't believe she's coming from Cody to help us today," Cheyenne said.

Everly wrapped her hand around Cheyenne's, pulling it away from the hem she'd been picking at. "The people around here who know the real Ridge will do anything to help him. Jenny loves this community as much as we do, and the people of Blackwater are going to save this program."

Cheyenne's phone dinged with a text. "That's Jaden."

Everly put her laptop away. "Let's go get her."

They got out of the car and walked into the hangar. Ridge had chartered a flight for Jaden, and as far as he knew, they were spending the day showing her around Blackwater. And while that was part of the plan, they had bigger goals.

If the plan worked, the people who knew and loved Ridge would provide enough credible testimony to save the program. If it failed, they could bring more awareness to Ridge's past.

Cheyenne and Everly walked inside the huge building with plain beige walls and stopped at the front desk. Cheyenne introduced them and asked for a man named Danny who would escort them to Jaden.

The polite receptionist waved them toward three chairs that sat against one wall to wait. Cheyenne started picking at the hem of her shirt again, and Everly placed a steadying hand over hers.

"This will work," Everly said.

"I hope so. I'm just so glad Jaden agreed to help us. Again."

"Jaden is a good woman who got caught up in the wrong job. Well, she was actually good at her job, but she had a bad boss. She stepped up when it was time, and I know she'll do anything she can to help us."

Cheyenne gripped the arm rests to keep herself from fidgeting. "I trusted the wrong person before, and I just pray we're not making the same mistake twice."

"Jaden isn't going to double cross us. I know she's been unhappy working for David for a while, but I'm glad she stayed as long as she did. She saw signs of the things he was doing, and she stayed so she could find out enough to leave with a bang. That takes a lot of courage."

Cheyenne nodded. "Of course. You're right. I do trust her. And I hate that she had to work for him for so long."

"We were all tricked by David at one point or another. He's a master manipulator. But that shared experience makes us uniquely qualified to give him what he deserves."

A tall, dark-haired man with broad shoulders walked in the room. "Ladies, I'm Danny." He extended a hand to Cheyenne first.

"I'm Cheyenne. This is Everly."

Danny tilted his head toward the door. "Right this way, ladies."

Cheyenne and Everly followed Danny through a short hallway and into the massive hangar room. Danny walked with purpose until they reached the wide opening on the other side of the building.

"Thank you for helping us," Everly said.

Danny looked back over his shoulder. "It's no problem at all. Ridge helped me out a few years ago when a tree fell across the road near my mom's house. He went and bought a chainsaw and spent hours cutting up the tree and clearing the road. I would have been out there all night if he hadn't stopped to lend a hand."

"Did you see the news the other day?" Cheyenne asked. She'd missed the original airing, but Everly had helped find a clip online. The broadcast had painted him in such a bad light.

Danny rubbed his jaw and kept his attention on the path toward the plane. "I did. I saw the news about the arrest when it happened years ago, but I like to think I have plenty of discernment. Ridge didn't strike me as a brawler when I met him, so I just put that notion behind me."

"You knew about the arrest?" Everly said.

"Well, yeah. Anyone who followed professional football knew. It was all over ESPN."

"Right, but no one here has mentioned it. At least not that I've heard," Everly said.

Danny shrugged. "I guess anyone who knew was like me. People make mistakes, and his happened to land him here. I've always known him to be a good guy." He pointed toward a small plane idling on the runway. "There's your friend."

"Thank you so much," Cheyenne said. "Would you be willing to sit for a short interview about how you know Ridge? We're working on a news spotlight with a reporter from Cody."

"Sure." He pulled a card from his chest pocket. "Here's my number. I'll grab your friend's bags and escort you back out." He veered off toward the back of the plane.

"Thank you, Danny," Everly said as they walked toward the door to meet Jaden.

Cheyenne grabbed Everly's arm. "Did you hear that? What if more people already knew?"

"That needs to be a question we ask first when we start the interviews." Everly checked her phone. "The church ladies are getting together now. They should be ready by the time Jenny gets there."

"I can't believe so many people are willing to stand up for him," Cheyenne said. "I wish I had been as quick to trust his true character when I met him."

"The past is the past, girl. That's the whole premise behind this plan," Everly said.

Cheyenne pointed toward the door of the plane as it opened. "Here she is."

Jaden stepped out onto the stairs and smiled. Her straight black hair blew in the wind, and she pulled it to one side.

"Jaden!" Everly shouted as she ran for the stairs.

"Hey!" Jaden tucked her purse to her side as she descended the stairs.

Cheyenne and Everly took turns hugging Jaden. They met up with Danny, who carried her bags, and headed back toward the hangar.

Jaden took a deep breath. "I can't believe I'm here," she said.

"Me either. This is weird. I've only seen you at the Lang Corp. office," Everly said.

Jaden rolled her eyes. "I practically lived there."

"You're free now!" Everly shouted.

"I can't wait to see the town. Cheyenne, you made it sound like a dream."

Cheyenne nodded. "It is. I'm sorry we won't get to do the casual tour."

"No, no." Jaden waved her hands. "This is better. I get to actually talk to everyone, and that'll be fun."

Cheyenne's phone dinged. She'd reached out to dozens of parents in the last twenty-four hours. It seemed that anyone whose kids had already attended the program were impressed with Ridge's management or their kids had great things to say about him, but the willingness to help was fifty-fifty.

She read the message while praying and breathed a sigh of relief when the response was a good one. "That's another parent on our side. She'll be at the church tonight."

"Does Ridge have any idea about this?" Jaden asked.

Cheyenne rolled the phone over in her hands. "No, and I'm still not sure he'll be happy when he finds out, but it'll be worth it if we can save the program."

"I agree," Everly said. "I know he didn't want the word to get out about all this, but now that it has, I think we have to speak up too. He certainly isn't going to do it."

"Why not?" Jaden asked.

Cheyenne rolled her eyes. "He says they're right to not trust their kids with him. He said if he was a parent, he'd feel the same."

"But they don't even know the truth," Everly said. "And no one can teach those kids the way Ridge can."

"I agree. He puts his life experiences into the work and teaches the best lessons." Cheyenne swallowed hard, pushing through the emotion that gripped her whenever she thought about losing the program. "He's such a good role model and teacher."

"He used to always get recruited for the charity football camps when he was a player. They loved him."

Jaden pulled her phone out and started tapping. "I found some great interviews he did about those camps. We can see if Jenny can track them down to use in the segment."

Cheyenne responded to the parent, thanking her for her help. As soon as she sent the message, a text from Ridge came in.

Ridge: Did Jaden make it?

Cheyenne: She did. Thank you so much for sending the plane.

Ridge: You're welcome. Have fun today. I love you.

Cheyenne typed her response, but the three words didn't come close to the wave of emotion that filled her heart for the man she was planning to redeem in the eyes of the people of Blackwater.

Chapter Thirty-Two

Ridge

Ridge lined up a cut of wood on the stump and lifted the ax over his head. He swung it down in a rush, splitting the trunk in two. He lined up another cut and swung again. He needed the mind-numbing labor of chopping firewood. The precision kept his attention on the wood, and the monotony allowed him to turn his mind off.

Lincoln picked up the split pieces and stacked them in the back of the UTV. Lincoln had been at the ranch for three years, and the two men had an unspoken agreement: don't talk. Ridge welcomed that reprieve today. Everyone had been pushing optimism in his face, and he wasn't holding out hope that the program would still be in his hands come next spring.

The ache in his shoulders was growing into a warm burn, and he pushed harder against the pain. That physical wall had been his old friend and enemy as long as he could remember, and right now, he let the fire run wild. If his muscles hurt bad enough, maybe he'd forget about the program.

That was a stupid thought. Teaching the kids had been first and foremost in his mind for over a year, and he'd gotten a taste only to have the dream stripped from him.

Lincoln stepped up to the cuts of wood on the ground and propped his hands on his hips. "You got three months?" Linc asked.

Ridge didn't look up as he readied another cut. "I thought I wouldn't have to talk about this today."

Linc stared at the ground but didn't move to pick up the wood. "I had six months, then another four years."

Ridge let the ax fall but didn't move to lift it. He wiped the sweat off his brow and turned to Linc. "For what?"

Lincoln finally met his gaze. "Theft, then arson."

Leaning on the ax handle, Ridge gave Linc a once-over. The guy had always been quiet, and Ridge had never thought for a second he needed to know anything about who Lincoln North really was.

Now, the gates had been opened, and Ridge wanted to close them back up along with everything he'd just heard. "Does Mr. Chambers know?"

"Yep." Linc looked to the right, then the left. "My parole officer knew Mr. Chambers, and they worked out a deal. He agreed to give me a job when I got out."

"What was the catch?" Ridge asked. Mr. Chambers was a good man, but he always had a trick up his sleeve. The man had expectations, and he always had a safeguard to make sure his plans worked out.

Linc huffed. "I had to go to church. Every Sunday. The old man hasn't put me on the Sunday schedule since I came here."

"He's hardheaded," Ridge said.

"Yeah. I'm still not sure I believe all the grace and mercy talk."

Ridge wanted to ask, but he wasn't sure he wanted to hear the answer. "Why not?"

Linc shrugged. "Some things are too wrong to be set right."

"Are you talking about me or you?" Ridge asked.

"Maybe both of us. Maybe just me." Linc bent and started piling the split wood in his arms.

Ridge stood still for a moment, mulling Linc's words around in his head. The panic that came with the doubt had his head spinning. "I don't believe that."

Linc stood and stacked the pieces in the UTV trailer. "Didn't think you would."

Ridge's phone rang, and he pulled it from his pocket. Cheyenne's name lit up the screen.

"Hey. You make it back?" he asked.

"We did. I'm just showing Jaden around the cabin, and we're going to head over to the barn. She wants to see the horses, and I'll feed them while we're there."

Ridge looked at the dwindled pile of logs. "How long will you be there? I'm finishing up at the woodshed."

"Probably a while. She's never seen a horse before, and she's excited," Cheyenne said.

"Do you two have plans for supper? We could meet up with Blake and Everly."

"That's what I was hoping. Everly already said she wanted to get together this evening. She was supposed to be asking Blake while I asked you."

Ridge looked down at his red T-shirt. Dirt was smeared over one side, and a dark sweat spot covered his chest. "I'll finish up here and run home to get a shower."

"No rush. Well, rush a little. I'm ready to see you."

Jaden let out a long "Aww" in the background of the call.

"I'm ready to see you too," Ridge said. "Tell Jaden that Nathan Fox called me earlier."

"Really? What did he say?" Cheyenne asked.

"Just that he thinks the contract for Jaden's protection should be extended. Ask her if she wants me to have him meet her when she leaves the ranch."

Cheyenne squealed. "I'll talk to her and let you know at dinner." Cheyenne whispered, "She's been talking about him. I think he wants to do more than protect her."

"Oh, so I'm a matchmaker now. I'll add that to my resume," Ridge said.

Cheyenne laughed. "I have to go talk to her about this. See you soon. I love you."

"Love you too," Ridge said. The echo of Cheyenne's laughter hung on the call until she ended it.

Linc stepped up to the log and crossed his arms over his chest. He'd picked up all of the cut wood and stood waiting for Ridge to do his part of the job. "Looks like you get a second chance."

Ridge pocketed his phone. "Not saying I deserve it."

Linc stayed quiet while they finished the wood. With the UTV trailer full, they headed to the woodshed and stacked it. Most of the tourism stopped during the winter months on the ranch, but about a quarter of the workers stayed on site to maintain and repair anything that was needed for the upcoming tourist season.

Ridge and Cheyenne had talked recently about her plans for the winter, and she seemed content to stay. It would be the perfect time for her to learn more about the horses before next year.

But would there even be a program next year? The realization that her job here was on the line hit him in the gut. Maybe Mr. Chambers would let someone else work with Cheyenne to keep the program open.

Selfishness tasted like acid in the back of his throat. He wanted to be the one working with Cheyenne. They'd made a great team this year. But he could put his wants aside to save the program and Cheyenne's job at the ranch.

Ridge stacked the last of the wood and pulled off his gloves. "I need to run. I'll put in a work order on the UTV if you drive it to the maintenance building. I think Brett is over there today. He can give you a ride back."

"Got it." Linc threw his gloves onto the short wood stack next to the door as he walked out.

Ridge headed for the main office and parked in the back to avoid the guests milling around in the front parking area. He took the back entrance and headed for Jameson's office.

The door was open, and he didn't knock. "You got a minute?"

Jameson pushed away from his desk and leaned back in his chair. "Anything to save me from more paperwork. What's up?"

Ridge leaned against the wall beside the door. "I thought paperwork was Ava's job."

"It is, but she's taking a day off. She wasn't feeling good this morning."

"She okay?" Ridge asked.

"Yeah. I took her lunch earlier, and she said she was feeling a lot better. What can I do for you?"

"What's your plan for the program?" Ridge asked.

Jameson's jaw worked from side to side before he spoke. "Not sure yet. I think all of the schools dropped out for this fall."

Last Ridge had checked, there had still been two schools who hadn't dropped their field trips. "Right. I was thinking it might help if I dropped out and you got someone else to co-manage, it might work."

Jameson shook his head. "I've thought of that, but I don't know anyone else as qualified as you. You and Cheyenne made a great team."

Made. Ridge didn't miss the past tense in that one word. "I'm the only problem with the program. Get rid of me, and things might still work for next year."

Ridge's phone rang, and he pulled it out of his pocket. "Why would Remi be calling me?"

Jameson shrugged. "Not sure."

Ridge answered the call. "Hello."

"Hey, who is at the west barn?" Remi asked.

"Cheyenne and Jaden."

"Oh. I recognized Cheyenne's car but not the other one."

Ridge gestured for Jameson to follow him and backed out of the office. "There are two cars? Jaden didn't rent a car."

"Well, there are two parked at the barn," Remi said. "You want me to check in?"

The cold warning slid down Ridge's back as he stalked toward his truck. "No. I'll head over there."

"Why do you sound worried? You think it's David?"

"Don't go over there. I'm on my way," Ridge ordered.

"Too late. See you in a minute," Remi said matter-of-factly.

Ridge growled as he slid the phone back into his pocket. "I'll drive. You call the police."

"You sure?" Jameson asked as he slid into the passenger seat.

"Sure enough that I want them on their way," Ridge said. Trying to ignore the fear rising in his head, he sped toward the barn.

Chapter Thirty-Three

Cheyenne

Cheyenne opened the old door and stepped to the side for Jaden to enter. "This is the tack room. It's where we keep all the saddles and equipment."

Jaden walked in and ran her fingertips over a saddle horn. "It smells like leather and dirt. Am I crazy to think it smells good?"

Cheyenne laughed. "No. It sounds strange, but I think the same thing. Wait till you get close to a stall. That's not a good smell."

"So you're tearing this barn down and building another one for next year?" Jaden asked.

Looking around, Cheyenne sighed. "I don't think they'll tear it down, but the plan was to build a new one. I don't even know if that's happening anymore."

Jaden tilted her head. "I'm sorry. I really hope our plan works. We can still create enough positivity around this place that people might come back. Plus, you might get new registrations too."

"We already lost all of the schools for the rest of the year. The program is dead." Voicing the sad truth brought back the guilt. Losing the program was all her fault. She hadn't said the program was everything to Ridge, but anyone who heard the phone calls she'd made to Jaden would be able to tell how hard Ridge worked to make the program the best.

"Don't think like that," Jaden said. "Wait until the spotlight airs. Jenny was so sweet, and she really cared about what we're trying to do."

"I hope you're right." Cheyenne jerked her head toward the door. "Let's go see the horses. I need to feed them too, so I'll let you help with that."

"Sounds great, but is there a restroom I could use first?"

Cheyenne covered her smile with a hand.

"What?" Jaden asked. "There's no restroom?"

"There is, but it's out there." Cheyenne pointed to the opening leading out of the barn.

Jaden's eyes widened. "You have an outhouse?"

Cheyenne fell into a fit of laughter. "That's what I call it, but it's actually just a building with the bathrooms in it. The barn didn't have plumbing, so they put in a septic system."

"You just described an outhouse," Jaden said.

"Well, let me show you to the outhouse." Cheyenne waved her hands toward the exit.

"You said this place was charming. Does the toilet at least flush?" Jaden asked.

"Yes, there is a real toilet. I promise." Cheyenne stopped in the barn doorway and pointed to the little shack next to the barn. It was newer and sturdier than the old barn, but the practical building merely served its purpose. They'd coated the wood in a light stain, hoping to preserve it until the new barn could be built, but that was the only extra feature the outhouse boasted.

Jaden hummed. "Okay. I'm doing this. My mom will never believe I used a real outhouse."

Cheyenne laughed. "I'll be in the office. It's that room." She pointed to the door across the breezeway from the tack room.

In the office, Cheyenne checked her texts. A few of the parents were still sending encouraging messages. They'd all been wonderful during the interviews, and after hearing all the nice things the people said about Ridge, she was starting to think they actually had a shot of saving the program.

The low hum of a vehicle raised Cheyenne's attention from the computer. It wasn't Ridge's diesel engine. The only person she'd expect to stop by would be Ava, but she'd been feeling sick when Cheyenne spoke to her earlier.

She headed toward the door to let whoever was coming know where to find her, but her steps came to a halt as soon as she peeked out.

David stalked toward the entrance, looking over one shoulder, then the other. The fake friendly smile he'd used on her during her interview was long gone, replaced by the scowl he'd worn in Mr. Chambers's office last week.

Cheyenne ducked back inside the office and closed the door. She flipped the lock and prayed. What was he even doing here? He should be under investigation on the other side of the country right now.

"Cheyenne!" David yelled.

The single word turned her blood cold. He was right outside the door.

He pounded on the old wood. "Cheyenne. Open up!"

Cheyenne lunged for her phone on the desk. She quickly dialed Ridge's number.

He answered on the first ring. "Are you okay?"

"David is here," she whispered. Keeping her voice down was useless. He knew she was hiding in the office.

His pounding started again. "Open this door!"

"I'm on my way," Ridge said on the other side of the call.

"I'm in the office, but Jaden is out there. She went to the restroom–"

"I have Jameson with me. We'll handle everything. Stay on the phone with me, and don't open that door."

"Cheyenne!" David yelled. The heavy thuds on the door rattled the walls.

"There's a pistol in the top drawer of the filing cabinet. The key is in the top desk drawer," Ridge said.

"I can't use a pistol." Panic and heat raced up her throat at the thought of having to use it.

"I can walk you through it," Ridge said. "I need you to get it out."

"I know *how* to use a pistol. I just… can't."

Tears welled in her eyes as David pounded again. Jaden was out there somewhere, but David must not have noticed her yet.

Ridge's words were calm now. "Listen, Cheyenne. If there's a choice between you and him, choose you. I choose you. I will always put you first. I'm on my way, and I'll make sure he never tries to hurt you again."

Cheyenne nodded. He couldn't see the movement, but everything he said made sense. Of course, she had to protect herself. She could use the pistol if it meant life or death.

She tucked the phone between her shoulder and ear while she looked through the drawer. The key was clearly labeled, and she darted around the desk toward the filing cabinet.

"You still with me, baby?" Ridge asked.

"Yes. I'm opening the cabinet now."

David pulled and pushed the door, rattling it on its hinges. "Open the door or I'll knock it down!"

Her hand shook as she jammed the key at the lock. She gasped for breath, but the key missed the mark every time.

The door rattled and shook the walls as David rammed into it. Another thud had her heart pounding against the walls of her chest.

"Cheyenne, breathe. I'm almost there," Ridge said in her ear.

"Okay. Okay." She wrapped her left hand around her right, steadying it enough to unlock the drawer.

She pulled open the cabinet as the wooden door splintered, sending shards flying around the room. The phone fell to the ground as she reached up to shield her face from the debris.

David stumbled into the office, falling into the side of the desk. He righted himself and stood. His brows pulled together, and his jaw was set hard enough that the veins in his neck bulged.

Cheyenne reached into the drawer and pulled out the gun. The metal was heavy in her hands as she straightened her arms, pointing the weapon toward David.

David took a step toward her, clearly unafraid of the gun she held. She took a step away from him, and the back of her legs hit the desk.

Please, Lord. Please, Lord. The prayer tumbled in a rush in her mind, though it was the most fervent request she'd ever brought before God. She couldn't bring herself to pull the trigger, and David knew it.

David reached for her, and his lips pulled back over his teeth as he spoke. "No one betrays me. If you thought I had a grudge before, you haven't seen anything yet."

Remi darted into the room, and her red hair whipped around her as she swung at David. The impact knocked David off-kilter, but he quickly regained his bearings and lunged for Remi. She lashed out at him again with the horseshoe she clung to, but it did little to thwart him as he pinned her to the wall. Her head landed hard against the wood with a sickening thud.

Jaden ran into the room and gasped when she saw David pinning Remi against the wall. "Let her go!"

The heat of anger pushed Cheyenne forward. She might have been reluctant to use the weapon before, but she wouldn't stand by while anyone hurt her friend. Cheyenne pressed the barrel of the gun to David's head, causing him to still. He kept a tight hold on Remi, who gasped for breath and stared at the pistol with wide eyes.

"Let her go," Cheyenne said. "Now."

David's gaze darted back and forth between Cheyenne and Remi. She registered the moment when his pride won, and she jerked the gun back in the same moment he lunged for it. When he stumbled toward her, she slammed the butt of the pistol into the side of his head. The sickening crunch rolled her stomach.

David fell to the floor, and Cheyenne lunged for her friend. Remi sank to the floor, holding the back of her head. Jaden crouched beside her, and her shoulders shook as she kept David in her line of sight.

"Are you okay?" Cheyenne asked as she searched Remi for injuries.

Remi reached up and touched the back of her head but didn't take her gaze off David. The hand she lifted from her head was covered in red. The blank look on her face tensed, morphing into a scowl that she aimed at David.

"Cheyenne." Ridge rushed into the office, and Jaden backed up to make room for him to crouch next to Cheyenne and Remi. He looked back and forth between them, searching for injuries. "Are you okay?"

She'd never been happier to see anyone in her life, and as much as she wanted to sink into the comfort of his arms, the danger wasn't gone. "I'm fine. Remi is–"

"I've got her," Jameson said as he quickly pulled Remi from the office out into the breezeway of the barn.

There was a fire in Ridge's eyes as he pushed Cheyenne toward the door. "Stay outside. The police are coming."

David tried to pull himself up on the side of the desk, but he still had a dazed look in his eyes. Cheyenne looked from David to Ridge and back to David.

"Go," Ridge said with another push.

Cheyenne lifted the gun to hand it to him when David crouched low and barreled across the room, tackling Ridge at the waist. Cheyenne stumbled back, losing her grip on the gun and falling through the doorway onto her back. The impact jarred her to the teeth and sucked every ounce of breath from her lungs. The pain in the back of her head jolted through her body as she gasped for air that never came.

Chapter Thirty-Four

Ridge

Ridge braced for the impact as David ran in for the tackle. Ridge's arms lifted instinctually, and the power in his legs and lower back exploded toward David as they collided.

The blow wasn't anything close to the hits he'd taken on the field, and Ridge's defensive push sent David flying back into the desk. The hard wood held as David crumpled.

Ridge looked for Cheyenne. She'd been right beside him before David attacked him. When he found her, wide-eyed on the floor in the doorway. All logic and self-preservation died as he lunged for her.

"Cheyenne. Cheyenne!" he shouted as he leaned over her.

With her mouth gaping, she clutched at her throat. She couldn't breathe. Ridge frantically looked for Jameson. The foreman had been a paramedic before his time at the ranch.

Jameson was running toward them. "I've got her."

A siren grew louder as Ridge moved to Cheyenne's side to give Jameson space. What if she'd broken a rib that punctured her lung? What if she couldn't breathe until it was too late?

Jameson examined her with a calm professionalism, but the urgency in Ridge was about to explode.

"What's happening? What's wrong?" Ridge asked.

Cheyenne inhaled, and it sounded like she'd gotten at least part of a breath that time.

"She just got the wind knocked out of her," Jameson said. "Solar plexus syndrome."

Ridge exhaled a deep breath and squeezed Cheyenne's hand. He'd gotten the life knocked out of him more times than he could count, but he remembered getting his breath back quicker than this. Could it be more serious than Jameson was letting on?

Cheyenne gulped another half breath and squeezed his hand back.

"Ridge. Get David," Jameson shouted as he leaned over Cheyenne.

David? But he couldn't leave Cheyenne. He didn't know if she was okay.

"Ridge. Now," Jameson demanded.

The sharp words broke Ridge out of his indecision, and he moved back into the office. David was on his hands and knees, coughing and spitting blood onto the floor. Ridge set his jaw as he reached for David's collar. He wouldn't be fighting back in this condition.

The second before Ridge had the man in his grip, David whirled, grabbing the gun off the floor and pointing it at Ridge.

The shot rang out in the instant Ridge grabbed David's wrist, and a scream followed the echo of the explosion.

Without any time to process where the bullet had landed, Ridge tightened his grip on David's wrist and pushed him to the floor. Another scream filled the air as Ridge pressed his knee into David's back.

"Drop the gun," Ridge demanded.

David resisted, but an extra twist of the wrist released the hold. Jameson ran into the room and kicked the gun out of reach. He helped pull David to his feet while Ridge twisted David's arms behind his back. He cried out in pain, spitting blood into the room.

"Shut it. You're done. It's over, and you lose. Got that?" Ridge growled.

David gasped for a breath. "She can't be trusted," he said low and ragged.

"No, you're the one who can't be trusted," Jameson said. "What did you think you'd do? You'll be behind bars this time."

David scoffed. "That won't happen."

Two men in law enforcement uniforms ran into the small room. The first one said, "I think you're wrong, Mr. Lang."

David spat blood. "Who are you?"

"Officer Asa Scott. This is the fourth time I've introduced myself to you. I take it you ignored my advice to stay away from the ranch the last time I escorted you out."

Ridge transferred his hold on David to Asa, while David rattled off more threats. Ridge looked around the room and spotted the hole where the bullet had gone through the wall. He didn't want to think about how close David had come to winning.

"You have the right to remain silent," Asa told David.

"Get your hands off me!" he screamed.

Asa led David out of the office where the other officer, Dawson Keller, was crouched in front of a bench talking to Cheyenne, Jaden, and Remi.

Ridge walked up just as Officer Keller asked, "What happened when he attacked Mr. Cooper?"

Cheyenne picked at a bandage on her elbow. "I don't know how, but I got pushed, and I landed on my back just outside the doorway." She pointed to the area and caught sight of Ridge. Her eyes widened, and she rushed toward him.

"Are you okay?" Her shoulders started to shake as soon as she finished the question.

Ridge wrapped his arms around her. "I'm fine. Are you okay?" he asked, clinging to her with every ounce of strength he had. He kept an eye on David as Asa escorted him out of the barn. The department would have their hands full with that lunatic.

She buried her face in his shirt and cried. "I'm so sorry."

Ridge brushed a hand over her hair, feeling for any bumps or cuts. "Why are you sorry? I'm sorry you got dragged into this mess. Are you sure you're okay?" Something in him wouldn't rest until he had undeniable proof that she was okay.

"I got us into this." She sobbed and sniffed. "But I'm glad you got here so quickly.

How did you know? You asked if I was okay when I called you."

"Remi told me there was someone else at the barn. I had a feeling it was him."

She wiped her tears on his chest and looked back to where Remi sat on a bench. Jameson examined the back of her head, and Officer Keller squatted in front of her asking questions. "I'm glad so many people around here are looking out for me." She sniffed and wiped her face. "I'm so sorry."

Ridge cradled Cheyenne's face in his hands and tilted her chin up. The pain and sadness in her eyes tore him in two. "Listen, this isn't your fault. He did this, and it has nothing to do with you. Okay?"

"How can you ever forgive me for telling him things about you?" she whispered.

Ridge wrapped her in his arms and pulled her close. "It's in the past, and I've forgiven you ten times over. It's you and me now. Nothing can come between us."

420 | MANDI BLAKE

Chapter Thirty-Five

Ridge

Ridge flipped the patty on the grill once more before scooping the spatula under it and placing it in the pan beside the grill. "Burgers are ready!"

Colt popped up beside him. "Remi likes hers a little burnt."

Ridge picked up one of the patties and laid it back on the hot grill. "I'll give it three more minutes, but I'm not serving a black burger off my grill."

"Thanks, man." Colt looked at his watch. "Take these in so everyone else can get started. I'll finish Remi's."

Ridge passed the spatula and grabbed the tray of patties. Inside, everyone was huddled around the bar in the kitchen. Everly opened bags of chips on the counter, and Cheyenne refilled glasses with water.

She looked at home in his kitchen. When had she inserted herself into his life so fully that she'd become a part of his home?

Cheyenne *was* his home. She was the only exception to every barrier he'd fortified against the world, and now she was the queen of his castle.

He stepped up beside her and kissed her cheek as he set the patties on the counter. "Dinner is ready."

Remi whirled and leaned over the tray. "Did you burn mine?"

Ridge shooed her away. "You're dragging your hair in the food."

"Burnt. Burger," Remi repeated.

"Relax. Colt is working on it."

Remi smiled. "I knew I kept him around for a reason."

Cheyenne chuckled as she stirred the chip dip. "I don't think you had much choice."

Blake whistled loud, getting everyone's attention. "It's time to eat. Fix those burgers and head to the living room."

Ridge frowned. "Let's eat on the patio. It's nice outside."

"Nope," Everly said as she whirled around him, gathering condiments. "We're eating in the living room."

Ridge looked to Cheyenne for support, but her attention was glued to the burger she was constructing. Resigned to eating indoors, despite the perfect weather, Ridge built his burger and piled chips on the other side of his plate.

The living room was big enough that everyone had plenty of room to sit, and an ESPN special played on the TV with the volume low. He usually kept the TV off the sports channels when Cheyenne was around. Not because she'd asked, but because he didn't know how she'd react if Jerry Keeton suddenly showed up for an interview.

It didn't seem right that the retired football star was her dad. He'd met the man plenty of times, and he'd gotten the impression he was a stand-up guy. Maybe he'd been different when he was younger.

"Bless the food!" Remi yelled as she tucked her legs beside her on the couch and rested her plate on her thighs.

"Ridge, do us the honor," Blake said.

Ridge bowed his head and thanked the Lord for the food and friends. He'd never had this many guests in his new house, and the company brought a sense of peace after the run-in with

David earlier in the week. These people had shown up on the frontlines when Cheyenne needed help, and he'd never forget that loyalty.

When the amens quieted, Everly changed the channel to a local news station and picked up her burger. She'd gotten enough exposure to sports over the years, and now she was married to a former player and agent.

Blake had left the business when Ridge did, and it seemed neither of them had looked back. As much as he loved playing, Blackwater fit them better than the gridiron.

Cheyenne leaned over, bumping his shoulder with hers. "This burger is delicious!"

Remi raised her hand. "I second that."

Everly turned the volume up on the TV and shushed everyone. "It's starting."

"What's starting?" Ridge asked.

Cheyenne set her plate to the side and threaded her fingers through his. "We did something. To try to save the program." She pointed to the TV where a young reporter stood in front of their church.

"Our spotlight tonight takes us to Blackwater where a community is rallying around former Colts offensive lineman Ridge Cooper."

Ridge looked at Blake, then Cheyenne. "What?"

Cheyenne pointed at the TV, drawing his attention back to the news.

Everly stood in front of the church with the reporter. "The recent news circling my brother is without context." She looked at the camera and laid her hand on her chest. "He did it all to protect *me*. I know Ridge Cooper isn't a violent man. I've seen him walk away from many confrontations *to prevent* a physical fight."

The next scene was a group of people talking in the church community center while the reporter narrated. "Ridge Cooper started a youth learning program at Wolf Creek Ranch this year, and the future of the co-op program is at risk following the allegations regarding an assault charge from six years ago."

Silas and Anita Harding, the owners of another ranch not far from Wolf Creek, stood together in the next scene. "Ridge has been a help to us more times than we can count," Anita said. "When we needed an extra hand, he never hesitated. He just showed up and started working,"

The next scene was Hudson Jett with his dad. "Mr. Cooper is the best guy. We had so much fun at the ranch this year."

Then the reporter was back. "Hudson Jett attended the youth learning program at Wolf

Creek Ranch before the news about Mr. Cooper's former charge was brought back into the light."

Hudson stood with his dad again. "I heard about what happened back then. I was too young to know what was going on at the time, but then Miss Everly told me what he did for her, and I think he was really brave to stand up for her."

The scene cut to Everly talking with a woman he recognized from the post office, but the reporter spoke. "New information regarding the man Mr. Cooper allegedly assaulted has recently come to light."

"He was protecting me," Everly said. "There was a man who Ridge thought was stalking me. And when he confronted the man, Ridge didn't know he had a weapon."

The reporter was back again as grainy surveillance footage showed the parking garage where Ridge approached the man. "This video shows the man pulling what looks to be a gun on Mr. Cooper."

Ridge looked at Everly, Blake, then Cheyenne.

"Jaden helped too," Cheyenne said.

Laughter drew his attention back to the screen where Hudson Jett rode Burgundy along the trail behind the barn. The horse stopped next to Ridge in the video, and he reached up to run his hand along its neck.

"Did you take that video?" Ridge asked.

Cheyenne chewed the inside of her cheek. "Hudson's dad said I could use it. I guess I should have asked you too before I let them put it on air."

Ridge leaned forward and rested his elbows on his knees. He watched as different kids who came to the program over the summer talked about all they'd learned and their thankfulness to Ridge and Cheyenne.

With one hand covering his mouth, Ridge listened as kids, parents, and people he knew in Blackwater advocated for the youth learning program. Everyone interviewed seemed to really care about what they were doing at the ranch and wanted their kids to be able to come back next year.

The reporter appeared again, with Cheyenne by her side. "Miss Keeton, what was your experience with Mr. Cooper and the program at Wolf Creek Ranch this year?"

"It was so much more than I expected. Ridge taught the kids and teens so much about horses, building, and working the land, but he also taught them patience, resilience, and dedication. He taught them to take pride in the work of their hands and what they could do to help others."

Ridge turned to Cheyenne, who sat rigid on the loveseat beside him. "You did this?"

Cheyenne nodded. "Well, we did." She gestured to the other people in the room.

Ridge rubbed a hand over his mouth. In all the years he'd been interviewed, filmed for commercials, and been the focus of hundreds of nationally screened football games, he'd never felt torn wide open like this. They'd pored over everything he cared about. The ranch, the program, the family, the friends–they were all laid bare in this news report.

If David had wanted to know what Ridge valued most, he could have watched the five-minute segment and gotten the whole story. He cared about all of it, so much that hearing the way everyone talked about the program settled the matter. He had to fight to save it.

"Please don't be mad," Cheyenne whispered beside him.

Ridge turned to her again and quirked a brow. "Mad?"

Cheyenne twisted one of her fingers. "I know you came here for privacy, and I know I've invaded that personal space before, but this time, I did it with good intentions." She laid a hand on his shoulder. "I want the program to stay as much as you do."

Everly scooted to the edge of her seat. "Now that everyone knows David's twisted story, they need to know the truth." She pointed to the TV. "This is the truth that can undo all of his mess."

Cheyenne scooted closer to him. "I don't know if this is enough to save the program, but I know the people here see the real you. Just like I do."

Ridge grabbed her hand, pulling her to her feet in a rush. He wrapped her in his arms and rested his cheek against her soft hair. "It's enough. It's more than enough." He placed his hands on her face, tilting her chin to look up at him. "Whether it works or not, it's enough."

Pressing his mouth to hers, he breathed in the freedom that came with that realization. He had everything he needed–the love and trust of a good woman, and a group of friends who would stand beside him when he needed them most.

Cheyenne wrapped her arms around his neck and pulled him closer. When they broke the kiss, she stared up at him with a wide-eyed excitement that had his fingers clenching tighter around her.

"I won't give up. I can't."

Everyone in the room cheered, but Ridge pressed his forehead to Cheyenne's. "We're in this together."

She smiled up at him. "I hoped you'd say that."

Chapter Thirty-Six

Cheyenne

Cheyenne watched as Jess led Star around the outdoor arena. Jaden clung to the reins, grinning like a kid on Christmas morning.

"Cheyenne, are you seeing this?" Jaden asked.

"I am. I knew you could do it."

Jaden had been eager to ride a horse until she found out how big they were in person. It had taken her almost a week of hanging around the barn to get up the nerve to ride.

Cheyenne lifted her phone and made a video of Jaden riding Star. "Your mom will love this."

Jaden's mom had been a barrel racer in her younger years, but they'd lived in a city Jaden's whole life and the love of horses wasn't passed on to her daughter.

An incoming text popped up on the screen, and Cheyenne ended the video to respond.

Ridge: You coming over?

She checked her watch and gasped. "I forgot I'm supposed to meet Ridge at his place for dinner."

Jaden let go of the rein with one hand long enough to quickly shoo Cheyenne away. "Go on. I'm having fun."

Jess shouted over her shoulder, "Yeah, she'll be here when you get back. Take your time. We'll have supper here and check out the rodeo."

Cheyenne backed out of the barn. "Thanks, guys!"

She waved her good-byes and looked down at the plaid shirt and jeans she wore. To change, or not to change? Deciding against it, she jogged to her car. Once she was in and the car was running, she texted Ridge.

Cheyenne: On my way. Sorry!

The summer heat was slightly fading, and she drove the back roads to Ridge's house with the windows down. She had one more week before her trip back to Tennessee, and as much as she missed her home there, she would miss Wyoming more.

The small blessing of the program dropouts was that she now had the time to travel back to the South. Ridge had found the perfect long-term care facility for her mom, and Hadley was taking a job at the ranch come spring.

She wouldn't be returning home to Blackwater alone. Her family was coming with her. Her heart wouldn't be torn anymore. Everyone she loved would be within a short drive.

She parked in front of Ridge's house and pulled the visor down to check her hair in the mirror. After a day at the barn, strands of hair had escaped her ponytail, and she quickly pulled all of the hair back into the tie. That was the best she could do, but Ridge always assured her she didn't need to fix up around him.

Ducking her chin, she jogged for the door. Looking up at the monstrous house always evoked unease, so it was better to trick herself into thinking the place wasn't as big as it was. She'd never get used to the large rooms and tall ceilings, but it was true that Everly had done an amazing job of making it feel like a welcoming home.

She walked in the front door and shouted, "I'm here! Sorry I'm so late!"

Ridge stepped out of the kitchen and met her halfway. "You're not late."

He leaned down and kissed her, but the connection ended too soon. She started to lean back in, initiating another kiss, but he grabbed her hand.

"I have a surprise for you."

Cheyenne pulled back a little. "Your surprises tend to be over the top."

Ridge shrugged. "This one is too. Prepare yourself."

"Ridge!"

"You'll like it. I think."

Allowing him to lead her, she closed her eyes as they entered the kitchen. Ridge stopped her and moved to stand behind her, resting his hands on her shoulders.

"Open up."

Cheyenne opened her eyes and gasped. Jerry Keeton stood in the kitchen by the bar, and a dark-haired woman who looked to be about the same age stood carefully poised behind him.

Cheyenne took a step back, running into Ridge.

Jerry linked his hands in front of him and shifted his weight from side to side.

Her dad–the one she'd never met and never cared to know–was looking at her like she might flog him at any moment.

She whirled on Ridge and opened her mouth to speak, but the words wouldn't come out. She couldn't think past the anger and hurt. Pushing by Ridge, she stalked out of the kitchen.

"Wait. Cheyenne," Ridge called behind her.

She picked up the pace as she neared the front door. Not that man. She didn't want anything to do with him.

Ridge caught up to her as she reached for the door, resting a hand on top of hers as she turned the knob. "Cheyenne, please wait."

"I don't want to wait for anything. I want to get out of here." She jerked the door open and walked out onto the stone entrance. She stopped her retreat and covered her mouth with both hands.

Ridge was behind her. She could feel the heat of his body before he rested a hand on her shoulder. "I'm sorry. I don't want you to be upset, but–"

"Then why is he here?" Cheyenne asked, rounding on him.

Hurt morphed Ridge's expression into a cautious frown. "Hear him out." He tilted his head toward the door. "I've met Jerry a few times over the years, and it didn't sit well with me that you said he didn't acknowledge you as his. I reached out to him, and turns out, he didn't know about you."

Her eyes widened along with her mouth. "What?"

Jerry cleared his throat behind Ridge. He stepped out onto the porch, and the woman followed him.

"Ridge is right. I didn't know about you."

"You didn't?" Cheyenne asked, but she wasn't sure she wanted to know the answer.

Jerry tilted his head and twisted his mouth to one side. The slight change in his expression flashed the dimples she knew so well in her own reflection.

"I'm sorry. I never knew about you at all. I…" He lifted his hands in the air, then shoved them into his pockets. "I never knew."

"You didn't?" she asked, still trying to catch up with the short conversation. "But Mom said she got a letter and a check."

Jerry looked down and shook his head. "I can't believe that happened. Well, I can believe it because my manager at the time did so many things I didn't know about or approve of, but this is…"

"Your manager?" Cheyenne asked.

"There was a man who worked for me a long time ago. He pretty much took care of everything for me. I never got any correspondence from your mom. I would have come back." He scuffed the bottom of his boot against the tile floor. "We talked before I left, and I wrote to her, but it doesn't sound like she got the letters. It's a fair guess to say my old manager intercepted them."

Jerry turned to the woman behind him and reached a hand out to her. She took it and stepped to his side. "This is my wife, Laura. We've been married for twenty years."

The woman reached a tentative hand out to Cheyenne. "I know this is all a lot to take in, but Jerry and I have talked a lot since Ridge contacted us. We'd like to get to know you, if that's something you'd be interested in."

Cheyenne shook her head. If what Jerry was saying was the truth, then she'd been terribly wrong in her assessment of him in the same way she'd been wrong about Ridge.

Jerry rubbed his jaw. "I wanted your mom to come with me. That was the plan back then. When I never heard back, I assumed she'd changed her mind." He squeezed his wife's hand. "I hadn't met Laura then, and I'm sure things would have turned out differently had I known about you. We might not have met at all."

Cheyenne stared at the floor, remembering her mom's tears and heartbreak over Jerry's dismissal. "I thought… I thought I hated you for doing that to her. To me."

Jerry looked down and rubbed a hand over his mouth. "I wouldn't blame you one bit." He lifted his attention back to her and set his jaw. "I would never do that. If I'd known about you, I wouldn't have written a letter. I would have been right there. For everything." He rubbed his mouth again. "I missed everything. I have two sons now, and I have a good idea of everything that I missed in your life. I would have been there."

Cheyenne bit her lips and looked back at Ridge. She believed Jerry, and with that truth came the longing. She'd always wanted a father–anyone but him. Now, she grieved the life she could have had with a dad who loved her. Her mom had struggled to keep their family fed most of her childhood. Things could have been so different.

"I'm so sorry, Cheyenne," Jerry said. "I know this is a lot to take in. I've been struggling with understanding it since Ridge reached out to me. But when he showed me a photo of you, I knew. Without a doubt. I've missed everything, but I don't want to miss any more."

The words rushed up her throat. *Me too.* She wanted the acceptance he offered more than she'd ever taken the time to realize.

"Would you let us be a part of your life?" Jerry asked.

Cheyenne looked from Jerry to his wife and nodded, still unable to speak. She covered her mouth, trying to hide the telltale sign of the tears that wanted to break free.

Jerry took a tentative step toward her and lifted one hand. She met him in that leap of faith and closed the distance. Jerry wrapped his arms around her, and she released a calming breath. His embrace felt so much like the comfort of Ridge's arms.

If she hadn't met Ridge and learned to accept actions as truth of the inner workings of someone's heart, she wouldn't have given Jerry the time to explain. Now, forgiveness had saved her, and she knew what it meant to extend that grace to someone else.

"I missed so much," Jerry whispered against her hair. He was tall and broad like Ridge, and she knew now that the two men were the exceptions to every label she'd tried to place on them.

She turned her face to his chest, wiping a single tear on his shirt. "You don't have to miss anything else."

Epilogue

Cheyenne

Cheyenne stood just inside the hangar at the local airport and searched the blue skies. "They should be here, right?"

Ridge put his hands on her shoulders and turned her to face him. The peace in his eyes made her tense muscles relax instinctively. "They're not due for three minutes."

She looked over his shoulder. "But I should be able to see the plane when it's three minutes away, right? I can see for miles."

Ridge leaned down, putting his face right in front of hers. "Stop worrying."

"Easier said than done. My mom is on that plane, and what if something happened during the flight?"

"She has a nurse on board with her," Ridge said.

"But what if–"

"What if she gets here safely?" Ridge interrupted.

Cheyenne narrowed her eyes at him. "Stop being so rational."

"Nope. It hurts me too much to see you worrying over your mom to just let it go. Hadley is with her. And the doctor said your mom is healthy enough to travel this way."

"But she couldn't have come on a regular flight. This is only possible because you have piles of money and can afford a private plane."

"You're never going to get used to it, but I wish you would."

She wasn't sure she would either. Ridge's money was beyond what she could understand. But he'd told her about so many of his projects outside of the ranch, and he did so much good with that money that she knew the privilege had never come to a better man. Now, he was making sure her mom would be safe and well cared for in the best place in northern Wyoming.

Cheyenne peeked over his shoulder again and gasped. "There it is!"

The plane was headed straight toward them. She started to move, but Ridge held her back.

"At least wait until the plane lands," he said.

She held onto his hand with a white-knuckle grip as the plane touched down. As soon as they got the all-clear signal, she took off running toward the plane. The fall wind burned her cheeks as she gasped in the cold air.

She could have Ridge and her family too. It all seemed unbelievable. She'd never experienced more happiness than this.

The stairs were positioned at the door, and it opened. Seconds later, her sister's smiling face greeted her.

"Is everything okay?" Cheyenne asked as she jogged up the stairs.

"She's fine," Hadley opened her arms and wrapped Cheyenne in a hug. "I can't believe we're here!"

Cheyenne buried her face in her sister's neck. "I can't believe you're here either." They'd started getting everything in place for the move when Cheyenne and Ridge had visited Bear Cliff a few weeks ago. They'd brought as much back to Wyoming with them as they could, but Hadley needed to stay a while longer to wrap up the closing on the old trailer.

Hadley pulled back, and her hair whipped around her face. "Let's go! I can't wait to see the ranch!"

Cheyenne and Hadley moved down the stairs to make room for the attendants to bring their mom off the plane. Jim pulled up beside the plane, and Ridge and Hadley said their hellos as the men loaded her mom into the car.

"Mom looks so good!" Cheyenne said.

"She's doing great," Hadley said. "It's hard to tell just how much she can do over our video calls, but she's improved a lot."

Cheyenne squeezed her sister's hand. "Thank you for taking care of her."

"What do you mean? Taking care of Mom isn't just on your shoulders. She's my mom too."

"I know, but you're my little sister. I'm supposed to take care of both of you."

Hadley shook her head slowly. "That's not the truth at all."

Cheyenne's shoulders sank. "But I want to take care of you."

"And I'll always be thankful for that. You're the best sister, but I'm not a little girl anymore."

Cheyenne pushed her whirling hair from her face. "I know, and I'll try harder to treat you like a grown woman. I just love you so much."

"I love you too, sis." Hadley gave Cheyenne a side hug as the men helping her mother into the car stepped back.

As soon as it was clear she wasn't in the men's way, Cheyenne darted toward the car. She opened the door and climbed in beside her mom. "Hey!"

"Flower," her mother said. The word was strong and clear in her mom's old, sweet voice.

Hadley shouted behind Cheyenne, "Scoot your boot. I want to get in too."

The three women adjusted into the backseat, while Ridge sat up front with Jim.

"Everyone ready?" Jim asked.

"Our stuff," Hadley said.

"Colt and Linc are loading it into a pickup. They'll meet us at the cabin."

"It's not that much. I sold most of it before we left," Hadley said.

Cheyenne turned to her mom. "Are you really happy with the move?"

Her mom squeezed her hand. The strength was another indicator of her recovery. "I am."

"And I can't believe I'll be working at the ranch!" Hadley squealed. "It's like my dream job!"

"You sure you're up for working with the kids?" Ridge asked.

"Totally. I can't think of a better job."

"You'll love Remi. She's great with the kids too," Cheyenne said.

Hearing about all her sister did to sell the trailer and pack up to move to Wyoming was another realization for Cheyenne. Her sister was mature and responsible but still carefree and happy. Maybe Cheyenne leaving when she did was the best thing to help her sister grow into the woman she was now.

They went straight to Cheyenne's cabin, and Hadley stuck her upper body completely out the window when they crested the hill leading to the western side of the ranch. "Shut up! This is it?"

Cheyenne laughed. "That's it."

Hadley slithered back into the car. "I might just sleep outside. The weather is amazing."

Ridge cleared his throat. "Um–"

"You don't want to do that," Cheyenne said. "Or go outside at night unless you absolutely have to. Bears, wolves, mountain lions. Need I go on?"

"Nope. I was adequately warned at 'bears.'"

When they parked in front of the cabin, Hadley jumped out first and ran up the new ramp Ridge had built to the porch. She danced on her toes, swinging her long hair behind her. "I can't believe it!"

Cheyenne helped Ridge and Jim get her mom from the car to the wheelchair. Then Ridge jerked his chin toward the cabin, letting Cheyenne know she could go ahead. He settled in behind her mom's chair. "I'll get her in. Go let your sister in before she falls through the porch from all her jumping."

Cheyenne darted up the stairs and unlocked the door. "Here it is."

Hadley barged in, then halted. "Shut up! This is adorable!"

"Ridge designed it. It's super cute for a tiny cabin," Cheyenne said. She looked back to see how Ridge was doing getting her mom inside.

Hadley grabbed Cheyenne's hand. "Come on. Show me the bedroom."

"It's this way." Cheyenne pointed toward the door on the far side of the living room.

"Well, I had a fifty-fifty chance of finding it myself, since there are only two doors," Hadley said.

"You signed up for this!"

Hadley raised her hands and smiled. "Easy, tiger. I love it. Mom will love it too."

Cheyenne opened the door to the bedroom and waved her arms at the two small beds. "This is home."

"We're roomies again!"

"And wait until you see Mom's place. It's the cutest, and all of the staff I met were so nice."

Hadley wrapped an arm around Cheyenne's shoulders. "Thanks for doing all that. I know you went to a lot of places to find her the best one."

"I'm just so glad you're both here," Cheyenne said.

Hadley lifted her chin and waved her hand gracefully in the air. "I'll have Mr. Jim bring my bags in here."

Cheyenne laughed and turned around to check on her mom. Ridge, Jim, and her mom were just inside the door.

"What do you think?" Cheyenne asked.

Her mom brought one hand up and laid it on her chest. "Love." Then she reached for Ridge, who took her fragile hand in his.

Cheyenne's heart overflowed at the small touch. She knew how much Ridge loved his family, and if he had even half of that love for her family too, they would be blessed.

Ridge looked down at her mother and winked. Then he sank down onto one knee.

Cheyenne froze, and the breath she'd been taking died in her throat.

"Cheyenne Keeton, you've changed my life for the better. I've never met someone who challenged me in the ways you do. I feel like we're an indestructible team, and I wouldn't want to have anyone else by my side. Forever."

Cheyenne inhaled the rest of the breath that had lodged in her throat. "Forever."

"Forever," Ridge repeated.

"Yes," she whispered.

"I haven't asked yet," Ridge said with a grin.

"Yes," she said louder. "Yes. Yes. Yes."

"You'll marry me?" Ridge asked. "Just making sure that's what you're agreeing to."

"Yes!" Cheyenne shouted.

Hadley hooted behind her. "Let's get hitched!"

"Not today, Hadley," Cheyenne said. Then she turned to Ridge. "You don't mean today, right?"

"Today sounds good," he said with a smile.

"Really?" The word was a soft puff of breath.

Ridge stuck his hand in his pocket and pulled out a ring. The midday sun shining through the window glinted off the single stone.

"Wow. It's beautiful," she whispered.

"Hadley helped pick it out. I wanted to get you something bigger, but she said you wouldn't want something gaudy."

Cheyenne laughed. "She's right. It's perfect."

Ridge slipped it on her finger and looked up at her. "One day, we'll have a place where your mom can live with us."

Cheyenne bit her lips between her teeth and looked at her mom. Being able to bring her home had seemed like an unreachable dream, but Ridge knew her deepest wants and needs.

Family. She'd thought she could take matters into her own hands and save the people she loved, but she hadn't done anything at all. Somehow, the Lord led her to the right place where the right man would point her in the right direction.

Ridge stood and grabbed her waist, pulling her in for a kiss that stole her breath and her heart.

Bonus Epilogue

Colt

Colt grabbed the braided rope and adjusted his seat on the bronc. The arena lights cast shadows into the cage, and the stirred-up dust had his muscles tensing. He lived for the rodeo.

And Remi. Always Remi.

He looked up from the bronc and scanned the edges of the arena. Three seconds. It never took him more than five seconds to find her. This time, he'd locked in on her quickly. He knew the way her red hair caught the light as well as he knew the back of his hand. She leaned one shoulder against the gate while she chatted with Cheyenne's sister, Hadley.

As if she'd felt his stare on her, Remi looked his way. She flashed him a playful smile, then turned back to her conversation with Hadley.

"Earth to Colt," Brett said.

Colt cleared his throat. "What?"

"You ready?"

Colt scooted closer to the saddle horn and took that last deep breath before firing off. "Ready."

The cage gate opened, and the bronc shot out of the chute in a high spin, sending Colt jerking backward. The force rocked against his back, and his stomach flipped as the bronc landed hard against the red dirt.

Another buck, and Colt was riding the wave again, holding on with all he had. The roar of the crowd throbbed between his ears. A few more seconds, and he could dismount.

A side spin jerked Colt in a hard right, and he lost his hold on the rope. The familiar moment of weightlessness gave him time to prepare for the impact, but it was never enough. This landing would hurt like all the others.

Instead of the loss of breath he'd expected, his left shoulder hit first and gave too much to the force of the ground. He felt the pop and ripping all the way across his back and down his arm.

His head fell back and rocked hard against the dirt. He couldn't even cry out around the grip of the pain, but his right arm instinctively grabbed his injured shoulder.

Look for the bronc. Look for the bronc. He worked to focus, but the pain seized him in its hold. It had been years since he'd dislocated his shoulder, and the pain seemed sharper this time.

"Colt!"

He turned, looking for Remi. She'd climbed the tall fence and raced toward him with her hair streaming behind her.

"Colt! You okay?" she asked as she slid to her knees at his side.

Jameson squatted on his other side. "Dislocated?"

"Yeah." Colt shook his head to wipe out the daze. "I'm okay."

Jameson offered a hand, and Colt pulled against the foreman, the rip in his back warning him every inch of the way.

"You think you can put it back?" Colt asked.

Jameson jerked his head toward the barn. "I'll get you fixed up."

"Colton Walker, everyone. Let's give him a hand," Blake announced.

The crowd cheered, and Colt waved his uninjured arm. He'd planned on helping with the mutton busting tonight, but it was looking like his evening would end early.

Remi walked by his side as they headed out to the barn. She didn't speak, but the warmth of her beside him was more than enough. Jameson led them to the main barn and into Jess's office. He pulled out a chair and gestured for Colt to sit.

Taking his seat, Colt winked at Remi. "If you're here to watch me cry, you'll be disappointed."

Remi's thin lips spread wide, but her teeth didn't show.

Colt tilted his head and furrowed his brow, sending her a silent question. *What's wrong?*

Jameson returned with the first-aid kit and started moving Colt's arm. While he had no plans to cry, the sharp pain begged him to cry out.

Not today.

He set his jaw and closed his eyes, giving Jameson full control of the shoulder. After what felt like an hour of torture, the pop radiated through the room and Colt's entire body.

Remi's quick gasp followed the sound, and Colt looked up. Remi stared at him with wide eyes, and her hand covered her mouth and most of the cute freckles on her cheeks.

"All done," Jameson said. He silently wrapped the shoulder in a sling and closed up the kit. "Pain meds?"

"Not today." Or any day. Addiction had ruined his dad's life, and Colt didn't plan to give the devil an inch of control.

Jameson put the kit back and gently patted Colt's uninjured shoulder. "Take it easy, and let me know if you head to the doc."

"You got it, boss."

Jameson walked out, leaving the door open behind him.

"Colt?" Remi asked. The word was quieter than he'd ever heard her speak.

"Yeah," he said as he stood, grinning against the pain.

"Are you okay?"

He turned to her and waited for the joke. She would pester him about being stupid enough to let the horse buck him off. She would make a comment about his defective shoulder. She would pretend she was going to slap him where it hurt.

But she didn't do any of those things. She pursed her lips and chewed the inside of her cheek.

"What's wrong?" Seeing Remi upset kindled a fire in his middle, pushing adrenaline through his whole body, tingling his fingers and toes.

"Nothing's wrong."

Lie. There was something wrong, but to his knowledge, she'd never lied to him before now.

Why now?

"Remi, come on. You can tell me anything."

Her gaze slid to his shoulder and quickly away.

"Are you worried about me?" he asked.

"No," she said quickly. "I just didn't like seeing you hurt."

That feeling went both ways. The unhappiness in her eyes right now was cutting its way into his heart.

Colt wrapped his uninjured arm around her shoulders and pulled her in for a side hug. "You can relax. It'll take more than a shoulder bump to take me out of the game."

Remi shook out of his hold and narrowed her eyes at him. "Can we just forget this ever happened?" she asked.

Colt looked down at her and grinned. "Not a chance, sweetheart."

About the Author

Mandi Blake was born and raised in Alabama where she lives with her husband and daughter, but her southern heart loves to travel. Reading has been her favorite hobby for as long as she can remember, but writing is her passion. She loves a good happily ever after in her sweet Christian romance books and loves to see her characters' relationships grow closer to God and each other.